The Moralist

AMS PRESS
NEW YORK

☆ THE MORALIST ☆

THE
MORALIST

BY

W. ADOLPHE ROBERTS

THE MOHAWK PRESS
NEW YORK   MCMXXXI

☆ THE MORALIST ☆

Library of Congress Cataloging in Publication Data

Roberts, Walter Adolphe, 1886-
  The moralist.

  I. Title.
PZ3.R5442Mo4 [PS3535.01793] 813'.5'2 73-18601
ISBN 0-404-11411-3

Reprinted from the edition of 1931, New York
First AMS edition published in 1974
Manufactured in the United States of America

AMS PRESS INC.
NEW YORK, N.Y. 10003

The Moralist

Chapter 1

USTIN BRIDE sat at the window of his room on West 29th Street, and basked in the April sunshine that had suddenly grown warmer and fuller that morning in a promise of approaching Summer. Boxes of flowering geraniums had made their appearance overnight on the ledges across the way. The street was decorous, empty and indolent-looking, because it was Sunday. Now and then, a woman in forenoon deshabille came hurrying from the Eighth Avenue corner, with bread and bottles of milk in paper bags. About one of the brownstone stoops a cluster of children played.

The room in which Austin Bride lounged was badly furnished and commonplace, a typical front parlor of the neighborhood. A great bedstead finished in imitation brass occupied the semi-alcove between the main part of the room and the now permanently closed folding doors that bisected the floor. There were a number of heavy chairs, a highboy with a stained marble top, and an uncomfortable sofa upholstered in shiny leather that had begun to crack. The broad desk in the middle of the room under the chandelier had been put in to meet Austin's special needs. It was littered with books and newspaper cuttings. There was an open book-shelf against the wall opposite the

3

mantelpiece, and the many small framed prints that had replaced the traditional parlor pictures were plainly of the tenant's selection.

When he had come to live there two years before, Austin had not been favorably impressed by the block, the house or the room. He had expected to stay for only a little while. Then he made certain discoveries which appealed to the ebbing romanticism of a temperament that, had he known it, was on the verge of maturing in a rapidly changing world.

The block, he learned, was practically all that remained of one of the French quarters of old New York. It had been called Lamartine Place until the municipal passion for masking the identity of streets behind sterile numbers had made it part of West 29th. Austin had deplored the disappearance of the poet's name, but had begun to have a friendly feeling for the block. He had written a Sunday newspaper article about its history, with comments on the literary importance of Lamartine which had been blue-penciled by the editor.

His reasons for growing to like the house and room were more definite. The landlords were a French couple named Boissy. Madame Hortense Boissy, a Parisian of the lower middle class, was a domestic tyrant, which meant, as far as Austin was concerned, that his bed was always fresh and comfortable and his furniture dustless. Paul Boissy was of military bearing, short and bullet-headed, with a gray imperial that made him look something like Napoleon III. He was very industrious, an energetic man who delighted in doing odd jobs of carpentering, steamfitting and paperhanging. He had fixed up a small office for himself under the staircase, but was seldom to be found there. When not tinkering with his own premises, he was likely to be helping his neighbors to beat the exhorbitant charges of union labor. He seemed to be a jack-of-all-trades yet his real business was highly specialized and exotic. He was a breeder of pedigree cats.

Because of the cats, Austin felt almost affectionate toward the Boissys and their establishment. The first time he had visited the animals, he had been attracted by indistinct mewing heard from the bath room window. The yard below was covered by a shingled roof with a low ridge pole, at either end of which stood a frivolous scroll of woodwork. A sumach tree in adjoining territory flung weedy branches above the roof. The effect was that of a cottage dropped surprisingly in those desolate reaches of fences and brick walls.

Austin had wandered to the basement and through the kitchen, vaguely possessed by the notion that there would be something beyond to interest him. His intrusion had led the kitchenmaid to cease polishing forks and turn toward him, but she said nothing. He had smiled at her, noticing that although she was slatternly and reddened by her work she seemed to have nice breasts under her dingy cotton blouse. She returned his smile; women of all kinds were flattered by Austin's facile observation.

He had then climbed a short flight of steps, pushed open a door and found himself on a cement floor, beneath the low roof, surrounded by magnificent cats. Maltese and Angoras, Persians and Siamese, stared at him from their cages. For a moment, he had been less impressed by the pageantry of their black and smoke-blue and white and orange fur than by the many shades of color in their jewel-like eyes. The great Persian male nearest to him on the left had orbs as bland and blue as sapphires, while the Angora in the next cage blinked clear amber eyes. There had been opals, garnets and emeralds in the inscrutable battery.

Austin still remembered how he had sighed with pleasure. He was very fond of cats.

Paul Boissy had come from the far end of the outhouse and extended a gossipy welcome. He had talked knowingly about his breeds, but he had irritated Austin instead of pleasing him by his manner of giving him a Siamese the color of burnt umber to fondle. Boissy seized the cat by the loose skin of its neck, as if it had been a kitten. He passed his hands of an amateur carpenter over its ears, and made a clucking sound with his tongue. "The creature isn't fit to own sensitive animals like these; he should breed goats," thought Austin scornfully.

Later, he had discovered it was Madame Boissy who understood the feline temperament and kept the cats happy with her petting. She sometimes gave her favorites the run of the house for a few hours. A blue female Angora with a ruff like shredded silk and a tail like an ostrich plume made her way straight to Austin's room on her first day of liberty, and the tenant had pleaded against her being ousted. Madame Boissy thereafter released the cat whenever possible, though she had pretended at the beginning to be annoyed.

His friendship with the Angora had been one of the factors in Austin's attachment to the house on 29th Street. Another had been the complacency of his French landlords in the matter of the visits paid him by his lover, Elizabeth.

Sitting by the window that Sunday morning, however, Austin Bride was unhappy. He knew that he was not depressed because of the delicate sensuousness of the weather, not suffering from spring fever in the ordinary sense of the term. The spring, as always, enchanted him, released him from a melancholia from which he was never free in winter. But the pleasure he took in the ripening season was harassed by a conviction that it found his life flowing too easily in the channels of habit. His mood was that of a man on New Year's Day, who feels suddenly that he should take stock of himself and make resolutions. It was impossible for Austin Bride to ignore the fact that he was thirty. He had had a ragged youth.

The circumstances by which he had been beset had been unfavorable, and though he had surmounted them it had never been in the most effective way, had never been equivalent to a real victory.

He remembered how his mother had wished him at eighteen to go to college and study law. She was an affectionate, level-headed mother, half Welsh, half French, but without a trace of the temperament characteristic of either race. The law seemed to her to be an eminently respectable and sometimes profitable calling, and she knew she had just enough money in a special bank account to launch her son. She had put the matter to him in those terms, and had reminded him that his utterly worthless Irish-American father would be unable to do anything for him. Austin did not think his father utterly worthless. The elder Bride was too impractical to earn his living, but he read the classics in the original and talked fluently on exotic subjects like heraldry and the doctrine of metempsychosis. His philosophy was sentimental to a degree, a traditional poetizing of the charms of vagabondage, a feeble mysticism. The boy had found it impressive in his adolescent years. Ironically, Stephen Bride, who was ultra masculine, if weak, was destined to be the only man to exert an influence in forming his son's character.

Austin had been outraged to feel that his mother wanted him to become a successful mediocrity—a sort of justification before the world of her blunder in marrying badly. The idea of being a lawyer was especially disagreeable to him. He saw lawyers as noncreative beings, as human moles engaged in burrowing through books devoid of beauty. He loved the written word too much to face an existence in which he would have to read not for the sake of the author's style, but to discover how some jurist had interpreted an issue in the comedy of human liberty.

He refused brusquely to study law, or even to go to college. The ambition to become a journalist had suddenly taken possession of him. He thought of himself as a member of a dignified Fourth Estate, not as a mere newspaper man, and played with the delightful illusion that the career would give him an opportunity to learn how to write in the manner of the masters he admired. It was his youthful belief that every article in a newspaper, not to mention the editorials, was carefully written and that old reporters being more experienced than callow ones were relatively better stylists.

The family was living in a shabby frame house in San Francisco that had been left by an uncle to Mrs. Bride. Austin had practically run away from home. After he had found it impossible to get work on one of the San Francisco papers, he had taken an opening in Sacramento, and though his mother had packed his trunk and given him forty dollars as pocket money, she had tried up to the last moment to persuade him not to go.

He wondered now in the room on West 29th Street why he had seen the adventure through. It was scarcely astonishing that he had been unable to forego the romantic start. But why had he remained for seven months on the absurd country sheet in Sacramento? Why had he continued in newspaper work through the following twelve years?

He had not made a good reporter. For one thing, he had failed to acquire a zest for the gathering of news as such. Personalities were usually interesting to him, the events that had brought them into notice only occasionally so. He saw the drama in crime, politics and sports, but was bored by the necessity of keeping to the happenings of the last twenty-four hours; his tendency was to draw character sketches and to clarify the history of the case. He could barely bring himself to report the conventions of Elks and Improved Red Men, projects for municipal uplift, the wails of charity societies concerning the city's neediest cases, or anything relating to banking, the labor movement or Church work.

Austin Bride's greatest drawback, however, had been his inability to march in step with the men who work on newspapers.

He had never quarreled openly with his superiors, but he had despised every managing editor and city editor he had known. They struck him as being ridiculous types of traders, seeing that they strove to uphold all that was profitable but mean in life, yet earned less for themselves than the smallest advertiser of the publisher's clientele. With certain fellow-reporters Austin had formed tepid friendships. His manner was not snobbish. Superficially, he was regarded as a fair mixer. But it did not amuse him to play poker all night, and he went cold with distaste when invited to share amorous confidences with the one-hundred-percent males of the city room.

He had found his compromise in journalism by drifting from news to special article writing. For six years he had worked only on Sunday magazine sections, in San Francisco for a few months and then at a jump on big papers in New York. And he had spent one summer in Paris.

His métier, he had discovered, was not a literary one, but it had its consolations. Being on the Sunday staff had relieved him of the hours of night duty he had detested. He had become like any other salaried employee, who could pretend to be too busy at his desk from nine to five to spare time for office acquaintances, and who could nightly resume his secret life unhindered.

He told himself that he had been a newspaper hack for the sake of books and women. It was the simple truth. But the results he was able to show for his obsessions seemed oddly negative.

Austin did not stop to review his reading, which had been disordered and continuous. He preferred to dwell upon his pursuit of love. Women had interested him to the point of enchantment. He had not spiritualized them much, not since his school days when he had been infatuated in a Tennysonian mood with a virgin threatened with tuberculosis, whose delicate features and dreamful eyes would have made the success of any Christmas calendar for which she had posed.

He had looked both sensuously and aesthetically on all later women. Every variation in their beauty fascinated him. He found them sensitive to his feeling for the art of living subtly, where men were crass, direct, lacking in imagination. There were no circumstances in which he did not prefer the company of women to that of men, but he was sure that the flesh was the final key to understanding. He desired realistically to possess the girls he admired. He offered them love and friendship at the same time. The one without the other would have seemed to him insulting or stupid. To this extent, he was an idealist, who shrank from the obvious truth that there are many women in the world who want only love.

It had not worked out uniformly well, this attitude of his. His wooing had more than once been met with a nuance of fear that had made intimacy impossible. On his side, he had often been afraid; it had taken him the experiences of seven years even to begin to control a form of shyness that was actually an over-refinememt of finesse. He dreaded making himself ridiculous by an ill-timed advance, and had credited the stenographers, minor actresses, artists' models, shop girls and waitresses of his early days with caring as much about tact as he did. Kidding, as a means to becoming confidential, had amused him in other people, but was a form of technique he had not acquired.

He had had four or five love affairs, certainly, that had not been lacking in a measure of charm. He did not count the score of swift contacts that had left only a blurred, collective memory.

Florence Tronchet would always be unforgettable. He had met her when he was nineteen and they had adjoining rooms in a cheap lodging house on Mission Street, San Francisco. Austin was asserting his independence by living away from home. He had not yet had a lover, and from his first sight of this ordinary French girl with her mat complexion, sloe eyes, thick eyebrows and kind, wide mouth, he had confessed a tingling hope to himself. One morning he had heard her singing and from his side of the partition had taken up the chorus of her popular ditty—a banal beginning, but he was too young to know or care. They had exchanged greetings, then, on the stairs, and a few evenings later he had knocked at her door and suggested timidly that they go up to the flat roof of the building. He could still sense the flood of moonlight that washed about them in the warm September night as they found a seat and leaned consciously, shoulder to shoulder. Austin had begun to kiss her, wordlessly. It had been an astounding experience. He had discovered that a passionate girl strained her body against one for long moments, went limp, resumed the fierce pressure. He learned that her lips were mobile instruments of pleasure, that their moisture was exciting. If novelists had mentioned these things, they had done it so badly as to give him no forewarning of what they would be like. And writers had not even hinted at the verities of the situation that awaited him downstairs, when he had guided her away from the direction of her room to his and closed the door behind them. Florence had been more experienced than he. She had laughed purringly and teased him with committing his first sin, and he had lied to her and said it was not his first. But that had been after the caress, and she had not believed him.

Their affair had lasted only a few weeks. He had managed it clumsily. Florence, who worked in a millinery shop and earned as much as he did, suggested that they take a flat and share expenses. But he still had the Christmas calendar girl at the back of his mind, and he had been afraid of the complication. They quarreled without malice, and Florence had wandered on to another city, another sweetheart. He had regretted her for years.

Austin's next attachment had been with the secretary of one of his long list of managing editors. She was several years older than he, a lean, unbeautiful woman of a harsh racial mixture—Norwegian and Scotch. He had made almost no effort to please her, but she had taken impetuous possession of him and overwhelmed him with a display of sensuality that the youth found flattering. At the end of six months he had tired of her, while refusing to confess it to himself. She, however, had also tired, and had escaped by means of an ignominious scene and a tragic view of the crisis that had led her to throw up her job.

Then, there had been Sally, a blond girl who ran her mother's theatrical restaurant in California Street, and who tormented him with her histrionic jealousies; there had been the model he had met just after his arrival in New York, and to whom he had given a shallow love for nearly a year; there had been the vaudeville actress, Erna Ull, who had quickly decided she preferred legitimate marriage with a member of a well known team of acrobats.

"Stages in my sentimental education," thought Austin, glowing faintly at his memories. But in leading up to his present lover, Elizabeth, had the others produced a climax? Was there nothing new for him to learn about beauty? Was he contented to accept Elizabeth Curran and her sweet, sticky devotion as the goal toward which he had been moving in his pursuit of love?

Two years before, he had been introduced to Elizabeth Curran at a bohemian party in a table d'hôte restaurant. He had noted her for her bright Irish coloring, her blue eyes, her mahogany-brown hair. Her chatter with the trivial youth accompanying her had seemed witty. She was a little too plump, perhaps, but Austin admired the sure taste with which she was dressed—all in black silk, a gown that was as trig as a tailor-made suit and a toque finished chicly with a frond of paradise plume.

He had flirted with her slowly and affectionately. A few evenings later, she had given him an opportunity to see her home, but he had pretended to be indifferent and had escorted her no farther than the subway. They were both coming regularly now to the table d'hôte restaurant. He learned she had been born in Philadelphia, that she lived alone, that she had a small shop on West 34th Street where she sold imported lingerie and laces.

Austin had angled in his own time for an invitation to visit Elizabeth. He had gone on a Sunday afternoon and had taken her a bunch of red carnations. Their heavy, sweet odor suggested her to him and their color, he thought, went with her hair if not her eyes. He had been visiting her regularly every Sunday since that day. Their intimacy had developed equably, like a middle class courtship, betrothal, marriage and honeymoon. For the past year it had not even pretended to ardor, but it had been lulling to the senses, harmonious and stable. Through the week, Austin met Elizabeth two or three times after work, and they dined in some quiet place. They seldom had definite plans as to what they would do afterwards. Occasionally, they sauntered on to a theater. More often, they slipped home, to her flat or to his room. Their life had become a model of domesticity, without the exasperations of house-keeping, free of the labels that invite society to present its bill of responsibilities.

A nice, reasonable life! Yet Austin Bride stirred rest-lessly in the golden Spring sunshine that streamed through the window. He got up and roved the room, pausing before several of his framed prints, but failing to distinguish be-tween the Goya "Capricho" and the Leda with a black swan from a recent Paris Salon, between the "Canicule" of Rops and the Three Fates of the Parthenon.

He picked up the Sunday newspapers, but he threw them back on to the desk without unfolding them. Ordinarily, he went through them diligently before noon. It was an old reporter's habit, lightly as he held the things printed in them, and he could not break himself of it. He often wondered why he did not confine himself to checking whether his own articles had been published.

"I must do something about my life," he said aloud. But, in spite of his New Year's Day mood, he made no resolutions.

He returned to the window, and immediately became absorbed in watching the children who were playing across the street. There were three little girls and four boys, a haphazard group from French and Irish families of the neighborhood. The soft weather had warmed them to gaiety, and they were free of the inhibitions that would have restrained Puritan children from raising their voices in bubbling laughter on Sunday. They were an eddy of youth, a shifting pattern of color, in the decorous block.

But Austin observed that in the evocation of beauty it was the little girls that counted. The boys threw themselves about with brusque motions, they rolled on the pavement and were indifferent to the grime that stained their clothes; yelling and snatching at each other, their mimicry was that of barbarous warfare. The girls moved lithely and with subtle restraint; mostly they stood in a small cluster, their arms curved suavely, their dresses falling in lines of intuitive grace. The voices of the girls were high and flute-like, and their laughter floated on a note of dignity above the clamor of their playmates. The girls appeared to be much older, to be conscious of their sex and so less blunt, than the primitive boys with whom they deigned to frolic.

"Look at them—women in control of their world, even at that age!" reflected Austin Bride, delighted.

Chapter 2

USTIN lunched in a restaurant on Eighth Avenue that had nothing to recommend it, except its nearness and its reasonable prices. It was an American eating house of the type that is giving way in New York before equally unwholesome, but much more pretentious-looking Hebrew restaurants with names like St. Remy and Coventry and Marmaduke. The Eighth Avenue place had a tin ceiling stamped with meaningless circles enclosed in diamonds; its wallpaper, a reiteration of large bouquets of rosebuds, would have been considered tasteful for a New England nuptial chamber. The table-cloths were never quite clean, and the knives had spots of rusted metal showing through their silver plating. Mashed potatoes were served with no matter what meat one ordered, served by good-humored waitresses who were either stout or emaciated. A girl with a medium, beautiful body had, somehow, never been known in the establishment.

Ordinarily, Austin talked to his waitress. He did not mind that his remarks seldom aroused more than a mild interest in her. Aware that she would prefer admiration to talk, he found it distinctly amusing to probe the feelings of the girl who happened to have his table, to ask her about her life, and to note that she thought him eccentric, that he intimidated her slightly.

That Sunday, however, he found nothing to say. He ate quickly and with distaste, then walked almost mechanically up the avenue to pay his habitual visit to Elizabeth.

He walked in the full sunshine of the April afternoon, responding slowly to the charm that New York had for him when winter was over. He enjoyed the dryness of the air, the tropical clarity of the hot light that seemed a prodigy of nature in a climate capable also of producing Alaskan snowdrifts. He liked even the thin coating of dust that blurred the sidewalks, for it was another harbinger of summer.

The family parties out for their weekly exhibit of clothes and offspring entertained him. He was never tired of wondering how the strutting middle-aged and middle class fathers had achieved the conquest of the wives who trotted beside them and pushed perambulators. Bizarre pictures of viol, or conjugal bribery, formed themselves in his brain. Playfully ignoring the maternal instinct, he told himself it was not to be imagined that women willingly collaborated with mates devoid of the least sign of emotional finesse. Couples of which both partners were young he saw less cruelly as amateurs engaged in acquiring experience at a high price. Nearly all would continue, of course, to do the goose-step of civic virtue in one another's company; but a few of these juvenile mothers would demand more finished lovers, would break away to become actresses, or businesswomen, or prostitutes, would weave bright strands into the pattern of New York's complexity.

Austin made swift note of the face of every woman he saw, classified it as being temperamental or dull, and then forgot it. His fantasy gave interest to the walk up Eighth Avenue and down the long blocks of 34th Street west of Sixth. Between Sixth and Fifth Avenues he passed Elizabeth's shop. It was one half of a ground floor front, and in spite of being small it gave the effect of luxury. The show window contained a few pieces of French lace underwear, and electric lights cleverly arranged behind it enabled the passerby to see the counter with its alluring display beyond. On the glass was lettered in flowing italics the name "Mlle. Élise." It was preferable in her business, Elizabeth had explained, to use a French pseudonym. The snobbery of smart customers demanded it.

Sauntering up Fifth Avenue, Austin turned into East 38th Street. His feet had beaten so familiar a path to the building in the middle of the block on the south side, where Elizabeth Curran lived, that it would have been superfluous for him to consult the numbers. He mounted the stoop of a brownstone house exactly like the others on both sides of it. It had been converted into apartments, two to the floor. There were letter boxes and bells in the vestibule, but the door stood open and Austin went in without ringing. At the head of the first flight of stairs, he tapped at the frosted glass of the door of the rear flat. His signal was special, a light rat-tat-tat, followed by a scratching at the rough surface. Immediately, some one could be heard stirring in the living room. The couch moved on its rollers, and feet touched the floor. A muffled sound of slippers on the hardwood boards announced the advancing footsteps.

Elizabeth opened the door and stood to one side, smiling. Her rather prominent blue eyes had a candid and affectionate expression. She was dressed in a wrapper of black silk, on which small flowers, like asters, were embroidered in white.

"Hello, dearie-dear!" she said in a cultivated voice that mitigated the banality of the pet name.

"Hello, yourself!" answered Austin lightly. After he had entered and the door was closed, he kissed her on the mouth, but he did not linger at her lips.

Elizabeth returned to the couch and leaned indolently on one hand, with her feet still on the floor. Austin took an armchair that stood beside a small oak desk of the folding variety. The flap of the desk was down and bore a few slips of paper with figures scribbled on them in pencil. The pigeon holes were stuffed with letters. On the narrow top were three framed photographs, of which one was of Austin Bride, and a vase containing a bunch of red carnations.

"Dearie-dear, it's terribly hot today," remarked Elizabeth plaintively.

"I like the heat," murmured Austin.

"I know you do. You're a salamander. But that doesn't make me like it."

Austin smiled, tilted his head back and glanced at the reproductions of paintings of the school of Burne-Jones,

Leighton and Alma-Tadema with which the walls were decorated. It was no longer necessary to pursue the tenuous subjects of conversation which came up between Elizabeth and himself. She talked about the heat, or styles in hats, or the latest society scandal, or her plans for next summer's vacation, and if he did nót wish to reply she gossiped on in a pleasant monologue, and then tried something else.

He interrupted her now, when he was tired of looking at her pictures, to pick up a copy of the Sunday newspaper on which he worked. Like the one he had left on his own desk, it was still unfolded. With a nervous gesture, he laid aside the news and rotogravure sections, discarded in a heap the several thick divisions given over to want ads, real estate and department store advertising, and retained only the Sunday magazine.

"Look, Elizabeth," he said, opening it accurately at a double-page spread of one of his stories. "I wrote this about a Colombian poet—José Asuncion Silva—who committed suicide more than twenty years ago because of the death of his sister. He was a poet of genius, one of the best in modern Spanish. The story got across on account of a relative of his, who is here on a diplomatic mission and who gave me an interview. The authorities in Colombia won't allow a monument to be raised to Silva. They say his love for his sister was incestuous, which it probably was. I had to tone the facts down a little."

"How interesting!" returned Elizabeth. She took the paper and ran her eyes over the screaming lettered title, the exclamatory subheads. A smudged cut of the noble head of the poet held her attention for an instant. "He was a terribly handsome man, wasn't he? What a pity you didn't have a picture of the sister, too! Well, I'll read it sometime."

She placed the Sunday magazine carefully in her desk, where Austin knew it would lie untouched for days, for weeks perhaps, and at last find its way unread into the waste paper basket.

A glum resentment pervaded him. The article was not sufficiently well written to be worth any one's serious attention. All his articles were journalism, quickly and commercially hammered out on the typewriter. But he could not reconcile himself to Elizabeth's lack of interest in matters with which his mind had busied itself. For that reason, if for no other—because his mind and not some one else's was involved—she should be eager to read his articles. It would not be expecting too much of her, even though her tastes were not literary. She was one of those well educated persons who early get out of the habit of books. A shelf near the mantelpiece carried about twenty volumes, some of which Austin had put there, and he was certain she had not read four of them in the past year.

"Are you moody today, dearie-dear? Don't be. Come over here and kiss me," demanded Elizabeth.

Every time they were together in her rooms or his, they followed the same programme. They would converse sketchily about unimportant topics. A more imaginative rôle would be vainly attempted by Austin. A moment of silence. They would slip into one another's arms. Elizabeth seldom put her invitation into words, so bland and expected had the ritual of the senses come to be.

That Sunday, Austin Bride crossed over to the couch in a jet of impulsive energy. He pressed his face to the woman's mahogany-brown hair, then kissed her on the throat and bared shoulder. His right hand passed feverishly down her body, while Elizabeth, faintly startled, responded with whispered and unmeant chidings. But he broke off and swung away from her. Stumbling to his feet, he made an erratic tour of the room. His eyes had an unhappy light in them, and the corners of his mouth were crisped.

A union of this sort was a lamentable habit, he said to himself. He was fond of Elizabeth, but that was all. Fond of her! It was not enough.

"Austin, what is the matter with you?" she asked sharply.

He came and stood beside her where she had raised herself on one elbow. "I am impossible. You ought to be tired of me by this time," he urged.

"But dearie-dear—why? Please don't say cruel things."

The face he had loved was flushed—too flushed. He felt himself harden at her proprietorial anxiety. His course now seemed beyond control and freed of subterfuges. He did not try to enlarge on his statement that Elizabeth ought to be tired of him, for it had had no significance other than a vague hope that she might have been led to forestall him.

"I think we should re-arrange our lives," he said. "I care a lot for you, but we are not really suited to each other.

We don't get enthusiastic about the same things. We just kill time together. I mean, we've fallen into the commonplace, like a married couple in a Bronx flat. If it goes on, we'll despise our love. It's been wonderful, but we should separate before it dies, while we can still be good friends."

His words sounded pitiably flat to Austin. He wondered whether in such circumstances such words were the best that any one found to use. Yet Elizabeth plainly held them to be sufficiently poignant.

She was looking at him, her eyes drowned in unshed tears. Her expression was that of a slapped child, whose humiliation was the greater because it had believed itself too grown up to be so punished.

"You—you are throwing me over, Austin?" she stammered.

He hated the popular cliché she had uttered. It chilled him almost to callousness.

"I happen to have been the first to see we should stop now. If it had been the other way around, you wouldn't have hesitated for an instant. And you'd have been justified —not because you were a woman, but because you were a partner in a love affair. Women and men should be equally honest, and equally good sports."

"But I never would have wanted to leave you, Austin," she wailed illogically.

"You do now, after what has been said," he replied a little sadly.

She covered her face with both hands and sobbed. Strange that Elizabeth should be crying, he thought, and that he should not go over and try to comfort her. But his heart felt empty, a heart made fallow to greet the new springtime that was burgeoning in the world.

Elizabeth fumbled for a handkerchief, then marshalled defiant platitudes against him.

"Only a fool would want you now. You have made up your mind to be free of me. Go, Austin! I shan't try to prevent you," she cried.

"I value your friendship, dear. Do I keep that?" he pleaded, as if grasping at a hope.

"No. I shall never see you again. I could not bear to see you again. Don't imagine that I want to be taken out to dinner occasionally, so we can talk about old times—and about your latest philandering, I suppose! No. This is good-bye, Austin."

He reflected mournfully that her superficiality was genuine enough. It was just as well that she did not attempt the possibilities in a comradely aftermath to love; she was made only for kisses. Why, she had not even tried to sound the realities of the abrupt crisis between them. She was taking the passing of love as a personal affront. But it could never be that.

Elizabeth rose and trailed heavily across the room. She looked about her in a quest the man knew was sentimental and obscure. Finally, she moved to the desk and snatched up his photograph from its place between those of her two sisters.

"Take it away with you," she said chokingly.

As Austin held the framed picture, he could not avoid the mental note that she possessed many others of him. Yet she had made a pathetic gesture. He wished she had not put the thing into his hands, and now it would be impossible to persuade her to accept it again. He forced it into his side pocket.

Tears were streaming down her cheeks once more, and at the last they touched him. He could not bid her farewell with a handshake.

"Let me kiss you, Elizabeth?" he begged, and tried to take her in his arms.

She stood back with dignity, beyond his reach. "No. You have kissed me for the last time."

But he captured her hand and pressed his lips to it.

"Good-bye, Austin," she said firmly.

"Good-bye, Elizabeth."

He turned and walked without pausing out of the room and out of the house.

In the street, he was invaded and calmed by the violent beauty of Spring. The knot in his throat softened. He refused to let himself think of Elizabeth left alone to her fluent tears. The break in their relations was a fatality for which no one was really to blame. Last April the unfolding season had left them both untouched. This year a subtle change had taken place in him. It was an act of life.

He wondered a little at his having found the courage to be ruthless. Adoring women as he did, how had he been able to strike at one of them? Yet that, too, was predestined.

He was blindly reaching out for other, more glowing, women. Leaving Elizabeth had been a revolt against the static passion of his uncomprehending youth.

Austin made his way home in the early twilight and sat by the window once more. He could not evade a threat of loneliness that hovered about him. But he had not been in the chair long when he heard a faint mew from the floor, and turned about in time to receive on his knees the blue-gray Angora that haunted his room. She looked like an unsubstantial cloud of ruffled fur, but her eyes shone enormous and golden, and her fine claws moved out and in, thrilling him with sensuous pleasure as they penetrated his clothes and touched his skin. He stroked her lovingly, and she responded with a soft clamor of rhythmic purring. Reaching up, she rubbed her head along his chin, then accepted the invitation of his outstretched finger and passed her head against and around it from many approaches. He spoke to her by means of a scarcely audible whistling through his teeth and the cat, trembling with delight, rolled on his lap, her purring keyed to a crescendo that broke at last in a catching of the breath and a deep sigh. She went to sleep flattened against him, her head thrust between his left arm and his side.

Rather than disturb his friend, Austin Bride did not go out to dinner until more than an hour beyond his usual time.

Chapter 3

MAKING his toilet with swift exactitude, the next morning, Austin paused to ask himself why he should hurry. It was half-past eight, and he was due at the office at nine. Being a few minutes late had never mattered on his paper, but he had preferred to be punctual. Another habit. A desirable habit, seeing that it helped to establish him as a privileged person who could take special leave when he wanted it. Today, however, he reflected, smiling mirthlessly, it was of no importance to him to be on time.

He left the washstand, drawing the curtain that had been rigged up to hide its salient ugliness, and strolled about the room. On the mantelpiece stood the framed photograph of himself which Elizabeth had forced upon him. No object could have been more personal, yet it struck him painfully as being out of place, a souvenir the presence of which he would be unable to endure. He wondered what he would do with it. And, wondering, he halted, leaned his head to one side and studied his pictured face.

Austin Bride saw a broad, high forehead that was saved from being portentous and dome-like by the way the black hair curled thickly above the ears and ruffled forward in the middle, leaving a large, triangular white patch below the parting and a smaller one on the right side. The eyebrows were sharply arched, well-defined toward the nose and thin at the extremities. The eyes were set far apart; one could not tell from the photograph that they were hazel-yellow and deceiving in their flickering change from an expression of amiable romanticism to one of intro-spection. Depressed at the upper end of the bridge, the nose was straight and undistinguished; it served to lead from the eyes down to the real point of interest. For, subtly, the mouth and chin combined to form the characteristic feature; they were as if cast in one mold, the lips full yet tight at the corners, the chin slightly pointed, and the whole preserving always the quality of a mask.

It was, taken all in all, a lean, clean-shaven face—mental and sensuous—of the type that aesthetic women admire and simpler women fear when they love, because it seems to the latter to be remote from common sympathies.

Austin's self-scrutiny failed to result in an appraisal. He shrugged his shoulders, moved the picture to an inconspic-uous spot on the mantelpiece and ended by locking it away in a drawer of his desk. He finished dressing slowly, and selected a brown palm-wood cane without a handle from a rack near the door where he kept half a dozen walking sticks and an umbrella. He longed intensely for a cup of coffee, yet did not hurry. Sometimes he had coffee served in his room, but when he was alone he disliked mingling the atmosphere of breakfast with that of bed. In the base-ment that morning, as usual, Madame Boissy served him with a light French déjeuner of rolls and coffee with a bitter tang obtained by roasting the beans black and adding a little chicory.

He ate abstractedly, and the moment he had swallowed the last mouthful of food he lighted a cigarette. A second was set going from the butt of the first. It was one of his inconsistencies to avoid smoking on an empty stomach, and then to use a meal as an excuse for smoking too much.

"You are late this morning, Mr. Bride," said Madame Boissy.

Austin turned on the waistless, middle-aged woman a look that was all deference and flattery. His eyes smiled at her and made her an accomplice. "I know," he whispered. "I wish I could blame it on a pretty girl, but I was alone last night, Madame—sadly alone. So it's my fault I'm late, and I should be ashamed of myself, but I'm not." It amused him to phrase naïve sentiments with short words to Madame Boissy. The method invariably thrilled her.

"Bad boy!" she sighed, lingering affectionately near his chair. "But I tell you, you should never have to be alone— a nice, bad boy like you."

He went through the basement door, swinging his cane, and turned down 29th Street to Ninth Avenue. Every day he took the elevated at 30th and Ninth. The station was one of the shabbiest in a demoded transportation system. It seemed a makeshift, a cramped shack perched at the top of dusty iron steps, a shack that vibrated crazily when the trains went by, a shack with a round-bellied stove for winter like the stoves one finds in country stores. In no other city, thought Austin, could one get a similar im-

pression of a structure that twenty years before had been
a monument of progress. New York, building her subways
with a magician's facility, treated the elevated as a relic
of primitive times, saw it with the changed values of
centuries rather than of the generation that had actually
elapsed.

For himself, Austin liked the old elevated trains when
the weather was fine. He took a seat near a window and
watched the kaleidoscope of tenement rooms, of women
struggling with bedding, of frowsy families eating in
kitchens, that flashed by him. Below Fourteenth Street to
Desbrosses Street and Franklin, he sniffed the odors of
fruit and raw Portuguese cork and strange chemicals from
the warehouses, and took pleasure in glimpses of docked
boats and shipping in the North River.

He got out at Warren Street and pushed through sidewalks cluttered with the bales and cases of a wholesale
neighborhood to City Hall Park. The tower of the New
York Forum, his newspaper, was a notable feature of the
eastern skyline. Austin had come to hate journalism, but
the physical aspect of Park Row held for him a certain
glamor of youth. He could not forget his optimism when
he had first passed that way in 1913; nor the satisfaction
it had been to sell a freelance article to The Sun a few
days later, and to join the queue in front of the cashier's
window on Friday afternoon—a green Californian doing
his best to look unconcerned at his début.

The memory entertained him now. His eyes twinkled
satirically, and he hastened across the square to the Forum

building. The editorial offices were scattered on several floors, in such holes and corners as the publisher could not lease advantageously to minor financiers, sales agencies or bucket-shop brokers. The back half of the second floor, however, was reserved as a minimum requirement for a number of departments, including the Sunday staff. It was reached by a narrow stairway behind the elevators. Austin mounted the steps, said good morning to the bleached-blond telephone girl in the reception room, nodded to two office boys of a Hebraic cast of countenance, and went on through the employees' entrance.

The floor was crowded with desks, on all of which were typewriters, pots of paste, many pencils and rubber erasers, and a tangle of copy paper and newspaper cuttings. The desks varied from old roll-tops to incongruously shiny, jerry-built, half-width affairs of the model provided in business offices for stenographers.

Although, at that hour of the morning, few of the desks were occupied, the characteristic racket was under way. An outsider would have been astonished at the nervous tempo in which the reporters hammered at their machines.

Austin's desk was a large flat one in a corner near a radiator, and so badly lighted that electricity had to be kept turned on all day. The nearest window was partly blocked by the roll-top desk of the Sunday editor, Saylor, whose idiosyncrasy seemed to be that he preferred artificial to natural light.

Austin sat down and went industriously through the pile of stuff on top, as well as the contents of every drawer of his desk. No one paid the slightest attention to him. He made things tidy and collected a number of personal belongings ranging from French and Spanish dictionaries to postage stamps and a cigarette case. He half filled a battered black handbag which had been in a lower drawer for months, locked it and then walked over to Saylor.

"I am quitting today," he remarked in a casual tone.

The editor was a man in his late fifties, a dyspeptic of the type that becomes red and flabby instead of sallow. His bald head was thrust forward like that of a turtle and bowed, as usual, between tall steel files on which innumerable papers were speared. But he came to life with a jump.

"Hey, what's that?" he demanded. "Quitting, hey! Are you trying to kid me?"

"Never more serious in my life," drawled Austin.

"Oh, you are! But where d'you get that today stuff? Goddamighty, Bride, you can't walk out on me with the next mag. just laid out!"

"I have no contract with the Forum. This paper is run on the old hire and fire basis, so I am as free to leave without notice as you would be to discharge me. You let Catherine Lacy go in five minutes last month because she thought Gaynor had been mayor immediately before Hylan. And it was on a Wednesday morning, if I remember rightly, when a short-handed staff was more of a problem than it will be to you today."

"I know, I know! Don't make me laugh, Bride. I might split my lip. If I put up a howl about you going, it's because I like your work. Sorry to lose you, hey!"

"Thank you," said Austin, smiling faintly at Saylor's turns of speech.

The Sunday editor removed one elbow from the desk and twisted his pink head around. "Don't mention it. But tell me, Bride, where're you going? Personally, I'd like to meet any raise you're getting. But it's no use; they're too damned stingy on this sheet. You landed with the World, hey? Or the Times?"

"I have no new job. I haven't the slightest idea where I can get one. But it won't be on a newspaper. I am leaving newspaper work for good," answered Austin.

"You're a nut," shouted Saylor in a sudden crisis of vehemence. "What have you got against the newspaper game? It's a grand game."

Austin looked steadily at the grotesque old man, and for the first time that morning asked himself what, indeed, were his concrete grievances against his calling. Though aware of the impulse, he had not come down town late for the express purpose of resigning. He had tidied his desk and resigned almost automatically. Why? Because, he supposed, he was disgusted with the bad writing and the rubber-stamp sentiments demanded by a great home journal. Because an anonymous journalist over the age of thirty was a case of arrested development. Saylor was an object lesson; he labored for ninety dollars a week to produce the world's worst five-cent magazine, and measured his enthusiasm for the result not by some perverted taste of his own, but by the grocer-publisher's O.K. A man or woman who signed any feature, whether it were the

Washington letter or a comic strip, was comprehensible. But newspapers submerged the personalities of nineteen out of every twenty who worked for them. An old age like Saylor's would be a horrible prospect.

"It is all right as a training school. But why remain in school for ever!" he contented himself with replying, maliciously.

"That's your idea, hey? Going to shoot at the Cosmopolitan and the Saturday Evening Post? Half the reporters I've known have quit jobs to do that. But there weren't many Richard Harding Davises and David Graham Phillipses among them. The most of them came back to the newspapers, Bride, the most of them came back."

"It is quite possible to graduate into some other field than the fiction magazines," said Austin pleasantly. "I know several politicians who were once newspaper men. I might also mention one of the most flourishing prize fight promoters and a man who keeps a second-hand bookstore on Fourth Avenue."

"Then you're not going to write?"

"I do it so badly now that my sense of humor may save me from trying to be a—a Richard Harding Davis. On the other hand, it may be too late to reform."

"I don't get you at all," complained Saylor, looking baffled and only remotely suspicious that fun was being poked at him.

"The fact is, I have not made up my mind about my future, Mr. Saylor. I am tired of the job, tired of newspaper work. I am going out into life to see what I can find. A change. Something new."

The Sunday editor's face cleared. "Spring fever, hey? Well, be good to yourself. And if you want to get back on the Forum later on, I'll see what I can do."

"Thank you."

They shook hands.

This had been his longest conversation with Saylor and surely his most personal one, reflected Austin, as he turned to pick up his bag. He made a brief tour of the office, saying good-bye to those he knew best and uttering non-committal statements about his prospects. There was no one from whom he minded parting, except a little from Marguerite Sims, the dramatic critic, a somber, black-haired girl who wrote gaudy journalese. She had taken him to the theater now and then on her passes, and they had talked about the Flemish school of art, her hobby. Yes, he liked Marguerite Sims. But she was not down that morning, and he did not get an opportunity to bid her farewell.

He left the Forum building an hour after he had entered it, and in the opulent sunshine of outdoors the meaning of what he had done surged through him like a revelation. Yesterday and today he had been tearing at bonds that had become more irksome than the ordinary bonds of habit. He had been swathed as in a chrysalis, and because he hoped to ripen into a new maturity, it had been necessary to destroy. Leaving Elizabeth had seemed the definitive gesture, but it had been just as essential to set himself free of his job.

It was done now, and he could throw himself upon the breast of New York. He was an aspirant, an adventurer, a newcomer in a sense. The realization stimulated him. It was a more exciting, because a more subtle, sensation than the romantic wonder with which he had greeted the city six years before.

Austin preferred to make no plans for his first day of liberty. He crossed City Hall Park and got into a Broadway street car, lured by the fact that it was one of the first open cars of Spring and he could smoke on a rear seat. He contemplated lazily the extraordinary jumble of signs which have stamped Broadway between Chambers Street and Union Square as the Yiddish paradise. Names ingenuously Anglicized competed with uncouth collections of syllables. Names set up in huge letters, solidly gilded names. But in block after block not more than a dozen closely allied products were offered at wholesale. Cloaks and suits, misses' suits, sweaters, raincoats, fur coats, pants, overalls, cloaks and suits—Austin read the words as on a reel of film shown over and over again. There would be a subject for an article in how many American citizens were clothed from lower Broadway without knowing it, he mused, and chuckled at the mental reaction that still led him to think in terms of Sunday newspaper articles.

At Union Square he left the car and explored the nondescript neighborhood. It had always had an attraction for him. He knew of the existence of odd, barnlike studios which could be had at a low rental, and he felt that soon he would want to take one of them and furnish it according

to the desires he had never satisfied in any of the places
where he had lived. The room at the Boissys' was as comfortable as such a room could be, but on the whole it
was drab. He might miss Madame Boissy's care; that could
not be helped. The blue Angora cat, however, need not
be lost to him. He could buy her and change her pedigree
name, Sultana III, to some suave, atmospheric French name
like Soumise, or Câline, or Grisette.

Austin's project for a studio apartment was too vague
to spur him to the point of entering the rusty brick and
brownstone houses where the boards of real estate agents
hung. But he wove in and out of the blocks in Fourteenth,
Fifteenth and Sixteenth Streets, east of Fifth Avenue,
lingered by the stoops and noted impressions of the buildings which appeared possible.

He had a late lunch, then drifted up Fifth Avenue and
northwest beyond Madison Square along Broadway. Since
its first fulfillment, the Spring had not faltered. The sky
was sapphire-blue, and the upper stories of the skyscrapers
were flooded with golden light. The jonquils and violets
of street vendors blazed at the main crossings.

Austin, for that day, had exhausted his need for action.
Tomorrow would be time enough to pursue with a fresh
heart the roadway of destiny. He went home and turned
lovingly to his books. His hand lingered on volumes of
Joseph Conrad, Anatole France and George Moore. But he
ended by taking down the poems of Swinburne and read
aloud, stricken exquisitely by beauty sublimated and the
magnificence of sound:

"Forth, ballad, and take roses in both arms,
  Even till the top rose touch thee in the throat
Where the least thornprick harms;
  And girdled in thy golden singing-coat,
Come thou before my lady and say this:
  'Borgia, thy gold hair's color burns in me,
    Thy mouth makes beat my blood in feverish rhymes;
  Therefore, so many as these roses be,
    Kiss me so many times.'"

Chapter 4

THE New York that Austin Bride explored afresh was that of 1919. The war, to which he had not been drafted because an over-cautious doctor had mistrusted his tobacco heart, was being forgotten with extraordinary speed.

With no precise ambitions and free of revolts other than his distaste for daily journalism, Austin made up his mind quickly to look for work on the staff of some monthly or weekly magazine. His years as a special writer for the Forum had given him certain connections of a vague character with men in the world of periodicals.

He went to see the noisy editor in chief of the Lumley group of fiction magazines. His name was Morgan, and he was known familiarly as Tom to writers who had barely shaken hands with him and to many who had not so much as seen his burnt-brick face with its snapping eyes and perpetually surly mouth. He gave Austin a belligerent welcome. Secretly delighting in his own work and easy reputation, he declared that the wise ones wrote for magazines instead of editing them. However, he would bear this latest voluntary slave in mind for the next vacancy.

Austin found Tom Morgan amusing. He was bored by

the air of shrewd pedantry, of idealism viewed as good business, worn by most of the other editors on whom he called. They gave him the impression of being impractical persons, in fear of being found out. They were a different tribe from the robust egoists bred by the newspaper atmosphere to which he was accustomed.

On the south side of Bryant Park, one afternoon at the end of the week, he ran into Frederick Hagen, a German-American from Ohio, who had had a sketchy career in advertising and the motion pictures. Hagen's thirty-five years had taught him no pessimism. When his projects went wrong, he was downcast in a jaunty, sentimental way. The future, he assumed, must be rosy because it was the future. He could not believe that anybody was his enemy, and he took a warm-hearted joy in helping others to realize on their credit in the bank of hope. Between Austin and himself there was a desultory friendship. Neither of them remembered clearly how they had met, nor found it odd that they should not have seen each other for months at a time.

"I've been managing editor of Sloat's since February fifteenth," announced Hagen, after the first greetings.

The news interested Austin, less on Hagen's account than because the name of the publisher Walter Rupert Sloat had the unfailing power to stir his curiosity. The man was supposed to be a towering genius among publishers, and certainly his string of magazines as well as newspapers had been converted rapidly from insignificance into the principal purveyors of mental narcotics to the American people. His commercial success was neither here nor there to Austin, but behind it he sensed a bizarre personality. In its outer, official aspects, Sloat's life was a triumph of reticence and hypocrisy, yet his indifference to gossip of a contrary nature seemed to be complete. Every one knew his greed for power was a lust. His sensuality was legendary. He signed platitudinous manifestos by the score, but never used the publicity he knew so well how to manipulate for others to present himself as a heroic figure.

"How did you land there?" asked Austin.

"Guy Bent took me on. I once did an advertising job for him, and he promised we'd work together in a big way some day. Guy's a prince."

"He is editor in chief, isn't he?"

"Oh yes—boss of the whole show! I'm only responsible for making up Sloat's Monthly. Managing editor doesn't mean so much on a magazine as it does on a newspaper."

"I know," replied Austin. "But I am glad to hear you are going ahead. You consider it that, don't you?"

"You bet!" cried Hagen cheerily. "Managing editor of Sloat's! With a prince like Guy Bent! I'll say so!"

Austin smiled covertly. "I got tired of newspaper work and quit it," he remarked. "I am looking for something else."

"You are? This falls just right, Bride. I don't like one of my assistants and am going to make a change. Would you work under me?"

Austin considered the final question seriously, without appearing to do so. He was not sure whether it appealed to him to work under Hagen. A subtle feeling of disappointment connected itself with the idea, as if it meant the re-acceptance of things he had been trying to escape. Yet that was absurd, he told himself. He would be in an entirely new milieu, and Hagen was a friend. He smiled again and nodded.

"Thank you, I'll be glad to try it," he said.

So it came about that Austin Bride found himself, a few days later, a part of the elaborate machinery which utilized a seven-story building in West 42nd Street for the production of the Sloat magazines.

The editorial department in which he worked occupied a floor laid out in imitation of some downtown factory of finance, such as an insurance office or the inner regions of a bank. An ornate suite in one corner isolated Guy Bent and his secretaries. Otherwise, there were no partitions. Flat-top desks in a uniform shade of light walnut were arranged in symmetrical groups. The desks of the more important employees had glass tops, and in obedience to the latest shibboleth of efficiency they were kept as bare as possible. A few manuscripts, proofs from the printer, letters awaiting signatures—these were the maximum impedimenta not consigned to the neatly closed drawers. The stenographers had been trained to hide everything except a notebook, a pencil, a rubber eraser and a glass bowl for clips. Tall, narrow cases with reference books broke the monotony and stood like company sergeants in the regiment of desks. The effect was that of an organizing for activity, extravagantly in excess of the work to be done.

With variations, the other floors presented the same appearance. The one given over to the advertising department had a more feverish atmosphere, the floor used by the cashier and bookkeeping staff was more cluttered.

Assuring himself from the beginning that he did not like it, Austin nevertheless found the system interesting. He had seen such offices before and had put them down broadly as the normal framework of American business. It had not occurred to him to connect them with publishing. Still less had he imagined that he would ever work in such a setting. But now he observed closely and with a certain zest.

The preponderance of women at the ranked desks had a meaning he was sure most people missed. Their presence was not wholly explained by the lower wages they were willing to accept. They had become a feature of the machine as it was run, for they did by far the greater part of the labor required on a given job and did it in a special way that could not be dispensed with. Men still did most of the planning, but the execution was largely left to women assistants, secretaries, stenographers. He wondered what the inevitably profound difference would be when the management of whole enterprises fell into the hands of women.

On the social side, the life at Sloat's struck him as being singularly arid. Here was a world free of the turmoil and harsh demands of journalism. These crowds of girls and men were seldom really busy, and the discipline of neat desks under which they worked was for appearances only.

Their opportunities for adroit flirtations were unequalled. Yet almost nothing of the kind occurred.

At lunchtime, the girls flocked out singly or in large groups, the men solemnly made appointments among themselves for smaller parties. Austin knew that this was a typical procedure, but he did not understand it. The probable disapproval of department heads afforded no explanation; such disapproval was humanly intended to be evaded. For himself, now that he had broken with Elizabeth, he wished that he might lunch every day with a new girl until he found one whose appeal lured him on to maneuver for intimate friendship.

The duties of his position under Hagen were not inspiring. He prepared copy, read proofs and studied the pages from the point of view of their general appearance. Makeup was regarded with an exaggerated seriousness by the editors, but no two of them held the same opinions. They insisted on innumerable changes until the final result was submitted to Bent, who approved a page or ordered it changed again according to his caprice of the moment. Austin's preliminary work had practically no weight, and the futility of his making decisions as though they were to stand kept his nerves constantly on edge.

He found a secret diversion in the varied physical types of the girls imprisoned with him. He saw them first as a pageant of bodies severely dressed, of white hands fluttering over papers, of bent heads. Then he picked out individuals of special charm—Irish girls with cream-colored skins, showing the first freckles of summer if their hair was red, flushed warmly and gray-eyed or blue-eyed if their hair was black; blonde Nordic girls with opulent breasts; swarthy Jewesses with strong eyebrows and ripe lips.

Impersonally as yet, Austin noted them and speculated as to how large a part love played in their lives. At times, when he had had more than enough of the ritual of magazine make-up, he invented an excuse to visit the circulation department, or the floor ruled by the strange creatures of the advertising staff, or some other subdivision of the Sloat machine. It pleased him to glance at fresh hosts of women, similar generically to those he had left, yet offering surprises at this desk or that as one looked closer.

Austin was talking pointlessly on a Saturday morning with Miss Clamart, the assistant cashier, when the middle-aged woman asked suddenly:

"Have you met Miss O'Neill?"

She waved her hand at a slender, tall girl sitting with her back toward them, and Austin realized that though he had observed Miss O'Neill he had had no positive reaction concerning her.

"I have not," he answered, "but I'd like to."

"You ought to know each other," chattered Miss Clamart. "She writes poetry, and you're an editor. Maybe you could put her in your magazine. Maude, Maude, come here and let me introduce Mr. Bride to you."

The girl had already risen and Austin, faintly embarrassed that she should have been summoned rather than he, stepped half way to meet her. She had a sweet, rich voice;

he remarked it before he took count of her hazel eyes
spaced widely apart, and the way her mouth relaxed after
she had spoken into a half smile that was appealing and
a little sad.

"Don't think I really expect you to publish my verse,"
she said. "I know they want only big names in Sloat's."

"Big—yes," replied Austin. "Big in the sense that Wrigley
in the chewing gum sign is bigger than any one ever
thought it worth while to advertise the name of Poe. But
I am not a real editor, anyway. I am first assistant make-
up editor, which does not amount to much when it comes
to accepting manuscripts."

"I see," murmured Maude O'Neill. "And I keep books
for the first assistant cashier."

They laughed frankly.

"But there is nothing in the world I care more about
than poetry," said Austin.

"So? I love poetry, of course."

"Will you show me yours?"

"I might do that."

A subtle current of attraction was running between
them. The slight things they had said to one another had
glowed with a life not usually present in the casual conversation of new acquaintances. Austin knew that this
girl, though she might dissimulate, would accept happily
the prospect of seeing him again. But it was beginning to
be awkward to continue talking in the cashier's department. Miss Clamart had gone back to her work, but

various clerks were watching Maude O'Neill and himself as they stood in an open space of floor among the desks.

"Are you a train-catcher?" he asked. "I mean, do you have to rush madly to Jersey, or Long Island, or some wild place like that when the whistle blows?"

"Oh no! I live downtown, in a woman's hotel in Abingdon Square. Why?"

"Because people from the suburbs make their engagements so far ahead. Because I hope now to tempt you into having dinner with me soon, so that we can talk about poetry. Will you?"

"All right. I think that would be nice," she answered steadily.

"Monday evening?"

"All right."

"Shall we meet at the door of the building at five-thirty?"

"Yes."

Their voices had been low and neutral, like the voices of persons discussing trivial office details. Only their eyes smiled, and they parted without touching hands. Austin's last glance recorded that her neck was too long for beauty, her shoulders too sloping. A gauche girl physically, but charged with repressed ardor. A girl who was restless because her emotions—mystical or fleshly, perhaps both—were so near to the surface.

Through Saturday afternoon and Sunday, he wished that he had tried for an earlier engagement with Maude

O'Neill, but it would have been a mistake, he knew. He had been bold enough.

On Monday, he made ten pages of the next month's number of Sloat's conform to his own typographical ideas, and then held them until five o'clock before he gave them to Hagen. He shook with inner mirth at the earnestness with which the managing editor threw himself upon the proofs and commenced to indicate changes. But it was too late in the day to affect his own plans. Hagen would not be ready to call one of his absurd conferences until the next morning.

Austin lighted a cigarette and read a short story on which his opinion was wanted. Liking the story, he wrote a report which he knew would run counter to the reports of all the other editors; he had found a piece of fiction that reflected vividly a phase of modern American life, but had not been constructed according to the Sloat formula. At twenty-five minutes past five, he took his hat and cane, rode down in the elevator and stepped to the prearranged spot on the 42nd Street sidewalk near the main entrance.

The rush of employees going home began in a moment. The men hurried by unseeing, their faces intent upon the suburban time schedule, the subway, or the drink they expected to have at the next corner. The women were lighter hearted, more effervescent; their babbling talk did not prevent their eyes from roving in an eager search for the faces of friends, or for the novelties of the passing scene.

Then Austin caught sight of Maude, slender and tall in

the throng, and observed that her hair was indefinite-colored, a rather lustreless brown. It was coiled at the back under the lightest of straw hats. He wondered whether it would be more effective bobbed.

"Miss O'Neill."

"Hello!" she answered softly.

He touched her arm to guide her across the street, and they sauntered toward Broadway. She was carrying a yellow-bound French book, he noticed, and he took it as a promising sign. So few of the girls one met in offices read French.

"What is the book?" he asked.

She handed it to him. "Gourmont's *Le Pèlerin du Silence.* Do you know it?"

"I should say I did," exclaimed Austin, as happily startled as if an exotic personage had materialized before his eyes. "I discovered it without the help of the learned critics who are making a fad of Gourmont. This is the book of his most worth reading, and the one they talk about least. The *Litanies de la Rose,* eh?"

"Yes, yes. I am glad you like that. The roses are not real flowers. They are cut out of tapestry and velvet, and are scented with incense. But they are the most beautiful roses on earth."

"We must read it together this evening."

"Oh, we must do that!" she murmured, with naïve enchantment.

With the exchange of a few sentences, they had drawn immeasurably closer. Austin was conscious of a curious ex-

citement. He asked himself flatly whether he were falling
in love with Maude O'Neill, and answered the question
with a reasoned denial. But already she was giving him
something that had been lacking in his amorous experiences, a thing he had needed without being able to define.
She was helping him to approach possible intimacy of the
body through a new gateway—an intimacy of the mind.

They pursued eagerly the subject of books. Her interest
in the printed word was not the passion that it was with
him, he discovered, but she was widely read. They walked
down Broadway without knowing exactly where they were
going, and in Madison Square they strolled aimlessly about
the pathways of the little park.

"We must decide where to have dinner," said Austin
at last.

"Anywhere at all will do."

"What about an Italian table d'hôte? It is fun once in
a while."

"I'd enjoy that. But not in Greenwich Village. I'm tired
of the Village places."

"My idea is one of the real, old-fashioned table d'hôtes.
They are doomed, I suppose, now that prohibition is coming; I cannot imagine them without their red ink. I'll
take you to a typical one."

They turned back to 27th Street, where between Broadway and Sixth Avenue Austin pointed out the name Ber-
tini on an electric sign that hung at right angles above the
doorway of a brownstone house. In the basement was a
forlorn bar and a few tables for diners, but Austin and

Maude climbed the stoop and entered the restaurant that occupied the front and back parlors thrown into one. The first impression was of garish red wallpaper, of napkins folded like zanies' caps erect upon the tables, of Italian bread-sticks curving in bouquets from tall glass holders, of dark pint bottles beside each plate. The hour was early for the regular patrons, and only three or four were seated —men with bilious faces and mustaches so black they seemed dyed. The waiters, shabby as crows, hovered about the entrance leading to the kitchen.

Austin selected a table in a far corner and placed Maude where she could look down the room, while he sat opposite to her. He ordered a quart bottle of chianti, round-bodied in its wicker casing, to replace the house claret.

"I like red ink better as a stage prop. than as a beverage," he told the girl.

"Chianti is nicer, of course."

She spoke the words in a vague tone, as she looked at him, her eyes illusioned and burning, her lips shaken by an involuntary tremor. He saw that it meant nothing to her to talk about wines, or to discuss the local color of Italian restaurants. The room for her was localized at their table. His hand, lying on the cloth, moved forward and for an instant their fingers clung.

"Do you write, too?" she asked him.

"A little. Not seriously. I have manufactured hundreds of columns for newspapers, but I do not count them."

"Perhaps some of that work was good," she said slowly,

as if jealous of a hard judgment. The contrast between her attitude and Elizabeth's forced itself upon Austin.

"You are good to leave me a loop-hole," he told her gratefully. "I am afraid my stuff has never been anything but journalism, all the same. Let's not waste tears on it now. I want to read your verse. Did you bring some?"

She at once produced a crumpled sheet of paper from her handbag, and gave it to him. A short poem was typed on it—a gnarled little poem in which severe, dry words were combined to form a plaint of discontent with beauty. It was studiously unhackneyed, yet it was immature.

"You felt this, and I like it," said Austin. "A clearer case against beauty and a more finished rhythm, though, would have made it a better poem."

"Thank you for being sincere. We can be friends if we are always so, both of us."

Their eyes met, gravely intimate. Then she put the manuscript away with a concise gesture that laid aside with it for that evening the whole subject of criticism of her work and his. They leaned toward each other across the table and exchanged disjointed confidences about their lives. Maude came from an Irish family in one of the smaller industrial towns of New England. Nostalgia crept into her voice as she spoke of the harsh fields on its outskirts where she had played on stony hillsides among weeds sprinkled with the simple blossoms of sorrel and wild daisies. When Austin touched on California, she pressed him with questions, like a child greedy to be assured of reality in the glamorous unreality of a fairy tale.

Their conversation did not lag as the meretricious courses of the dinner came and went. But it had a superficial quality, in spite of their interest in knowing more about one another. They ordered cordials after the black coffee, and talked on.

"We both know that we are talking to kill time," thought Austin. His hand shook a little as he raised a cigarette to his lips.

"If we are to read *Le Pèlerin du Silence*, we must go somewhere where it is quiet," he said at last.

"We must do that."

He found charming the trace of dialect that led her frequently to close a short sentence with the word "that." The skin at the corners of his eyes gathered into fine wrinkles as his eyes smiled at her.

"My place is near by. Will you let me take you there?"

"Yes."

They left the restaurant and walked through several blocks into which night had settled between the rows of gloomy loft buildings. The old houses of Austin's block on 29th Street west of Eighth Avenue were like an oasis.

"Is this quite all right?" Maude asked in sudden hesitation, as he took out his latchkey.

"Quite. My French landlord does not supervise my guests."

They entered the house and turned into Austin's front parlor room. The littered desk and the framed prints that had become to him more familiar than the faces of friends confronted them. But the setting seemed to be negligible to Maude. She stood, pallid and tense, her arms hanging awkwardly, her eyes following Austin as he drew two armchairs close together and arranged a reading lamp. When she sat, it was with a self-conscious rigidity; a cushion that had been placed for her slipped behind her back, and she did not relax against it.

She reminded Austin of a nun. "She is afraid," he commented to himself, but evaded a precise definition of what it was he thought she feared.

"Shall I read now?" he asked.

"Please—from the *Litanies*. Music, color, intoxication— all in one—the *Litanies de la Rose*," she answered, in a surprisingly rich, clear voice.

He took the volume from her, opened it with a sure malice, and read:

"Rose violette, ô modestie des fillettes perverses, rose violette, tes yeux sont plus grands que le reste, fleur hypocrite, fleur du silence.

"Rose rose, pucelle au cœur désordonné, rose rose, robe de mousseline, entr'ouvre tes ailes fausses, ange, fleur hypocrite, fleur du silence.

"Rose en papier de soie, simulacre adorable des grâces incréées, rose en papier de soie, n'es-tu pas la vraie rose, fleur hypocrite, fleur du silence?"

His voice stammered on the words. He threw the book aside, bent from his chair to hers and took Maude in his arms. She came, with a sharp cry, half way to meet him.

Her passion was avid and unrestrained. Her kisses burned his lips with the heat of a flux of life impatient of the incapacity of flesh. Austin's senses leaped to meet the ardor of hers, but the critical demon in his brain functioned relentlessly:

"What a contrast! A nun—an Irish nun—who grew up among sorrel and wild daisies, who loves them still, but who plucks the decadent flowers of Remy de Gourmont's garden. The link is her inherent mysticism. Whatever one thinks about love, passion can be mystical."

He drew her to her feet and carried her, limp against his shoulder, to the alcove at the far end of the room.

Chapter 5

A T THE height of summer, Austin carried out his plan for an apartment. His liking for the old neighborhood drew him to Union Square; it was a part of town where one could remain hidden from cliques and circles, yet be on the edge of everything. The bohemia of Greenwich Village lay immediately to the southwest, and the theatrical district was within walking distance by way of either Broadway or Fifth Avenue. On 14th Street the surf of the East Side broke about the steps of Tammany Hall.

Austin found two rooms in a weather-scarred house at 38 East 16th Street, a few doors west of the square. They were two flights up in the rear, and the windows opened on a wide and almost flat roof that covered an extension from the floor below. One of the rooms was of medium size, and square; it had been a bedchamber in the days when the house had been a private residence. An alcove had been divided into a kitchenette and a bathroom. The other was the hallroom; it connected, but had also a separate door at the head of the stairs.

The approach to this apartment was fantastic in its dusty pride. The street doors were massive and black, and though the stairs were uncarpeted their banisters were the original mahogany. Niches for statues gaped emptily at the turn before each landing. The single gas jet lighted by the negro janitor at twilight projected from the wreckage of a chandelier. Obscure trades had taken possession of the basement and ground floor; until one had mounted beyond them, he was aware of the odor of an illusory and faintly pleasant chemical. Yet the only product in evidence on the sidewalk, awaiting shipment, was a simple variety of wicker basket.

Austin arranged his rooms slowly and with a youthful sense of enjoying a fresh outlet. He bought ordinary furniture, because his tastes did not lie in the direction of novelty in the objects of domestic use. He wanted no more than an adequate setting for his books, his pictures and himself. A light buff wallpaper, green carpets and orange curtains pleased him as a color combination. The larger room proved to be commonplace, with its inevitable bed and chest of drawers for clothes. But he made a library of the small room, and achieved a curious individuality for it. The bookshelves he put up himself were in three groups, one on either side of the window and one beside the door. A wide table, serving as a desk, formed an L with a divan, the latter lying along the far side-wall and stopping against the lowest row of a bookshelf. Austin placed softly cushioned chairs in the open spaces inside the L and between the table and the door. He hung his prints on the two side-walls clear of books. The hermaphrodite Venus, whose calm face might be that of the Cytherean from Milos, gazed at an etching of Swinburne. A Pan with a nymph and a centaur with a nymph, both of the Munich school, flanked the portraits of Anatole France and d'Annunzio. The austere head of Joseph Conrad was set against the Three Fates from the Parthenon.

The little library was at once as cluttered as a museum and imperative in its assertion that nothing there could be spared. And it gave the impression of being large, or providing space for beauty, materialistic or precious. Austin knew that, somehow, it expressed himself.

His finishing touch was to bring down the blue Angora cat from 29th Street. Bluntly obliging, Paul Boissy agreed to sell her and would take only a nominal price. But Mme. Boissy wept. It was clear that parting with one cat among her multitude of cats caused her no especial grief. The ready tears of a sentimental woman of forty-five were shed because she could not bear to see her tenant go.

"She has a warm heart—for the beasts, you understand," said Boissy. "Me she drives about like a slave."

Austin smiled. "Deep down, Mme. Boissy is always thinking how she can be good to everybody."

"Yes, yes," echoed the Frenchman hastily. "One would look far for a better wife."

The Angora was placed in a basket, and Austin carried her in a taxi to 16th Street. With the tip of his finger, he rubbed her nose through the wire grill of the basket and soothed her nervous mewing: But as soon as she was safely upstairs and he had lifted the cover, he chuckled with delight at the self-possession with which she leaped out and started on a tour of investigation. She padded noiselessly from object to object, sniffing at the trailing ends of the bed cover, the seats of the chairs and the corners of the chest of drawers. She jumped on to the mantelpiece, prowled along it, and passed to the top of a bureau, treading delicately and displacing nothing. Returning to the carpet, she slipped into the small room, her tail fluffed out and quivering like a shaken plume.

"All right, Grisette," he said, renaming her on an inspiration. "I know you've got to find out what everything smells like and looks like, and where everything is."

She sauntered back presently, rubbed the whole length of her body against his leg, then made a deliberate choice among the armchairs and sprang into one with a yellow cushion. She licked her right forepaw and commenced to wash her face. She had accepted her new home.

"Will Maude like her?" wondered Austin, and his mind having turned to Maude he considered dispassionately her influence upon his life.

Through the past two months, he and Maude O'Neill had been lovers on a plane of sensuous exaltation more intense than he had known, and that had proved compatible with friendship and the needs of the mind. He perceived that she appealed to him largely because she was intelligent, and that she probably would not have accepted him so quickly if his method of approach had been purely physical. But he found it hard to decide if the relationship between them deserved the name of love. On the whole, he thought that it did. What was love, after all? When he was absent from Maude, he failed to throb with the glamor of a romantic devotion, but she made him long for her presence with a more genuine interest than other women had been able to arouse. Perhaps there was maturity and immaturity in love, as in men.

Austin sighed. He felt that there was a weak point in his reasoning. Nothing, however, could alter the fact that the feminine manifestation of life obsessed him as the poet is obsessed by intangible beauty. He was drawing closer to all women, he told himself, by discovering with one woman a new pathway of the intellect and the flesh.

When Maude came that evening and he had finished showing her the apartment, he seized her willing body in his arms. Their kisses, stabbed through with cries, affirmed that the bond between them had not weakened. The hours following were suave with talk of books and their own rôles in the comedy of existence.

It was a fortuitous chance that had placed Maude and himself in the same office. Frequent meetings were made easy. Austin liked to be able to join her for luncheon, and to walk downtown with her at half-past five. His position on Sloat's Monthly acquired thereby a measure of justification more important in his eyes than the practical advantage he might get from the experience.

Austin knew that he could never be contented with his work in the make-up department of such a magazine. He found it increasingly childish and boring. The good-hearted Hagen tried to widen his opportunities by giving him manuscripts to read and urging him to try his hand at the singular outbursts of editorial quackery which appeared under each title in a number, and which were known professionally as blurbs. Seeing that stories which did not falsify success or sex were doomed in advance, and seeing that the blurbs were invariably touched up to a unique point of hysteria by Guy Bent, the efforts of an assistant editor were thankless.

Austin did not admire Guy Bent. He was a product of the American business world, juggled by Fate into the management of a group of magazines instead of the advertising agency for which he would have been ideally fitted. He made good, nevertheless, this strutting, irritable little man whose mind was a collection of rubber-stamps of publicity. The magazines steadily gained in circulation, and apparently Walter Rupert Sloat asked for no other result.

Sloat spent much time at his newspaper offices, but he seldom visited his magazines. He was satisfied with looking at dummies made of the final page proofs, which were carried to him reverentially by one or other of the editors. His opinion was non-existent, so far as the lesser members of the staff knew. In the building on 42nd Street, as with the general public, his personality was veiled behind a fog.

A day arrived, however, when Austin was allowed a glimpse within the circle of the fog.

The September number, which went to press on July 20, had been giving trouble toward the last. A special article, thought to contain dynamite in the way of libel, had been altered again and again by the author, the legal bureau and the editors. It still seemed dangerous in its final form to Hagen, who darted with the proofs to consult Guy

Bent. He was back in a few minutes. His face wore a harassed expression.

"Mr. Bent thinks it's all right, boys," he announced, moving jerkily from desk to desk, his voice unnecessarily solemn. "But he says we'd better get the O.K. of the big boss. These pages have got to be taken to Mr. Sloat's house right away. I can't go myself—damn it! Appointment with the engraver. What about you, Bride? Do you know how to reach Mr. Sloat?"

"I know where he lives," replied Austin drily.

"Yes—but his secretary and the butler, they've never seen you. Well, it's all right. I'll give you a card."

Hagen scribbled a brief identification on a card and thrust it along with the proofs into Austin's hands. "Don't let 'em stall you, and be back quickly, there's a good fellow."

Austin rode uptown, his general curiosity concerning Walter Rupert Sloat stimulated. As he had imagined, reaching the publisher, in the circumstances, proved to be the reverse of difficult. At the small private palace on Park Avenue, he was at once shown to an anteroom, and after the telephone had been used he was told to walk into the study beyond. He saw there a tall man pacing beside a table and scrutinizing a pair of silver-mounted pistols which he held in either hand. Austin had heard of Sloat's penchant for ancient weapons. As he watched him now, the latter was apparently too absorbed in the fine points of his pistols to be aware he was no longer alone.

But Sloat looked up almost immediately and nodded.

His features were extraordinary. His eyes were set close
to a long, straight nose that ran down to a mouth baggy
yet tightly clamped. The chin was blunted, without reced-
ing. Unlike most long faces, the salient points were round
instead of sharp. It was structurally the face of a chipmunk,
but the expression was malignant and dissipated, as if the
soul of a ferret had taken possession of a chipmunk. A
muddy, dark complexion enhanced the effect.

Austin explained the problem of the dangerous article,
and Sloat rather listlessly took the page proofs. The publisher moved to a chair behind the table and read the
paragraphs which had been marked.

"No sense bothering me with this," he commented. "It
is only an attack on a man whose reputation would make
him look sick in a witness box. I print more risky things
in the newspapers every day."

He scrawled an O.K. and handed the proofs back to
Austin. His voice ran on with scarcely a break, as he
changed the subject.

"Mr. Bright—Bride," he said, searching his memory.
"You're on the staff of the Monthly, eh?"

"Assistant make-up editor, Mr. Sloat."

"Well, young man, you have to read the magazine more
closely than most people do. What do you think of it?"

"I think it is good business," answered Austin coolly.
"It never fails to be popular stuff—thirty-five cents' worth
of what its buyers expect to get."

Sloat's lips unclamped into a loose smile. "The newsdealers agree with you. But analyze the selling-appeal, if you can."

"The magazine is consistently easy reading," said Austin, "the ideas are predigested, and the illustrations catch the eye."

"You are right enough. You might add that it dishes dirt," sneered Sloat. "The public wants dirt with gilding on it. Why not give it to 'em? I take it, you don't advise me to go in for uplifting American literature."

"I am not attempting to advise you, sir."

"I see. You gave me straight answers to my questions from my point of view, not necessarily from yours. That was sensible. You are all right."

Sloat bent over his pistols and examined the chased silver mountings. Without looking up, he extended a soft, moist palm for a handshake, and the caller was dismissed.

Austin felt that he had discovered nothing about Sloat. An obvious assumption that he was cynical had been confirmed, that was all.

At the office, Hagen seized the proofs and rejoiced vociferously at the O.K. that made it possible to close those pages without delay. Then a flood of final proofs poured in from the printer and he wallowed at a momentarily untidy desk, suffering agonies because no changes except a few of major importance could be made.

"My God!" he exclaimed. "Here's a dull caption. We've simply got to have a line with more pep in it. See what you can do, Bride."

He threw a page across to Austin. It was from a story by a

well-advertised nonentity and carried an illustration showing a girl cowering on a chair, while two men in tuxedos,
their chests inflated, threatened to exchange blows. The
scene was a night club; scandalized onlookers were indicated in the background. The caption, a speech by the
more respectable-looking man, read lamely enough:

"What do you mean by bringing that girl here?"

Austin ran through the text and found the speech in an
adjoining column. With a wry smile, he altered it in both
places to:

"You'd force your mistress upon decent people, would
you?"

The correction pleased Hagen. He chirped "Good
boy!" and put the proof in the envelope for the printer. It
was understood that the September number must be closed
that day, and that all the pages would be cast in the foundry
before fresh proofs were shown. By working overtime, the
editorial department had ended its task at seven o'clock,
and was prepared to resume its normal leisurely pace in
dealing with October.

But two days later, a peremptory message was brought
by Guy Bent's secretary. Mr. Bent wanted to see Mr.
Hagen, Mr. Bride and Mr. Thompson, the second assistant
make-up editor, together and at once. As far as his cheerful
cast of countenance would permit, Hagen looked worried.
He signed to Austin and Thompson, and the three walked
to the inner temple of editorial power.

Guy Bent was sitting behind a desk that set an example
in naked orderliness to all other desks. The shortness of his

body was undisguisable, but he kept his shoulders squared and his head straight and rigid. Thereby, he achieved a sort of military effect. A clipped mustache hardened the line of his upper lip. By scowling and slightly drawing in his chin, he was able to create the semblance of jowls, such as one associates with the colonel of a militia regiment. Austin saw that he held the proofs of the September number, complete.

"I have called you here because one of you is responsible for a horrible blunder," snapped Bent. "Your duties make it possible for it to be any one of you, so I want you all to hear it thrashed out."

None of the three editors, standing like schoolboys in front of the desk, could well answer a charge that had not yet been stated, and after a pause Bent continued:

"I had been feeling proud as I looked over this number of the magazine. It seemed like the best we had ever turned out. Corking fiction, inspiring articles, splendid pictures. I thought of the pleasure it was going to give Mr. Sloat, the credit that it would earn for the whole staff. And then I came upon a caption—" he struck the paper with his fingers—"a caption which had been rewritten at the last moment, and in which a low, nasty word was used. The word was mistress! Something about forcing a *mistress* upon decent people! Who, in God's name, had the rotten judgment to do that?"

"I wrote the caption, Mr. Bent," said Austin. For the moment, he was too astounded to be either resentful or amused.

"Well, let me tell you, Mr. Bride, you have spoiled my day for me. When I think of the word mistress appearing under an illustration in Sloat's Monthly, I feel just sick. A magazine that lies on reading tables in the best homes, where innocent girls and children have access to it!"

"There are stories about mistresses in every issue," asserted Austin, beginning to go cold with anger.

"That is beside the point," groaned Bent. "Frank situations, even frank words, in the text are justified, because the author leads the reader along to a moral conclusion. There is no excuse for misunderstanding. But think of the people who might pick up the magazine and prejudge it as being nasty because of a suggestive caption. The Vice Society regards the way illustrations are handled as being very important. Please get it into your head that, as a first requirement, Sloat's must *look* clean."

"As the head of the department, I am really the responsible one. I ordered the original caption rewritten, and I put the page through," said Hagen, impressed and grave.

"I know, Hagen, I know," answered Bent. "Everything I have told Mr. Bride applies to you, too."

Austin felt sorry for Hagen. He reminded him of a boy at the head of his class, who has unexpectedly incurred the teacher's wrath. Of course, Hagen was responsible, and of course he should resign after the humiliating way in which they had all been treated. But he appeared to have no idea of doing so.

"Mr. Bent, did you ever hear any one say that a popular magazine should dish dirt, that the most profitable stuff to put in a magazine was discreetly gilded dirt?" demanded Austin on a sardonic note.

Bent looked startled. "That is no way to phrase our policy," he declared hastily. "But this whole incident of the caption is closed. Don't let a blunder of the kind occur again."

"Absolutely no chance of it occurring through me. Your eloquence has convinced me I should be quit of this job at once."

"I said nothing about your doing that. Don't sulk," cried the editor-in-chief irritably.

"I prefer to look for something else—for my own peace of mind, shall we say?"

Bent shrugged his shoulders, and Austin turned and walked from the office. Before he had reached his desk, Hagen had overtaken him.

"Don't mind Bent," pleaded Hagen. "He talks in that violent way because he thinks it is good for discipline."

"He can go to hell," replied Austin in bland tones.

"But what will you do, old man?"

"Look for another job."

"You have nothing in mind?"

"No."

"Well, I'll write you, or run down to see you some evening. I may be able to give you a live tip."

"All right. It's good of you to bother."

Austin shook hands with Hagen, and going on to his desk he collected his belongings for another migration.

Chapter 6

THE evening of the day he left Sloat's Monthly chanced to be one for which Austin had no engagements. Maude was dining with an aunt from Boston, and on account of his love affair he had been neglecting the few acquaintances who would otherwise have shared his time. He rejected the idea of looking up any of them. He was not in a mood for casual company.

On the whole, his mood was gay, with the humor of a personality that was detached from the main currents of existence and that took a spectator's pleasure even in those comedies in which he played a rôle. Austin was conscious of a somewhat malicious satisfaction in having been able to throw up his job in just the circumstances that had arisen. Scorning all moral propaganda, he did not regard his action as a protest against the hypocrisy of Guy Bent. But it had been priceless to hear him rage at the word mistress—a word that had been vulgarized, to be sure, but that described admirably the frailer heroines that twittered through the pages of the magazine. It had been a salve to his boredom to resign after a sermon on virtue by Guy Bent, the representative of Walter Rupert Sloat; it had been a thing to remember and put into a novel some day.

When Austin was not employed in the service of women or books, he was drawn by the magnetism of crowds. It amused him to go to a summer beach resort, or merely to walk up Broadway from Herald Square to the Circle, and to find every time a new cinematograph of obscure impulses portrayed by the twitching facial muscles, the gestures, of people he would never know. He liked to go to genuinely popular entertainments in search of another form of wordless drama—the response of the audience to the arena or the stage. Crudity in individuals repelled him, but he enjoyed the gross humor of crowds. He had always been attracted by vaudeville.

That evening, Austin took the Broadway subway at Union Square and got out at 42nd Street about nine o'clock. The long summer day was not fully over. The sky in the west was a luminous green, and the streets had a hard clarity, as if they were giving out a little of the sunshine they had absorbed. The electric signs glittered and throbbed in a disorderly pageant along the upper line of the buildings. In half an hour they would dominate, but for the moment they were like fireworks released too early.

Austin drifted with a tide of women in muslin and georgette, of straw-hatted men in serge and palm beach suits. His eyes lingered on the necks and bare arms of the girls and took no count, for that once, of their faces. It was surprising how few skins were bad, no matter how ill-shaped the bodies might be. He had often remarked the point, and given New York the credit. Even the hordes of young Jewesses, with the Ghetto one generation behind them, had smooth, sweet skins. They might be huge-breasted, short-thighed and thick-ankled, but they had been bathed in the wine and milk of the air of Manhattan.

Continuing up Broadway, Austin crossed at 47th Street to Seventh Avenue. The facade of the Palace Theatre blazed in front of him. The photographs af variety stars in large frames were set on either side of the lobby. An illuminated programme to the left of the entrance proclaimed a wealth of headliners, whose appearances had been calculated to the minute. Miss Patricola, "The Scintillating Melodist"— 9:45; Joe Cook—10:05; Cleo Mayfield and Cecil Lean, in "Look Who's Here!"—10:25.

Austin bought an orchestra seat and entered the Palace. He caught the tag-end of a dialogue between two lesser comedians.

"I've admired women for their youth, their beauty, their intelligence, and their wit. But my feeling for you, Mother, is just plain love," declared the male actor.

The woman, made up as a caricature of a feministic wife, protested that the requirements of her sex had become complicated, and obtained the answer:

"The first duty of a woman is to be a mother. Her second duty is to be a *good* mother."

The audience rocked with an enjoyment that shaded from naïve approval to an appreciation of low-brow satire. Austin wondered which of the two motives was the stronger, in which of them the comedians placed most confidence for the applause they got. The perspiring faces in the half-light about him were at the same time simple and unsentimental, the faces of urban wiseacres in fear only of not laughing in tune with the mob spirit of their mercurial generation.

The act was over before he could form an opinion, and a thin, ardent girl, with hair as pale as flax, took vehement possession of the stage. She offered herself as the incarnation of Times Square, as the mouthpiece of all the unsung damsels who bring ambitions to market. A single form of expression did not suffice her. She recited a monologue that parodied adroitly the technique taught by some school of dramatics, then danced to a syncopated number composed for her glory, and at the periods in her imaginary song when the chorus would have been due she sang a quatrain modernized from an old hit. "I'm the Only Star that Twinkles on Broadway," she exulted, and put into the words a nuance of illusion, of new-born dreams embraced as being already true because she dreamed them.

It was art of a kind, and Austin leaned forward in a mood of superficial admiration such as vaudeville often gave him. The girl was throwing her long legs about the stage. Her gray eyes shone in her childish, pointed face. Her flat chest and fragile arms were somehow pathetic.

The audience was silent and attentive. Heads were being nodded, and there was a facile sparkle in a number of eyes. "They find romance in this," thought Austin. "It is odd. They lack sentiment, but keep a place for romance in their hearts. There is a difference between the two emotions."

He took no pleasure in the following act, which gave

five sturdy acrobats an opportunity to swing on trapezes and build pyramids with moist, pink bodies from which muscles bulged unbeautifully. But he laughed at the wild antics of "The Scintillating Melodist," the savorous vulgarity of her songs, the irony with which she built up the conviction that she was not yet middle-aged and then produced an adolescent son to share her applause. He listened happily to the curious drawl in Cleo Mayfield's voice, and was glad that in her case no flame of temperament had burned scars upon her blond comeliness.

The luxurious night, as caressing as a night in the tropics, but with an undertone of northern vigor, encouraged him to walk home after he left the theatre. He loitered down Broadway, his flesh responding to the warm breeze, his eyes enchanted by the faces of women that stood out for an instant and were gone in the surge of humanity under the lights. Only after he had passed the zone of night life, and was between tall, dark buildings in the Twenties, did he begin to hasten his steps.

The short block in East Sixteenth Street, where Austin lived, had only one lamp on either sidewalk and made a somber appearance. As he approached the house, he saw a dim figure leaning against the railing at the top of the stoop. It was vaguely familiar, and he watched it until he had mounted to its side and found himself with Maude O'Neill.

"Austin, I thought you'd never get here," she said, with an unexpected note of tragedy in her voice.

"We did not have an engagement for this evening, my

dear," he answered tranquilly. "Why should I suppose you'd come down? Has anything happened?"

"Anything happened! You have left the magazine, Austin."

"Yes. But how does that figure as a tragedy—between us, I mean?"

"You walked out of the office without even stopping off downstairs to tell me," declared Maude obliquely.

"I know. You don't understand the situation. I got into a sort of row with Guy Bent, and resigned on the spot. Every one had his eyes on me. It would have created a peculiar impression if I had run straight down to you. Give me a chance to tell you the whole story."

"Oh, but I'm not angry! Really, Austin! Just worried a little. This may prevent us from seeing so much of each other. One of the girls told me you'd left, and I could think of nothing else during dinner with my aunt. I escaped about ten o'clock and came here. When you didn't answer the bell, I knew you were out, so I waited."

"I see. Let's go on up, now."

Austin was conscious of a certain ennui at her illogical worrying. He had intended to telephone early the next morning, a move she might well have taken for granted.

He opened the street door, and before climbing the stairs he looked in his letter box. There was a special delivery letter from Hagen, which he slipped unopened into his pocket. Preceded by Maude, he went on up the ill-lit flights to the apartment, humming under his breath the air of one of Cleo Mayfield's songs. Grisette leaped from a

chair and ran, crying in feeble, staccato mews, to greet
him. He lifted her against his breast and offered Maude
her back to stroke. But the girl touched the cat listlessly.

"Where did you go this evening?" she asked.

"To a vaudeville show."

"And do you mean that? The name vaudeville makes
me think of negro minstrels and ventriloquists and men
dressed as tramps who come on the stage and give long,
stupid monologues. Does it amuse you?"

"Certainly," smiled Austin. "I mean, clever vaudeville
acts amuse me—not the things you mention, which are
somewhat out of date at the Palace Theatre, my dear."

She did not pursue the subject. Sitting very straight
on the edge of a chaise-longue in the large room, her hands
clasped on her knees, she was silent for a while. Then she
asked, her real preoccupation showing itself again:

"You won't take a job that will make it harder for us
to meet, will you Austin? Newspaper work, or anything
at all like that?"

"Newspaper work—no!" he protested. "I shall never go
back on a newspaper."

"What, then?"

"Oh, something connected with a magazine, or book
publishing! I don't care much."

"You are sure you will stay in New York?"

"Of course," answered Austin, surprised. "I hate all other
American cities, except San Francisco, and I can't imagine
a job that would take me there." He played with the
memories awakened by his mention of San Francisco. "It

would be like going back to school, to return to San Francisco now," he added.

"I'm glad you—you would not leave New York," she stammered. "If we could only find a way of being together even more than we've been! The evenings I don't see you, I'm so wretched." A note of extreme discontent was in her voice. "The stupid hotel for women, where I live. And all that." Her words trailed off, ineloquent and sad.

Suddenly, Austin perceived what was passing in her mind. She was making an indirect plea to him for a closer relationship. Not marriage, perhaps, but its practical equivalent. She would be satisfied if he pressed her to come and live with him, if in that way he gave her proof that his love was deep enough to make him want to risk the common identification of their lives. He thought quickly, and without conscious selfishness. The problem seemed to him to be a clear-cut thing, a matter for the reason rather than the heart. For the first time, he realized that he shrank from responsibilities in love. Other women had not wanted him to assume them. Elizabeth, for instance, in her shallow, kind way, had avoided placing the least responsibility upon him. He had been spoiled, maybe, but the result had been to give him a distaste for sacrificing any part of his freedom. How feminine it was of Maude to derive an impulse toward a domestic arrangement from the first convenient crisis—his leaving the magazine, as it happened—a crisis that had no real bearing on the question. Feminine, and dangerous! He must say something that would make it difficult for her to become more articulate.

"My dear, we can see each other as often as we like now. It's an advantage that I have left Sloat's," he told her. "You know how we did not want our friendship to attract too much attention up there. We sometimes did not make engagements on that account."

"Yes, it will be easier so. I had always to be thinking of gossip among the girls," agreed Maude, hesitantly.

"We might find it better for me to move farther down town, near you," he went on, as deceptive himself as a woman.

"You would give up this apartment, Austin?" she exclaimed, an obvious doubt of its permanence as a possible home stealing over her.

"If there seemed to be any advantage. Not right away, of course. A new job is what I must think of first." ·

He remembered the letter from Hagen, and took it out of his pocket. A typewritten letter with a meticulous note in the lower left-hand corner, "Dictated but not read." Austin could picture the amiable German-American telephoning here and there in his behalf and calling his neatest stenographer at the last moment to transmit the result.

"If you don't lose any time, I think you can land with Charlotte Moore as a publicity man," wrote Hagen. "Go to see Ed Crampton, the head of her press department—602 Seventh Avenue. He is looking for an assistant, and would take some one who had never done that sort of work before, so long as he had had newspaper experience. Ed is a good scout. Tell him I sent you. I can't say whether Miss Moore butts in a great deal. It may be you would find yourself working under a woman, and you might not like that. But I advise you, if you can get the job, to give it a trial."

Austin's interest was sharply piqued. Charlotte Moore in the past fifteen years had made her personality felt in grand opera. The public adored her, and the critics disputed whether she should be considered the best American woman singer. It was admitted that she brought a finer intelligence than any one else to the dramatic phase of an art grown stiff with conventions. Austin had seen her once in "Carmen," and from in front of the footlights had found her a keen flame of temperament. He had hoped to interview her some day for his newspaper, but had not done so. He smiled now at the obtuseness which had led Hagen to suggest he might not like to work under a woman like Charlotte Moore.

"I am always surprised and grateful when a man does anything for me, because I put myself out so little for men. Here is Hagen writing me about a good job," he told Maude, replacing the letter in its envelope.

"In town?" murmured the girl, her head very straight on its long neck, against a background of shadows.

"Yes—in New York," he answered, and kissed her, a trifle absent-mindedly.

Chapter 7

WHEN Austin Bride arrived at the offices on Seventh Avenue to see Ed Crampton, his ears were assailed, even in the corridor of the building, by the laughter of a patently crude and jocund man. Brief interjections cut into the clamor of merriment some story had aroused. The sounds suggested the bar of a club of sporting tendencies, rather than the headquarters of a prima donna.

Austin was standing in front of a door, on the frosted glass of which the name Charlotte Moore was lettered modestly. In the lower left hand corner appeared the further information: General Offices—Press Department. He found it a little odd that a singer should need an elaborate business establishment. The press agents of most singers functioned from a hotel.

He turned the handle and entered a reception room, where a plain girl in a high white collar and cuffs asked what she could do for him. Austin gave her a card for Crampton. A few minutes later, two men, both laughing immoderately, came from an inner office and shook hands at the door. The more hilarious one had iron-gray hair and a rosy face cast in a mold that suggested he might once have been an ideal type for the pulpit or the stage.

This individual said Good-bye to his friend, and then addressed Austin.

"Mr. Hagen sent you to see me, I believe," he said, his voice calming down in perceptible jerks.

He led Austin to his private office and asked a number of questions about his experience. They were perfunctory questions, and the man who posed them said so freely.

"It don't matter whether you're a sharp on grand opera, so long as you know what will make a good story and how to sling the English language. If you've worked on newspapers, you oughta be on to what they'll print. Oughta, I say, because there's no way of telling until you've tried. Publicity is a funny thing, boy. It comes natural to some of us to put it across, and others never will learn. When I hire a man, it's with the idea of trying him out. I take a chance and he takes a chance, and if he don't make good I fire him and there's not much harm done. That's fair enough, ain't it?"

Austin assumed that this bizarre person wrote less colloquially than he talked. He had met press agents before, and was aware that many of the older school associated an uncouth patter with the professional air. Why, however, he asked himself, should Charlotte Moore have chosen such a press agent?

"We're branching out here, I'd have you know," went on Crampton pompously. "Miss Moore is figuring on starting her own opera house. I'm about ready to spring that news, and there's no reason why every newspaper and magazine in the country shouldn't run our stuff. I need a bright young assistant. Sixty dollars a week, huh! Want to take a whirl at it?"

"Yes. I can start any time you say."

"That's the way to talk, boy."

It jarred Austin to be addressed as "boy," but it was clear that Crampton thought it the comradely thing to ascribe extreme youth to all his associates. "What story have you got in mind for me to do first, old man?" he asked, with studied rudeness.

The sarcasm went over Crampton's head. He even beamed at what he thought to be the democratic spirit. "Well, I'll tell you. You can just sit around and twiddle your thumbs for a few days," he said. "Miss Moore is in Washington for a conference with some big guns who may back her. When she returns, she'll maybe have a new slant on the campaign."

"I should think Miss Moore would be very easy to publicize. Editors know that the public wants to read about her," stated Austin, half to himself.

"That's right. Or it oughta be right." Crampton leaned forward confidentially. "But she makes it hard for her press agent. Let me give you a tip about Charlotte Moore. She's full of highflown ideas, and there's some of the regular tricks of this game she won't stand for. She passes on every piece of copy before it is released. Pull any rough stuff, and she's off the handle in a minute. Temperamental as hell."

"You mean, she won't let you pretend, for instance, that she has received a black-hand letter from the Mafia, threatening her with death unless she consecrates her voice to Italian opera?"

"That's about what I mean. Of course, when any one is as close to her as I am—" Crampton composed his features artificially and assumed a measured tone more equivocal than a wink—"a fellow who has her confidence and all that, why he can manage her pretty well. But she don't know a thing about you. You'll have to deal with her direct sometimes, and it'll help you to bear in mind what I told you."

Austin was familiar with the cheap vanity of men like Crampton, who lose no chance to infer that women the world desires have looked with favor upon them. In this case, the maneuver seemed more preposterous than usual. A wave of disgust passed over him. He could not believe that Charlotte Moore was wanting in good taste, and suddenly he formed the opinion that Crampton, from more points of view than one, was playing the great American game of bluff.

He arranged definitely to come to work the next morning, then wandered to the street with no plans for the afternoon of liberty before him. Seventh Avenue near 54th Street, where the office building stood, was a highway of little charm. But Austin went on to 57th Street and turned east. He liked the serried brownstone houses that had begun to surrender grudgingly their basements and first floors to trades connected with the modes. All the phases of the persistent, the colossal, rebuilding of New York had a fascination for him. He drew a parallel with

San Francisco before the earthquake, where he had been brought up. Most of the houses in San Francisco had been of wood, flimsy frame structures that their owners knew were temporary, and that gave way by the thousands every year to the permanence of stone. But New York, which generations ago had pushed the frame building to the outskirts of Brooklyn and the Bronx, was in as furious a haste of metamorphosis as San Francisco. It experimented, like a frontier town, with architectural makeshifts. The square miles of brownstone would go, and no less surely the earlier skyscrapers were doomed. Only a few vast monuments, such as the Pennsylvania Station and the Woolworth Tower, were certain of surviving in the unimaginable future city.

Austin walked down the broad sweep of 57th Street as far as Third Avenue, where smaller houses of discolored, sun-scaled brick began to appear. Beyond lay a vague, poor neighborhood. The Manhattan end of the Blackwell's Island Bridge started there. But a trip to the bridge did not appeal to him. He remembered that there were second-hand bookstores on 59th Street near Park Avenue, and he strayed with a quickening interest toward them.

Among the several bookstores, he chose one where former visits had proved to him that the attendant possessed the rare virtue of knowing books. She was a woman of thirty, the daughter of the proprietor, an unemotional, dusty woman, with a bony chest but delicate hands. She greeted Austin by his name, smiling distantly. He wondered whether she had ever had a lover.

"What has been written about Charlotte Moore, the singer?" he asked her.

"I do not know of any biography. Nearly every volume by a music critic has at least a chapter about her."

The woman rummaged through a block of shelves and brought him half a dozen books. He leaned against a counter and read a page here and there. But the criticism was technical and dull. He had often noticed that writers on music moved in a devitalized world of their own, employed a difficult terminology in an effort to create drama out of abstractions. The personality of Charlotte Moore had escaped them all, though the verbose hack, John Willoughby, succeeded in painting a florid picture of a beautiful body with a good voice which he declared to be America's pride and glory, and revealed by his naïve rhapsodies as being, incidentally, his own hopeless lust. Austin bought the Willoughby book. It would be amusing later, he thought, to compare its Park Row impressionism with the living woman.

He spent the rest of the afternoon in a leisurely circuit of the shop. Assailed by the temptation to select armfuls of volumes he might not read for years, he controlled himself by the boyish pretense that from all those shelves he was allowed one more book that day. He ended by taking two, an item of Americana dealing with the Huguenot settlers on Staten Island, and the poems of Nora May French. The last was a find, a copy of the only edition attained by the young genius who put an end to her life's fever at Carmel-by-the-Sea, in 1907. Austin already had a copy of the poems, but he could not resist buying another, because it was rare.

Nora May French and Charlotte Moore. The dead and the living. A characteristic coupling for one who loved books and women, he thought.

He found in the next few days that the press agent had been right when he had said there would be no work to do until Miss Moore got back. Sitting by a window that looked down on jumbled roofs stretching to the Hudson, Austin had abundant time in which to think about his new calling, while Crampton entertained a procession of theatrical and sporting friends.

Then, one morning, the office was abruptly restored to dignified activity by the prima donna's arrival. She passed by Austin's desk—a tall woman, dressed quietly in a blue serge suit and a small, smart hat that seemed to have molded itself about her brown hair. He observed that her features were so proportioned as to make a handsome, strong face, rather than a pretty one. Her eyes were exceptionally steady. One divined the torso and thighs of a Greek marble.

Austin was not presented to her. She had noticed him only in so far as she had included him in her general smile of greeting. He contented himself with dwelling on his first impression and fixing it in his memory, while Crampton, who had become businesslike and grammatical, made frequent trips from his room to hers with documents.

It was Friday, and Charlotte Moore did not come to the office the next day. On Monday, she was there early.

Crampton joined her for what he announced as an important conference. Conference was one of his favorite words. But after he had conferred for less than ten minutes, he hurried back.

"Look here, Bride," he said, "Miss Moore wants to try you on our new campaign. I guess there's going to be enough work to keep us both busy from now on. Go in and talk to her. Show her you're a live wire, boy."

A subtle sharpening of his gift of observation possessed Austin as he entered Charlotte Moore's office. He felt analytical, but not impersonal. This woman, he speculated, must be interesting in a degree altogether out of the common. He was glad of the chance to move closer to her.

She was at a small mahogany desk, and at once he noticed that she had it placed so as to give her the best light instead of taking advantage of the usual executive's trick of sitting with her back to the light and rendering her face almost invisible to a caller. She did not need to fear close scrutiny. Nothing could detract from the beauty of her broad forehead and her features which sketched simple, bold lines, like those of a medal in high relief. Her skin was rouged and powdered with an adroit parsimoniousness that smoothed it without troubling to conceal the fact that she must be forty years old. An infinitesimal sagging of the cheeks on a level with the upper lip gave her an air of fatigue, but there were no wrinkles visible.

"This is Mr. Bride?" she said, shaking hands, then motioning him to the chair at the opposite side of the desk.

"Yes, Miss Moore. I hope you will regard me today as

some one who has come to interview you. I do not know
your plans, or what you want me to write. But if you'll talk
to me as you would to a reporter you felt was eager to
find out all about you and print everything you said, I
may be able to get a certain freshness into my work. Editors
refuse to use a lot of press agent material because it is cut-
and-dried. I hope to avoid that." He spoke slowly, develop-
ing an idea that had crystallized in the moment he had
been with her.

"Very interesting," she replied, staring hard at him.
"Let us try it. Do you want to ask me questions?"

"Please tell me first what project you intend to put before the public. Assume that Mr. Crampton has not even
dropped a hint to me."

"An American theater—a really national theater, where
I can produce good operas, intelligent plays. I would appear in some of them, of course—those in which there was
a suitable rôle for me. My trip to Washington was for the
purpose of getting the support of rich men. A non-com-
mercial venture in art cannot live on popular subscrip-
tions: a patron is as necessary as he was in the Middle
Ages. Maybe, you had better not say that in our publicity,
but I tell you what I think in order that you may understand me. Senator Arbuthnot of Delaware has pledged me
fifty thousand dollars, which I shall use to take an option
on a site in West 57th Street. I shall build my own theater
there."

"You do not feel you could work through the New York
Opera Company? In order to hold you, would they not

provide for almost anything you demanded in your next contract?"

"I hate the New York Opera Company," she answered, with startling vehemence. She panted, then smiled with an enigmatic tightening of the corners of her lips.

"Why, Miss Moore?"

"You are right. I should explain my hatred. The directors of the Opera have got the usual view of success. They want to break records every season, in a popular, superficial way. The longest list of traditional masterpieces. The best-advertised foreign novelties, as long as these are not so radical as to shock their subscribers. An occasional American score in the good-Indian manner, to show that we can imitate Grieg or Puccini. If I were to insist on experimenting, they would allow it—yes, but they would feature the eccentricity of Charlotte Moore, not her art or the value of the opera she had discovered."

"Their methods probably bring the largest possible number of New Yorkers to the box office," asserted Austin dispassionately. "Would you mind if, in your own theater, the audiences proved to be small?"

"No," she answered. "I would be quite fatalistic about it. I sing and act in order to create an aesthetic thrill between myself and the people who admire me. I like to be applauded, and so I prefer big audiences to little ones. But if I were doing exactly what I wanted, I'd be satisfied with the sense of freedom that carried me along and the knowledge that my backers would never deprive me of the money I needed to continue experimenting. My following would enjoy itself with me. Some day I might find the thing that appealed to a great public. And if I never did, I would leave the work to a successor."

"You would try to be modern and original?"

"Not necessarily modern, but always original."

"What theme interests you most?"

"America. I am looking for the right composer to do an opera in jazz. It's not very clear to me how it could be handled, but I'm certain jazz is our contribution to music and that it could be used to express America."

"You would not be afraid of the critics, if you sang jazz?"

"No. The critics laugh at all experiments in art. I would expect to conquer them."

"You have an epicurean attitude toward life, and yet in art you are a fanatic," said Austin, astonished and charmed at the contrast.

"A fanatic? Yes, Mr. Bride. I do not mind admitting it to any one shrewd enough to call me one."

"It is only another term for concentrated energy."

"That is a good definition."

She kept her gray eyes steadily on his face, and he returned her look, wondering at her scorn of reservations.

"Anything more?" she prompted him.

"Only some figures, Miss Moore. The fact that you have an option on the site in 57th Street is news that the papers will surely be glad to print. But we must also tell them what this and that is going to cost, provide rows of ciphers for them to play with. The bare news story will lead up to the article about you that I think can be syndicated in Sunday magazines all over the country."

They bent together over contracts and plans, and she showed him what figures could be made public.

"Remember, my theater cannot be rushed like a new apartment house," she said. "It may be a year or more before I can build. I must sing for the New York Opera Company next season."

"Yes, and please trust me to write like a reporter who's tremendously interested, but who's really serving you and not a newspaper."

She nodded and smiled. "I'm sure you'll know how not to be indiscreet. Take as much time as you like, but let me see it as soon as it's finished."

Austin left her and returned to his desk. He staved off Crampton's curiosity concerning the interview by making entirely noncommittal replies to the volley of questions with which the press agent was primed. Miss Moore wanted to test out the value of his newspaper experience, asserted Austin; yes, she had fully explained what she required in the way of publicity. Crampton bored him. He felt that he must get away from his neighborhood, in order to concentrate on his ripening plan.

Excusing himself, he walked downtown to his rooms, and began to sketch out on his typewriter an article about Charlotte Moore. The next day, he telephoned to the office to say that he would not be there. He had finished the article by the middle of the week. It was in the form of an exploitation of her personality, her views, such as the

Sunday magazines of newspapers spread lavishly before their clientele of sensation-seekers. But though Austin drew on his experience to produce an example of the preferred formula, he introduced a subtle thread of propaganda which a reporter would have had no interest in devising. Going beyond what she had said to him, he quoted the singer as believing the things that he believed of her, the things that would be glamorous to a special public.

He titled the article, "Charlotte Moore to be First Woman Impresario," and added the subhead, "Diva Talks on the Fun Millionaires Miss." The exclamatory journalese of the words caused him to grin sardonically at himself.

Charlotte Moore, he had written, was about to give New York grand opera and plays in a new way, and for new motives. She was not going to furnish art for the profits it might bring. Profits would always be incidental with her. She was going to manage her own theater because she did not want to be hampered in entertaining the public and herself at the same time. A performance well executed, fully enjoyed, was a result in itself, the most satisfactory possible result of an artist's efforts. If the reader thought this quixotic, it was because he had a habit of mind formed by the dreary commercialism of the masculine age in which he had been brought up. It was, on the other hand, distinctly practical—due to the fact that a woman would carry it out. Women had proved in business that they could be just as efficient as men, but any one who had observed the workings of an office ruled by women must have noticed that they found their intrinsic reward in the work accomplished, to a far greater degree than did men. Men had commenced by inventing units of money as the counters in the game of finance. But they had become obsessed by the counters, and had partially lost sight of the game. Millionaires continued to work for money, instead of using it to produce things of intangible value which might happen to seem beautiful to them. Charlotte Moore, it was true, had received some backing from rich men, but her backers constituted a very small proportion of the millionaires of America. The majority were not getting so much fun as they might out of their fortunes. They should relinquish the idea that every dollar spent should be justified by economic or obviously educational returns, to themselves or even to the public. Let them build useless marble temples in the parks, if they liked architecture, or publish magnificent volumes below cost price to glorify their hobbies, if they liked books. Charlotte Moore intended to enjoy herself to the full with her theater and, seeing she was not rich, she would make it pay its way as a secondary consideration.

Austin felt that he had written an interview that would be published without an alteration by Sunday newspapers. Editors would be quick to see that the views it advanced would be eagerly read and discussed. It would flatter the men already supporting Miss Moore, and it might induce others to help her. But he was assailed by a newborn doubt as to whether she would approve of his methods.

"I have done my best for her, and it must stand. She can do no more than tell me to take lessons from Crampton. In that case, I shall resign," he thought.

He went to the office and left the article on Charlotte Moore's desk. She was not in. It was late in the afternoon, so he looked over some unimportant memoranda from Crampton, and then strolled out again.

"Was I sound in crediting women with being less mercenary than men?" he asked himself. "I have an instinctive feeling about it, and it makes a good story; but is it sound?"

The question occupied him, though not deeply, as he turned up Broadway on one of the long walks he liked to take in his half-conscious search for the essence of New York. The upper stretches of the great road, planted with trees, lined with apartment houses the ground floors of which were given over to shops, reminded him of Europe. Yes, Broadway above 72nd Street began to look like a Paris boulevard. There were no cafés, no tables on the sidewalk, but the shops were small and not too busy, and urban life flowed with a special charm because of the dappled shadows of green leaves.

When he had passed 96th Street, Austin felt hungry and glanced about him for dinner. He avoided a Hebrew chain restaurant that flaunted the name St. Remy, and was not attracted by the hygienic fittings that made a Childs restaurant look like a clinic or a tepidarium. He chose an eating place with a nondescript entrance, and was pleased to find that it was staffed by Irish girls. He wondered whether it was a form of romanticism that led him to prefer the service of waitresses. What difference did it make—especially in a lunchroom one might never revisit—whether a man in a hideous black coat and a false shirt front, or a woman whose hands were likely to be large and red, hovered about one and took one's orders? He had never considered the matter. He watched the waitresses from under lowered eyelids, and before he had finished dining he decided that there was a difference. At least, in a second-rate place like this one. The work was harder on girls than on men; it strained them physically, but they controlled their nerves more gracefully, were more polite. They were paid lower wages, yet they were too proud to stand at a customer's elbow and maneuver for a large tip, in the manner of their male competitors. They brought a certain dignity to a calling that men had made ignoble. He understood now why he had always found waitresses sympathetic, and had classed waiters with valets and Italian barbers.

He perceived, also, that his observations were not without their bearing on the feministic theories he had ascribed to Charlotte Moore.

Chapter 8

FOR four or five days, Austin got only brief glimpses of Charlotte Moore—a tall woman of infinite poise, who looked straight at him as she passed his desk, who said nothing, but never omitted a smile of greeting that set a new note of beauty upon her face. He began to make a cult of her strong torso, her thighs like those of a goddess of the Parthenon come to life. She had a body and mind which fulfilled the Greek ideal, he thought. Or why not the modern American ideal, which was too self-conscious as yet to express itself in the terms of poetry, but which worshipped fiercely, to the exclusion of all other gods, the principle of human energy. What was that but life worship, and could it find a better symbol than this woman of genius? Thus he intellectualized his feeling for her—his more than admiration.

In realistic moments, he mused on the strangeness of this rapid falling in love with one who must be ten years older than he. Earlier, he had had the usual tendency of the cerebral, shy youth to seek women who were rather beyond his age than under it. But of late it had not been so. And he had never imagined it likely that he would want to be the lover of a woman of forty. An emotional discrepancy between the sexes was said to widen with each year that

separated them, if the man were the younger. He had
accepted that judgment without analyzing it. An inhibition
had raised itself, but now it seemed a foolish inhibition. The
heart pursued its desire wherever it was to be found. He
speculated again, as he had speculated in regard to Maude
O'Neill a few weeks before, whether maturity in one's
conception of love did not flower from experience.

Remembering Maude O'Neill's part in his life, he felt
dejected and a little ashamed. He had been seeing her
almost every evening. She had been coming to him in her
avid, discontented way, an amorous girl who clearly was
seeking to prove each time that she had chosen well. He
had met her feverishly on the plane of the flesh, and stilled
her questioning. But how little he loved her now! She had
enflamed him because she was more intelligent than Elizabeth. She was a link between the attachments of his un-
discriminating youth and his dreams for the future.

His dreams! He found it extravagant to suppose that
intimacy with Charlotte Moore might some day be a reality.
Her life was crowded with many interests. According to
popular gossip and the insinuations of those who had
written about her, she had had a succession of picturesque
amours. It might well be that her latest lover still reigned.
She had shown no sign of extending even friendship to
Austin. There was small reason why she should do so.
Probably, she thought him an insignificant person. His
article had drawn no comment from her, though the newspapers on his desk told him that she had released the news
about the site for a theater.

She paused unexpectedly beside him, as she entered on the fifth day. Her smile was a shade more warm.

"Will you come to my office, Mr. Bride?"

Austin rose immediately and followed her. They sat in the same positions they had occupied for the interview. He had the illusion that the interview had never been interrupted.

"I must tell you that I dislike having to scheme for publicity. I resent the need of a press agent. One should not have to practice so oblique a method of reaching the public," she began.

"It is journalism grafted on to advertising. A horrible combination. The age in which we live makes it necessary." He was watching her eyelids that fluttered with a curious, regular beat above steady eyes, as she listened to him.

"Of course, Mr. Bride. But I've had to put up with press agents who were more stupid than their profession. Why should not a publicity story tell the things about one that one wants told?"

"If it doesn't, you might better pay for straight advertising," replied Austin, downcast.

"I've had men whose only idea was to get my name into print, desirably or otherwise. Cramptons—Ed Cramptons—all of them. You are the first to use any rational psychology, to try to understand me."

Austin straightened and stared at her in happy astonishment. "Why, I thought you were going to tell me how rotten my article was," he exclaimed boyishly.

"Rotten!" She repeated the word, laughing. "Oh, no! It was sensational, a little yellow perhaps. I don't believe I'd have signed it in just that form for a serious magazine. But I liked the opinions you invented for me. I was converted to them at once. I do think that millionaires miss a lot of fun, and I wish they would start building marble temples in the parks."

There was a new timbre in her voice, a note of almost affectionate banter, which did not escape Austin. He pressed the advantage with a response that was dictated by the second nature her sex evoked in him rather than by craft.

"Only the personality of a woman like you could have lifted me out of the hackneyed stuff I've had to write for newspapers. I never before enjoyed working for any one," he said.

"How nice of you!" She gave him two firm, white hands impulsively, and then was too proud entirely to withdraw the gesture. With her arms still resting on the desk and almost touching him, she leaned forward.

"Now I must explain the delay in your hearing about the article. I knew I liked it, but I wanted an editor's judgment. I asked the man at the head of the Transcontinental Syndicate to come to see me. He was here yesterday afternoon, and as soon as he'd read the copy he begged for it. He was worried lest I might give it to some one else. It will be published by more than a hundred Sunday newspapers."

Austin's eyes sparkled. "The opinions of Charlotte Moore!

Why not? You have an enormous following, you know," he declared, and could see the tribute pleased her.

"Perhaps. But I want the publicity statements I make in the future to be as good as that one. I've been leading up to a dénouement. Mr. Crampton is no longer my press agent. You are, if you'll take the position."

"Will I take it? I did not expect such luck!"

"Luck for me. A woman is fortunate when she finds a sympathetic man who will work under her. The Twentieth Century world is not a matriarchy."

"It is moving in that direction."

"Do you think so? I wonder!" Her level gray eyes caressed him. "In the meantime, please reform my office."

"I have cost poor old Ed Crampton his job," he commented, without genuine remorse.

"He is a fool," said Charlotte. "I employed him because I could not find any one better, and I have endured him long enough. Please straighten out my office—quickly, quickly, please."

Austin held for an instant the hand she placed in his, hesitating whether to raise it to his lips in the European salute. But in the end he pressed it lightly and went out.

He found that Crampton had already gone.

At his 16th Street rooms that evening, he told Maude that he had been promoted, and perceiving that her interest grew sharply, he sketched the history of his article.

"Miss Moore is in love with you," said Maude, a dry, angry catch in her voice.

"Absurd!" He was irritated by the conventional retort.

"You don't know anything about her, and you say that!"

"She's drawing you nearer to her, because she wants you near. I'd do the same thing if you were with me in an office."

"She is an artist, and in matters that concern her work she has no sex."

Maude studied him miserably. "It doesn't matter, if you love me and not her," she urged.

He sought for an answer, and found that he was dumb. It was much easier to kiss her on the throat and cheeks and mouth. In the convulsions of an ancient strife, the need for words vanished or was postponed.

But although Austin had been sincere at the moment of repeating the platitude, he was not convinced of the sexlessness of work. His daily association with Charlotte had a quality of intuition, of finesse, that was due in part to his love. Why, he asked himself, had men of action placed a tabu on one of the motive forces of achievement? The Caesars and Napoleons had taken passion brutally, had rejected the collaboration of lovers. But the women tyrants had not done so, from Semiramis to Catherine the Great. Charlotte might not be aware that he served her better because he loved her, but it was true nevertheless.

He did not openly woo her. Something of his old self-consciousness had returned, to hold him back. No sign of it showed on the deceptive mask of his face, which was always that of a zestful, yet slightly impersonal, friend. He admired Charlotte too sincerely to risk disturbing the balance between them by a premature display of his heart. He

waited for her reserve to falter, if ever it were destined
to do so.

The weeks wore on through August and into early September. She invited him at last to have dinner with her at
her apartment on West End Avenue, and afterwards they
lingered in a deep, cushioned window-seat that looked out
on to the tops of bronzing maples. They talked about the
robust plays of the Restoration dramatists, while Austin
watched the changing expressions on her face. Its beauty
seemed more sculptural than ever in the half light. She
might be expressing enthusiasms, but as far as he was concerned she was aloof, he thought. So he continued to discuss
Congreve, Wycherley and Vanbrugh. Veering to poetry,
he read aloud a scene from Swinburne's "Atalanta in Caly-
don," and went home at ten o'clock.

The next day she asked him whether he had an engagement for the evening. He said that he had not, that he
intended merely to go through some catalogues of old editions, a plan of no importance.

"It might amuse you to see Sothern and Marlowe's opening with me—" She interrupted herself and looked at him
curiously. "Stupid of me not to consult my engagement
book before speaking." She glanced at some memoranda
and shook her head. "Sorry. Another evening, if you will,
Austin."

She had dropped into the way of calling him by his first
name, but it still sounded unfamiliar from her lips and
gave him a keen pleasure.

"I'd love to," he answered.

He dined alone and was at 16th Street early. The catalogues awaited him. They were of mediocre interest, he found. So he read for a while, then succumbed to the suave coquetting of Grisette. The cat jumped on to his lap and uttered soft cries that were neither mewing nor purring. They were lyric and affectionate, brief exclamations that ended with a muffled click of the jaws, a sound that no cat deigns to make to human beings who do not love her kind. When she had said her say, she reached up with her paws against his chest and sniffed his chin. He stroked her, the whole length of her body, and she lay down purring, shifting her position voluptuously once or twice and finally curling herself into a perfect ring.

Austin felt as happy as Grisette. He was thinking of nothing in particular, as he smoked and occasionally caressed the cat. The ringing of the doorbell startled him.

"She manages to get here every evening, appointment or no appointment," he murmured, and did not stir for a while.

But when he went to the door, it was not Maude O'Neill he found on the landing. It was Charlotte Moore. Uncertain at which door to knock, she was glancing about her. Her face broke into a smile as she saw Austin, and her gloved hand went out.

He was astonished beyond words. Scarcely aware of what he was doing, he did not release her hand, but drew her into the room, his eyes glowing.

"I hurried through some tiresome business—in this neighborhood. Then I thought I would drop in to see you, Austin," she said on a casual note.

"I can't tell you how glad I am," he replied ineptly, covering his agitation with brusque movements as he stepped behind her to close the door. He knew she had understated her motive. Incredible that she should visit him carelessly, like a bohemian. Her adjustment to the social framework was rather formal than otherwise, the only graceful attitude for a woman as well known as she. That fact in itself would permit her safely to make exceptions. Exceptions! He remembered how she had asked him in the afternoon whether he had an engagement, and he wondered whether she knew then she would come, having discovered he would be alone.

"I like your place, Austin. It is the sort of place I expected you to have. Books, pictures, a cat!" She moved slowly about the room, before sitting down in the big armchair where he had been dreaming with Grisette.

He drew up a chair for himself, and they made small talk, while she held his eyes with her steady, impenetrable gaze. The things they uttered were of no significance, and led naturally to an oasis of silence. Charlotte allowed it to last. Subtly, she restrained him from speaking until she spoke:

"I might have telephoned you to come up to my apartment. But I preferred not to. You were there only last night, and the bell boys gossip."

It was certain, then, that he could at least kiss her. He became suddenly keenly observant, almost critical, of details. There were the mere beginnings of pouches under her eyes, and a tightness at the corners where crowsfeet would some day appear. The powder did not fully hide a line about her throat. Ah, but it was a strong, worn, beautiful face! The face of a woman among many. He thought disparagingly of his affairs with other women; they seemed like the adventures of adolescence.

"I love you," he said with intensity.

"Austin!" Her voice was edged like a fine blade. Her body stiffened against the back of the chair, but the gesture had no reproof in it.

"I love you, love you," he reiterated without stirring.

"But Austin—I wanted you to say it!" she cried, as if explaining away a doubt. "I've come to you selfishly."

"Selfishly!"

"Because I may have little for you. I've thought myself tired—so tired of everything but work."

He strove against her forty years. "You are not tired of love."

"No?" She moved her shoulders ambiguously. "Civilized faun, prove it to me."

He had been chilled. But in her arms the breath of disillusionment passed quickly. "This is the only proof," he muttered.

Eventually, they reached the point of calm where they could exchange the confidences after the event that lovers do not omit. She had questioned him with deliberate guile in the afternoon, Charlotte told him, yet she had not been sure whether she would go to see him, so she had given him no hint. She had kept her liberty until the last moment. Was one ever sure?

He answered that, for his part, he had been sure for a long time that he wanted her. But she laughed, and said that was not the same thing.

"You could have kissed me last night, Austin, only you were not sure you could," she teased him. "I was glad. It was nicer to make plans about coming here."

He reflected that she was adding materially to his wisdom in the lore of love. And while he was searching for a barbed answer, the doorbell rang a second time. Charlotte interrogated him with drawn eyebrows.

He shrugged his shoulders. "When I do not want to be in to callers, I am not in."

But the bell continued ringing, loudly, persistently.

"It may be a telegram," she said. "Surely you had better see."

Austin knew it must be Maude. "I'll open the door of the little room," he said at last.

As he went, he closed the connecting door behind him. He was already sorry that he had not kept to his first resolution. An unjust resentment against Maude choked him when he greeted her on the landing.

"Were you asleep, that you did not hear the bell, Austin?"

"Yes," he answered drily. Embarrassed beyond measure at the necessity of telling her she could not come in, he stepped aside to point to some imaginary work on his table. And as his tongue fumbled over the lie, she walked past him and sat down. He became infuriated, fearing her voice would be heard in the next room. But her words shocked him into a state of complete panic.

"I felt I could not stand my hotel tonight," she said. "So I ran over to stay with you."

He forced himself to speak nonchalantly: "Sorry, Maude, but I've been nervous as the devil all day. I want to be alone."

"Nervous!" she exclaimed. "I thought you said you had been sleeping just now."

"That's just it. I was forcing myself to rest. But now I feel wide awake, and in a rotten temper."

She stared at him, wounded. The actual situation did not seem to occur to her. There was no sound from the large room, and it was not essentially odd that there should be a light there. Austin was in the habit of roving from one room to the other.

"What you really mean is, you don't want me any more," she said, her voice hardening.

It was horrible that he could not say anything to ameliorate the truth of her accusation. It had been true for a long time. He must not risk starting a scene, giving an excuse for noisy weeping. The situation was such that he must invite her to consider him the traditional male, callous at the ending of an affair. Horrible, but he deserved nothing better from her. He watched her head droop on its long neck and her eyes fill with tears. He thought she would upbraid him, but at the last she spared him even the terms of her bitterness.

She arose and left silently.

Austin rejoined Charlotte, his face as noncommittal as a mask. Her steady eyes pierced him.

"I could not help overhearing a word or two. I see you have your complications."

"That one is ended."

"If it is ended, it does not matter. I have no claim on your past," she said.

Chapter 9

A T THE close of the operatic season, Austin Bride was a press agent who had won victories. His own name was not known to the public, but he had put that of Charlotte Moore into the everyday talk of middle-class breakfast tables and the chatter of shop girls. The magazines published interviews with her and competed for signed articles. She was quoted in the editorial columns of newspapers. Austin knew that he had had the advantage of starting with a woman already famous. But the Charlotte Moore of the summer of 1919 had been no more than one of a number of stage favorites whose managers spent money for advertisements, and who was consequently in line for a share of free publicity. The serious appraisals of her talent by writers on music had been only for the initiated. By the late winter she had become an American heroine, a personage who was automatically placed on those lists of the Twelve Greatest Women, so beloved by the readers of journals that reach the home. Except for the few behind the scenes, no one could tell how or why this had come about.

Charlotte Moore was being taken seriously because Austin had focussed attention on Charlotte Moore herself, instead of decking out a lay figure after the pattern consecrated by the press. He had found a mind, a positive ego, to interpret and, within limits, to romanticize. Her scheme for a national theater had been popular stuff. On the wave of discussion it had caused, he had floated a series of articles sufficiently well written to have been bought on their merits. Some, indeed, had been paid for by editors too dignified to accept publicity material as such. Offered free, the others had been easily placed. Austin had blandly assumed for Charlotte the leadership of American women. He had quoted provocative views, which marked her as a post-war feminist, proud of her sex, as against the older school that had imitated men. Interviewers, determined to see Miss Moore and relieve him of most of his work, commenced to flock to the office. She was implored to become a writer herself, and thereafter the articles he prepared and had her sign were certain of being printed unchanged. Babies and perfumes, race horses and summer cottages were named after her.

Austin lounged in his office on a day in March. He considered his work without vainglory. He had had an ideal subject, and he had been lucky in understanding the psychology of editors. It was much more interesting to ask himself why he enjoyed working for Charlotte, why he fitted so harmoniously into a position that, after all, was subordinate to hers? He had hated his former jobs, had felt that they crushed his personality. His resignation from the Forum had been, in part, a revolt against anonymous work. Yet now he was happy in his anonymity. He perceived that the drawback had been his dislike of men and their methods. Men had invented the commercial structure of the world, and had become slaves to it; he remembered how he had put that into his first article about her. It was true. Women were less traditional, the moment they set domesticity behind them. The wine of life was in them. As executives, they stimulated instead of boring him.

"When men were freer, they bound women with home duties. They taught them to look upon washing and cooking as sacred. But the Twentieth Century finds men caught in a ritual of business organization more absolute than the washtub and the stove. Women who break away from housekeeping have no gods, and they will do the original things," he said.

He told himself that he understood women better than did most men.

And following his thought along this line, he judged the passional phase of his connection with Charlotte. She had given herself to him without reserves except the unconscious ones of her wearying flesh. There had been a charm of autumn in her weariness. So their love had run deeply, but with little commotion on the surface. At times it seemed a sublimated friendship, at others a creative intimacy in which ideas rather than feelings germinated as in a hothouse. It had caused him to formulate a theory about love. According to Austin Bride at this period of his development, civilized love was founded upon reason. The swift passions that tore at the young and the chronically immature ceased to be satisfying as one became less primitive. They were illusions through which it was fatally easy to see. But with a mental basis for their choice of one another, lovers could practice sensuousness as an art that was godlike because its nuances could not be matched in any other combination of woman and man. He had refined to this point his early instinct for amorous comradeship with the beloved.

Outside it was snowing. Austin stepped to the window and watched the flakes dancing downward in the light of a wan day. He could see the tops of the buildings as far north as Columbus Circle and south to the upper triangle of Times Square. They jutted in irregular masses, like granite crags that had been planed to flat surfaces. A moderate wind had banked the snow on one side only of towers and sloping roofs. The streets gave the impression of being trenches chiseled deeply into the rock. A pale, hard luminosity rose from them to combat the snow. The circle of the sky had narrowed to the interior of a steel bowl that had been clamped upon the city.

Austin loved New York less in winter than at any other season. He was still enough of a Californian to shudder at harsh challenges to eyes and skin. But days when snow falls are relatively mild, and with the collar of his ulster turned up he enjoyed tramping through the drifts.

Charlotte was giving an informal reception that evening, and as she expected him for an early dinner it would soon be time for him to go home and dress. He must meet people, she had said, in sudden disapproval of his attitude of a spectator of all human contacts except that of love. She had made a problem of the discovery that he had few friends. Austin smiled as he remembered the energy with which she had set about revising his existence.

"If you isolate yourself, who will blow your trumpet when you write the book I expect you to write some day?" she had demanded.

"You will, darling."

"I am only one person. For a press agent, you don't ask much."

"When I am ready to boom myself, I shall hire a bright little girl, a female Austin."

"Be serious. On general principles, you should know interesting people. I am going to see that you do."

"You are a reckless woman. New acquaintances are dangerous in a menage," he had warned her playfully. But Charlotte had laughed and had said she would know whom not to invite.

There had already been an evening, at which he had been bored by a collection of musicians and actors. He was antipathetic to males on the stage. The musicians were relatively harmless, but he detested the actors for their mannerisms and childish vanity. They were effeminate in a disagreeable way, like priests gone wrong. Curious that it should be so, but decidedly miming was an art that only women could practice with dignity.

Charlotte had promised that the company tonight would be of a different stamp.

He walked down to 16th Street, his shoulders hunched against the snow, which had begun to fall more thickly. Huge impressions etched themselves on his brain—the cross currents of bowed, overcoated figures, like beetles on stilts, in Times Square; the dim elevated trains hurling diagonally across Herald Square; the imitation Campanile of the Metropolitan Tower, its summit lost in the storm; the prow of the Flatiron Building, the soaring prow of a vessel in drydock; the gesticulating bronze statues of Washington, Lafayette and Lincoln in Union Square, which were losing their silhouettes now under the wadding of white flakes.

The tramp had taken Austin longer than he had anticipated. There was danger of his being late, and he hurried with his dressing. But before he had finished, Charlotte telephoned to say that her cook was in rebellion, and that he must not come until nine o'clock. Hating temperamentally to rush himself, he was glad of the respite. He dined alone at the Brevoort, and in good time took a taxi to West End Avenue.

Several guests were ahead of him. He noted instantly a couple whose exoticism Charlotte was already adroitly featuring. They were sitting with her on her favorite Louis XIII settee to the left of the fireplace. The woman might have been one of the cousins that Zuloaga has painted in many canvases. She was so saliently Spanish that the fact held one absorbed longer than the ordinary first impression. Bobbed blue-black hair curved luxuriantly about her head like the plumage of a bird, and came down on her forehead in a short bang. Her eyes were large and black with long lashes, and her skin was a warm olive. She had the features of an Andalusian gamine, unclassical, blunt. Her lips flamed with rouge. No other woman, thought Austin, could paint her lips so heavily and be effective. Hers was the mouth of a precocious little girl, greedy for kisses, who had plundered the rouge-pot in mistrust of the unaided appeal of her admirable teeth.

The man was her complement. He was a thoroughly artificial-looking person, about thirty-five years old, with a slender body, delicate hands and a bony, faun's head. He had a tuft of black beard, and his mustache was too slight to need to be clipped. He wore evening dress like a masquerade that suited him with almost uncanny fortuity. His effervescent talk and perpetual, sardonic smile held the attention of every woman near him.

"There is a fellow who probably gives his own sex as little of his time as I do," mused Austin, and walked over, interested.

Charlotte introduced him to Laura Beltrán and Eustace Lloyd.

He had known they were expected, but had not recognized them. Miss Beltrán was a playwright, who was beginning to be known on Broadway. The poet, Eustace Lloyd, plumed himself on his reputation being limited to a few hundred ardent admirers. His verse was precious, not for the public at large. Those, however, who had only heard his glittering, worldly conversation found it difficult to believe this and credited him with being a best-seller.

At closer range, Austin found the girl insidiously stirring. He forgot the poet and addressed himself to her:

"What have you done with your *manto de* Manila and

your high tortoiseshell comb? It isn't fair that you should cheat us."

"Really! Do I look as Spanish as all that?" she answered with a naïveté of round eyes and mannered smile. "You know, I was born in Watertown, Connecticut."

"Watertown!" Austin was genuinely astonished. "Imagine your parents going into exile at Watertown, Connecticut!"

"Oh, but they did! They moved straight there from Sevilla. My father went into business. He manufactured thread. Didn't he, Eustace?"

Every one laughed. The question of Laura Beltrán's allegiance was seized upon and exalted into a fictitious importance.

"Don't hold Watertown against her. One's birthplace does not matter," said Charlotte. "She has adopted Manhattan between Washington Square and Central Park. She does not even know where Harlem is. She is a Gothamite."

"I am not, I am not!" cried Laura. "I shall live in Paris when I have made money. So I am already a Parisian."

"You are both wrong," declared Lloyd. "She is a Sicilian."

"A Sicilian! Now, I ask you! Isn't he mad?" said Laura.

"Not a mongrel modern Sicilian," explained Lloyd imperturbably. "Not even a descendant of any human being that ever lived in Sicily. But I am talking to poor unenlightened creatures, who do not understand the only true doctrine of metempsychosis. I learned it from the ghost of a mummy, one night when the guardians overlooked me in the Metropolitan Museum of Art and locked me in."

"You have our attention, poet," said Charlotte, amused. "You know how to capture it. We are waiting. What is the doctrine?"

"Incarnation—not reincarnation."

"That is too general. Remember we are poor unenlightened creatures. You said it yourself."

"Must I explain everything? Very well. The characters imagined by artists have no souls or bodies, do they? Yet they are real. That puzzles the gods, so the gods find incarnations for them. Laura is one of the honey-golden girls of Theocritus, perhaps gracious Bombyca whose voice was drowsy sweet. Obviously, then, she is a Sicilian."

"I love that, Eustace," murmured Laura. "And what is Miss Moore?"

"She is an Athenian—a niké by one of the great sculptors."

"Thank you, poet," said Charlotte. "You must tell us now what you are."

"Oh, I!" His face altered oddly. His mouth drooped and his eyebrows puckered—"I am a Pierrot posing as Mephistopheles, and sometimes mistaken in the dark for Pan."

Austin liked Eustace Lloyd. To be sure, everything the latter said was for effect. Laura Beltrán was nothing if not Spanish and civilized. Yet he had compared her to a wild girl of the Idylls, for the sake of the sound of beautiful words, no doubt. Was he altogether false, however? The warm brownness of Laura, her blunt features, were subtly Theocritan. If Bombyca could be incarnated through an Andalusian mother, might she not be like Laura? How just his picture of Charlotte had been—the statuesque Ionic vision that Austin had seen long since! And his bitter epigram about himself! Certainly, he would be a sympathetic acquaintance. For one thing, Austin had never heard anybody use the word metempsychosis since the days of his childhood when his own weak father had played with it.

He was about to speak to the poet. But Charlotte rose and took Lloyd away with her, to introduce him to some new arrivals. Austin restored his full attention to Laura Beltrán.

"I, too, am a seer, though a lesser one," he said. "It is my turn to tell you about yourself. You deny you are a New Yorker because this is a pioneer capital, and it won't be able to catch up with you in your lifetime."

"You think I am so terribly European?"

"Not merely European, but exquisitely decadent. The Spanish and French middle-class is as stolid as ours. That is not your world. You are of an old, old aristocracy, to be found in Paris, Madrid, Rome, Vienna, in palaces and studios—an aristocracy that collects sensations instead of membership cards in clubs for civic welfare."

"You have me all mixed up, you and that mad Eustace. He says I am a little goat-girl from Sicily. So I can't be decadent, can I? Decadent! I don't really know what the word means." She made the statement with provocative ingenuousness.

Austin feigned embarrassment and was silent for a moment. Then, "Do you care for Felicien Rops?" he asked almost formally.

"Oh, very much!"

"All right."

"I—I don't understand. Why 'all right'?"

"It is queer you should like Rops. Most unsophisticated girls have never even heard of him. Aubrey Beardsley is their limit."

She burst out laughing. "You are an impertinent person," she said.

"Guilty."

"If you have any Rops etchings I haven't got, you shan't be allowed to keep them from me."

"Let us compare our treasures. I plead for it as a favor."

He went through the American rite of obtaining her telephone number and inscribing it under the proper letter in his address book. He felt he had a great deal more to say to her, and much could have been said at once if Charlotte had not interrupted them. It was his duty that evening to meet people.

A novelist and his plain wife, a stout contralto from the opera, a theatrical producer of the tribe of Judah—these impinged on his consciousness in only a vague way. But he warmed to Theresa Glenn, a middle-aged woman who edited a magazine for motion picture enthusiasts. She had a wholesome brunette skin, wiry black hair, an ugly mouth and beautiful gray eyes. Her complete neutrality toward sex was obvious to him in an instant. He had never met any one like that who stirred in him the comradely, human feeling that she did. It was pleasant to chat lightly with her. She was simplicity itself after Laura, a calm, wise woman like an older sister, he thought.

Their conversation lasted for ten or fifteen minutes. He remembered of it only his remark that she suggested a gypsy to him, and her answer that it was not surprising seeing that she had gypsy blood. "Come to see me," she had added. "I should like to tell you about the American gypsies. Few people know there are any in this country." He had gladly promised to go.

Then Charlotte had called him again, and he was made to talk to newcomers, whose very names he failed to remember. Through their chatter, he was hoping to get a chance to recapture Laura, but the vivid girl was surrounded by admirers until it was time for her to go. He noted the matter-of-fact way in which she nodded to Eustace Lloyd, as a signal for him to fetch her wraps. Plainly, they were lovers.

Austin escaped from the couple he was entertaining and approached to say Good-bye. He obtained no more than a handshake from Laura, who had mysterious confidences to make at the last minute to Charlotte. But Lloyd and he bandied a few sentences, as they waited.

"You characterized our friends extraordinarily well," remarked Austin, indicating the two women.

The poet looked at him quizzically. "Phrases, phrases! I toss them as a juggler tosses colored balls at a show."

"They are real billiard balls, all the same, not celluloid."

"The harder they are, the better they toss." Lloyd

chuckled. "I did not include you in my vaudeville act. Shall I do so now?"

"Yes."

"Well, let's see. I don't know you at all; that makes it difficult." He cocked his head on one side. "Most people would take you for the wise lad who gets Columbine. You think so yourself. But you're a Pierrot, too. Have a prayer or a pistol ready for the day when you find I'm right."

Chapter 10

AUSTIN flirted all week with the idea of telephoning to Laura Beltrán. What more natural than that he should do so? he asked himself. They had liked each other, had found some tastes in common. But she made no secret of her intimacy with Eustace Lloyd, and probably she knew that Charlotte and himself were lovers. What of it? A telephone call, the visit he hoped to arrange, should cause no heartburnings to either Eustace or Charlotte. He sheered away from the implication in his having raised the question of loyalty. Bidding for Laura's interest was a pastime he chose to take seriously, and yet not seriously. It must not be hurried and blundered, nor must annoying considerations be allowed to color it beforehand in any way.

He unhooked the telephone receiver one afternoon and asked for Laura's number. Luck was with him, for presently her voice answered.

"Hello, this is Austin Bride," he announced.

"Oh, hello! I was just going to say I wasn't in."

"On general principles?"

"Of course. I am a busy woman. Most phone calls—you know!"

"Am I on your special list, or is it Rops?"

"Both of you."

They fenced for a while in the staccato with which telephoning is fast vitiating the American language. When Austin reached the point of asking to be allowed to call, he was invited carelessly to come the next day for tea.

He found Laura in a small apartment on West Eleventh Street, her setting a profusion of old carved furniture in dark woods, and walls covered with bookshelves from the ground to the highest point the arm could reach. The only pictures were Japanese prints—a false touch, he thought, but he was delighted to see the books.

Almost immediately, he discovered that Laura's artificiality was not a consistent manner. In a tête-a-tête, she was no longer the ingénue of Charlotte's reception. Rather, she had a direct, buoyant curiosity about his tastes, his impulse toward her and her own frankly admitted pleasure in knowing him better. He began to wonder whether she were not quite a normal girl, who occasionally dramatized her exotic exterior and enjoyed the bewilderment it caused. But it became clear that she could not be classified so simply.

"Why did you pretend you did not understand what I was talking about the other evening?" he ended by asking her.

"How should I know you really cared about civilized things?" she countered. "I prefer to be thought a cute little fool by men I'm not sure of. It encourages them to prove they are total losses. I haven't time for most men, you see."

"You find ideas more exciting?"

She nodded. "Something like that. If a man can talk to me about the things I like, or teach me to like something new, well and good. Otherwise, I prefer art."

Austin accepted this as a challenge. He held her attention for the moment, but the game between them was yet to be played. He entered upon it with zest. Laura seemed to him a justification of his theory that emotions should be approached cerebrally.

They began to see much of each other. In all respects, Austin was suave, calculated. Deciding that the damask rose was the flower that typified her, he never went to see her without taking a small bunch of full-blown crimson blossoms. He lent her books, the mere titles of which would have startled their mothers and fathers. Nonchalantly, impersonally, he matched his collection of etchings with hers. It astonished him to remember that a year before he had spent all his spare time with Elizabeth, who seldom read and whose preference in pictures ran to Watts and Alma-Tadema.

A sophisticated comradeship ripened between Laura and himself. If they were moving toward some deeper climax, he felt that Fate had played a certain part in it. There was significance, he thought, in two things affecting his life and hers. The passing days found Charlotte more possessed by her autumn energy for work, and work only, than she had been; she probably cared for him no less, but she cared less for passion. And Eustace Lloyd had disappeared mysteriously from the scene. Austin did not like to ask Laura why he had never met the poet at her apartment.

Innocent as the question should have been, he knew no way of saving it from appearing odd and pointed. Why be inquisitive? It was enough that Eustace was absent. She might not want to discuss him, any more than Austin would wish to be specific about Charlotte.

He brushed aside his scruples concerning infidelity.

With prohibition an incredible fact since the past January, Austin and Laura made a rite of obtaining cocktails and wine whenever they had dinner together. This became the most thrilling feature of an evening out. Like hundreds of thousands of other New Yorkers, they looked with contempt upon restaurants that refused to break the unpopular law, and delighted in speak-easies they would have found sordid in freer days. They investigated, one after another, the Italian places in the slum district south of Washington Square. It was amusing to ask, as they tramped through the freezing slush of late March, "Will dinner be wet or dry tonight?" And they laughed like children at some of the conditions imposed by timid hosts. There was a restaurant where cocktails in flasks were palmed into their napkins, and the waiter hissed in their ears that they must go to the telephone booth to drink them. The system of paying for police protection had not yet been perfected.

The spectacle of fastidious Laura, a product of old civilizations and modern beauty shops, eating and surreptitiously drinking in a spaghetti kitchen, her furs thrown back over a chair she would not have allowed in her pantry, symbolized to Austin the social vertigo with which reformers had plagued his country.

At Bori's, neither the least nor the most shabby of their strange resorts, she turned to him abruptly one evening and said:

"I am quite sure now that I like you. We speak the same language."

He looked at her intently, his eyelids drooped at their outer corners, and fondled her hand in reply.

"But you will have to decide. Is it to be friendship or love? Which do you want?"

The proposition, as she phrased it, astounded him. He had anticipated no such blunt dividing of claims upon the heart and brain.

"They are inseparable," he urged, after a brief hesitation.

"Oh no, they are not! If I give friendship, it is for life. I would do anything for a friend. But a lover!" She snapped her fingers. "Love is like that! Something nice that may last for a long while, or a little while. Who can tell?"

"We are friends already, Laura."

"Yes, ordinary friends. I think we can be more—the Greek ideal, you know. Throw it all into the fire, though, if you want. It will make a pretty blaze."

Austin was unfamiliar with this sort of feminine cynicism. It gave him an authentic thrill, like a new perfume. He had not expected anything like it from a Latin woman, for Latin women are fundamentally romantic. Laura, however, was not strictly Latin. Her environment had produced a temperamental composite.

"I refuse to admit we are just ordinary people, who have to be afraid of exhausting each other in any way," he said.

She lowered her head and traced with her finger tips on the table. Her plumes of black hair were almost brushing his face. "All the same, I have put it to you in the form of a choice. You must allow my right to think I understand myself."

"I choose love," he whispered, secretly clinging to his own theory. It would have seemed a barren thing to him to accept friendship with a limitation.

"All right," she answered. "All right. And now we will talk of something else, please."

They passed smoothly into a discussion of Gabriele d'Annunzio, whose iridescent corruption they both admired, and when Austin saw her to her door a sense of the subtleties of the situation led him to say Good-night to her with a mere fleeting pressure of his lips to the hand she gave him.

But he telephoned her in the morning, and they made another appointment for dinner. A complicity palpitated between them at the Brevoort, where they had gone because it was near and they had said they would return early to Laura's apartment to read d'Annunzio's "Tales of My Native Town." They lingered, nevertheless, over their coffee, and when they were in her small living room with the crowded furniture and the Japanese prints, they did not even touch the volume they had chosen.

Their kisses began with a voluptuous disdain of sentiment that Laura's terms had made inevitable. The flame of life lapped about them, and intoxicated but did not burn. In their rôles of wise adepts, they demonstrated to one another that flame is a charming plaything, the dangerous properties of which have been much exaggerated by the tragedians.

A vanity of the spirit possessed Austin, as he walked home through a powdery snow that fell in the light of a moon in its last quarter. He had made a cult of women, and he felt that he had attained the triumph of full contact with them. Charlotte and Laura were opposite types, yet both were among the least primitive of women, and he had known how to please them both. There had been a time, not so many years before, when they would have found him negligible, so timid an introspective youth, so self-conscious had he been. The time, for instance, when he had been glad to have an affair with Erna Ull, the vaudeville actress, she who had left him to contract a sagacious marriage with an acrobat. Austin smiled at this memory. Obviously, he had not been an expert lover in the days of Erna Ull. But the matter had been of supreme interest to him, then as now, and he wondered whether his will had not finally equipped him with a technique of love, as a painter who thinks incessantly about his art works out a technique. It might well be so. He knew there were men who emanated a spontaneous sex appeal, but he did not compare himself with them. "They are predestined husbands or ravishers, and they make no cult of women," he said. "Light love is an art."

He was in the mood to drift onward indefinitely in the pale, windless night. The mere dust of snow that was falling enhanced its beauty and tempted him. But it was absurdly late. He contented himself with stopping for a moment at the corner of 14th Street and admiring the empty northward sweep of Fifth Avenue, its parallel rows of lamps visible almost as far as the Public Library, converging to a point and curving at the end over the grade which once had been Murray Hill. Directly in front of him, black loft buildings made a canyon of the avenue. They had captured it on both sides from 14th Street to 23rd, had displaced old dwellings in a real estate coup which had been launched swiftly, like an army's occupation of territory, a few years before Austin reached New York. A scandalous invasion, an affront to the great highway. Yet, in its iconoclasm and its impotence to mar the whole effect, how characteristic of New York, he thought. Fifth Avenue surged scornfully past the loft buildings; they could be thrown down some day more quickly than they had arisen.

Austin's 16th Street house belonged to the eastern fringe of survivors. Approaching it from the direction of the avenue, skyscrapers flanked him half way down the block. Then, abruptly, he was between low brick and brownstone dwellings of the last century, and these gave way once more to skyscrapers on the Union Square corners. As always, he enjoyed the contrast.

But that night he could spare only a fleeting thought to the quaint block. He had Laura to think of, and Charlotte. How would he meet Charlotte the next day? He hoped he would not have a melodramatic sense of having betrayed her. She was no trusting virgin, no conventional wife; it would be astonishing if, in her time, she had never had the experience of sharing her own interest between two lovers. The situation was not novel.

And, in fact, Austin discovered he was free of compunctions with Charlotte. Outside of work and companionship, she had expected so little of him of late. Her kisses had been absent-minded. She was absorbed in her projects for a national theater. The morning after he had been with Laura, he found Charlotte making plans to go to Boston to see a rich woman who was thinking of becoming a patron. He was useless to her in connection with this trip, and as he sat watching her telephone and dictate letters, he felt like a son she had taken into her office, an affectionate son who saw no reason why he should tell her about his escapades.

After she had left for the Grand Central, he telephoned to Laura and begged her to break an engagement he knew she had. She refused, quarreling playfully with him over the wire and warning him it would be fatal if he tried to be a monopolist. They compromised on her giving him the following two evenings. But Austin would be entirely alone until he saw her, a state of affairs that did not fall in with his mood.

He remembered Theresa Glenn, the calm, friendly woman he had met the same evening as Laura, and decided he would at once keep his promise to go to see her. She had given him her office address, a number on Eighth Avenue, which Austin knew represented the home of the Cooke magazines. The latter included more than a dozen publications, ranging from a weekly which fed the popular appetite for the cardinal crimes rehashed, to two all-fiction monthlies of a fairly high standard. Miss Glenn's motion picture magazine hovered between the extremes.

The building impressed Austin as being more frankly a factory than the headquarters of any other publisher in a land where literature is a variety of trade goods. It was a huge, square factory, of somber brick, divided into eight stories, where presses clanged, type was set and engravings made, and editors read manuscripts. Without a guide, it would have been impossible to find the editors, because of the gigantic rolls of paper stored in columns in the very passageways that led to offices.

A boy took Austin's card, and returned promptly to shepherd him through the maze to Theresa Glenn. She was at a desk loaded with papers and the superfluity of expensive, shiny photographs which motion picture producers distribute in their frenzied gamble for free space in any publication. He contrasted her setting favorably with the aseptic neatness of the Sloat machine. Her desk looked as if it were used for work and not as a round table for conferences.

"You promised to tell me about the American gypsies," he said, following her exclamation of pleasure with an improvised reason for his call.

"Did I? But, of course I would have ridden my hobby. You make a hit with me when you show an interest in the gypsies."

"There is something romantic about the very idea," declared Austin vaguely.

"It bores some people. But you have a feeling for open air life, no doubt."

"I—no, I can't say I have. I have always lived in towns."

"You unfortunate man. You should pass a whole spring, as I have done more than once, in a gypsy wagon, following the trail from Maryland to New Jersey. It is good to break the habit of sleeping under roofs."

"But I like the country only for a day or two, as a novelty. After that, I feel depressed. And the birds twitter in the morning and wake me up."

Miss Glenn stared at him, as if wondering whether she had heard him correctly.

"Lunatic!" Frank laughter crystallized her reaction. "One goes to the country for rest from city people, for birds and green leaves. If you do not like those things, what do you like?"

He found himself telling her about his passion for women and books. He had never confided fully in one in whom he had no amorous interest. Curious, he reflected as he talked, that he should find Theresa Glenn sympathetic to the point of wanting to give her a true picture of himself. There was nothing specific in what he said. He mentioned no names, told no adventures. But within the bounds of tact where others were concerned, he was not reticent. The man he depicted was brought up to date—a more intellectualized, a more suavely sensuous Austin Bride than he who had pierced the shell of his chrysalis a year before.

"From my point of view, you are a very strange person," she said, when he had finished. "I do not approve, because you trifle with love, while I regard it as a sacred, exclusive thing between two who are meant for one another. I am traditional, perhaps. But I like you. Let us be friends—off and on, when you can spare time for an old woman."

"All right," he answered simply, and thereby flattered her more effectively than if he had insisted she was young and that they must meet often. "And I want to hear about the gypsies."

"What real interest can you have in them?"

"I have a literary interest, a human interest, too. Does that seem impossible?"

"No," she said. "My gypsies will give us a subject for a dull day. They would take more time than I have now. Will you have lunch with me on Saturday, at Madame Laurier's on William Street? I have invited some others—does that spoil it for you?—they are people I want you to meet."

Austin accepted. They shook hands warmly and he strolled away, astonished and pleased at the turn his visit had taken. Such surprises were of the warp of life. He was not sure that the luncheon party appealed to him, because most parties proved to be tiresome. But he could not have evaded it gracefully, and it was well to step sometimes into an alien world. With his slight knowledge of Theresa Glenn, he could not imagine what sort of men and women gathered about her.

The two consecutive evenings that Laura had promised him passed deliciously. They were tableaux in a Twentieth Century comedy of hedonism. Austin knew that he would never break Laura's heart, nor she break his. But he steeped himself in the charm of a companionship that was exotic only where love and the arts were involved. More and more, it was clear to him that Laura had a double personality, of which the one that faced the world of action was combative and practical. As much the adopted child of New York as he was, she was less the spectator. She wanted to be a successful playwright, and she worked hard to attain that end. Charlotte worked no harder.

He told her a little about his call on Theresa Glenn. But Theresa had not interested her, and she replied carelessly. So he omitted to mention the luncheon engagement.

On Saturday, Austin took the subway downtown and got off at the Fulton Street Station. Not knowing exactly where Laurier's restaurant was, he struck east to William Street and explored until he saw the name above the basement of a towering business building at the corner of Pine.

"A queer place for a French table d'hôte," he thought. "It looks more like a rathskeller."

But the restaurant proved not to be a table d'hôte. It was one of the many grill rooms that served the more prosperous office workers of the financial district, and assumed a French character only when the rush of business subsided in the late afternoons and on Saturdays. The walls were decorated with pictures of hunting scenes and stuffed relics of the chase. There was much dark woodwork. Pillars and a few semi-partitions created the impression of there being nooks and corners on the wide basement floor.

Austin entered and stood hesitating at the bottom of the flight of steps. At once, a waiter hurried up to him.

"Miss Glenn's party, sir? Yes? Over there to the right. She always sits there, sir."

Two tables had been set together to accommodate seven persons, and Austin was the last guest to arrive. He shook hands with Theresa and bowed, smiling, to the friends to whom she presented him in her emphatic way, making each introduction separately. The names slipped in and out of his consciousness, and the faces were a mere blur. It was always so with him for a moment, when he had to meet a number of strangers in quick succession.

After he had sat down, they emerged from their anonymity. There was an extraordinarily stout woman on his left, who resumed with energy an interrupted conversation with Theresa and punctuated her phrases with nods. Opposite there was a blond man whose vast, bare countenance suggested the Scandinavian type. He drooped silently, while at the end of the table a merry fellow who looked as if he might be a popular member of the Lambs Club entertained with quips and gestures an infantile dark girl.

Traveling around to his own right, Austin's critical glance was arrested by the gray-green eyes of a tall girl. He perceived in the next flash that she had the most bright, virile red hair he had ever seen. It luxuriated under her hat and looped down on either side as if it could not be controlled. It would be trivial to call her young, bold face beautiful, he decided. The nose and chin were positively arrogant. But the wide mouth was beautiful, and so were the high cheek bones and the long lines of her body.

He considered her keenly and in surprise. A girl he wanted to know well, a provocative, fierce girl, whom in a wave of desire he longed to kiss.

"Do you often see Miss Glenn?" he asked at random.

"No, very seldom. I scarcely know her, except by correspondence. She said she wanted me to meet some of her friends here. It was nice of her, so I came." Her voice soared sharply, in a half falsetto.

"She said the same thing to me. Perhaps she intended us specially to meet each other."

"Perhaps. Are you an editor?"

"No—a sort of writer."

"Oh, are you? I am writing a novel."

Austin thought a novel a large order for her. She had begun to impress him as being a girl who lived directly and vigorously, and who in all probability had found little time for studying the art of fiction. At her age, anyway— she could not be more than twenty-five—only the forced-ripe products of universities attempted novels.

"You are brave," he murmured, his eyes lingering on the cream-blond skin of her neck. "Do you write for Miss Glenn in the meantime?"

"No, I have had nothing published. But I asked her a few weeks ago to advise me about my life. I wanted to find out how editors replied to such letters. Our correspondence started that way."

"Remarkable!" mused Austin. "The gesture was that of a working girl, but not the motive. She is not ordinary.

"Well, don't join any stupid professor's class in short story writing," he said. "There is nothing to be learned that way, nothing that one can't teach oneself."

"I won't, I promise you."

He raised his eyes to hers and found that they were gleaming in an intent appraisal of him.

"That's right, Mr. Bride," called Theresa from the head of the table. "Talk to Miss Purcell about her work. She needs encouragement."

"If only I were an editor, Miss Glenn! I might be of some use to her in that case."

"Would you like to be one?"

"Surely. But I'd have to be in complete charge of the magazine," answered Austin.

"I shall remember that. I think you would make a good editor."

He turned back to the girl.

"What is your first name, Miss Purcell?" he asked boldly.

"Beatrice."

"It is one of the beautiful names. And do you really need encouragement about your writing?"

Her thin, fine hand sketched an unexpected gesture towards him. "I am doing the novel just to pass the time. I suppose it is no good, and I don't care much."

They drifted away from the subject and exchanged rude, but discreetly whispered, comments about the formidable stoutness of the woman who was haranguing Theresa

Glenn. The large-faced Scandinavian person across the table came to life and revealed that he had been a newspaper correspondent in the war. He talked heavily about the German leaders and declared he would like to be the first and only man to interview the Kaiser at Doorn. It would make his fortune, he averred, and paused with his mouth half open to answer any argument. But no one cared to decry the value of an exclusive interview with the Kaiser at Doorn. The jester from the Lambs abandoned his infantile girl and launched into a series of anecdotes for the benefit of the whole table. His snappy voice silenced other conversation.

The luncheon fell off into the commonplace for Austin. His thoughts strayed from Beatrice Purcell to Laura. Exotic Laura! His affair with her was so recent he could find no great interest in anything else. Why was he not with her that afternoon? But in the evening he would be. He did not hear a word of the last three stories by the member of the Lambs.

Then Beatrice rose to go. He said good-bye to her, and turned to watch her as she walked to the door. She was even taller than he had thought, a long-legged girl who walked swiftly with a free motion from the hips, her head and shoulders a trifle bent. He got a last impression of a coil of red hair seen from behind, incredibly vital against her white neck.

In William Street, when he also was on his way home, he shivered against the chill of a late winter wind. He cut across to Nassau Street and hastened toward the subway

station at Fulton. The weekday turmoil of these narrow
thoroughfares had subsided to a trickle of peddlers, wandering aimlessly as if they had lost hope of making another
sale. Clerks were putting up the shutters on haberdashery
shops. The mountainous sides of the office buildings on
either hand seemed almost to meet at the thirtieth story or
so, and to close away the sky.

Chapter 11

BEFORE Charlotte returned from Boston, Austin's intimacy with Laura had developed to the point where they confided in one another regarding such innocent questions as their work and their hopes for its advancement.

Laura, it appeared, had passed a short apprenticeship on the stage. She had hated the life, yet she had made a certain impression on Broadway in minor parts and had gone out with road shows. Feeling that the training would be valuable to her as a playwright, she had endured squalid dressing rooms and the banal companionship of the rank and file of the profession. She was now ready to use her experience in an original way.

"Olga Petrova did a comedy of mine last season," she told Austin. "It was too precious and failed in four weeks. But the critics praised it."

"I know," he answered. "I wish I'd seen it. I didn't, because I almost never go to plays."

"It gave me a start, anyway. And I have just finished a play that might be successful. It is about the life of the theater, and since I have lived that life I am thinking of filling one of the lead rôles myself. Do you fancy the idea? Playwright and actress in one—you know."

"It should be good for a lot of publicity," said Austin.

"I think so, too."

"Who is to produce the play?"

"Do I know? I haven't offered it to any one. But Petrova won't do it. I sketched the plot to her, and she said it was not for her."

"You are counting on your plan to help get you a producer. Is that it?"

"But of course."

Austin looked thoughtful. "In that case, your publicity should be started at once. Those Jews refuse to believe any one has a good idea unless the newspapers say so first."

"I see you know all about them, dear."

"I'd like to help you on this thing," he declared impulsively.

"If you only could! Can't Charlotte Moore spare you, now her season is over?"

"It isn't a matter of sparing me, or a question of seasons with her," he explained a little uncomfortably. "I have been publicizing her in connection with her new theater, and she may think I should not boom any one else."

"If you have scruples, don't ever speak of it again. You are my lover, not my press agent." There was a barb in the last phrase.

"*Her* press agent is going to ask her for temporary leave," he retorted swiftly.

"All right, but you must accept what she says—yes or no."

"Naturally."

They drifted away from the subject. Whether or no the reference to Charlotte had reminded her of him, Laura spoke about Eustace Lloyd. He was a brilliant cynic, she said, whose friendship had meant much to her. He had stiffened her will by showing her that life was nothing but a game, and that it was disastrous to melt into sentimentality.

"He is brilliant certainly, but is he really cynical?" asked Austin, recalling the poet's definitions.

"Eustace loves to mix up poetry and cruel realism until he has every one puzzled. At heart, he is disillusioned."

"I wonder!" What Austin actually wondered was why he had not met Lloyd at her apartment and whether they had ceased to see each other. He was as curious as a child who knew he should not ask a question. But the question nagged at his brain, and presently was uttered almost involuntarily:

"Do you ever see Mr. Lloyd nowadays, Laura?"

"No, but he writes to me."

Austin's face went blank with astonishment.

"If you must know," she went on, "when I began to get interested in you I told him to stay away, but I did not forbid him to write to me. He writes wonderful letters. I'm not answering them, and I shan't unless I decide I care for him again."

"I see."

He thought this Laura's crowning touch of artificiality. It shocked him for a moment, but he reached the conclusion that its logic was admirable. She assumed no responsibilities in love and imposed none. Hers, too, was a complete candor.

When he met Charlotte on her return the next day, the contrast between the two women reaffirmed itself and piqued him. He was proud to be loved by both of them. Laura was subtly exciting, but Charlotte was magnificent and sure. He kissed her with ardor, as they drove from the Grand Central.

Almost at once, she began to tell him about the outcome of her mission in Boston. The rich woman had been genuinely interested, but was one of those persons who hate to make a decision. She had half promised that she would contribute fifty thousand dollars to the national theater. A sum twice as large would be a trivial investment for her, yet she had temporized and made much of the necessity of consulting certain friends as well as her lawyer.

"There are others like her," said Charlotte. "They will all send me checks some day, but in the meantime my work is delayed. If I could only get a few more patrons as prominent as Senator Arbuthnot, the hesitators would quickly follow their lead. I must make another trip to Washington."

"A trip that will keep you away long?"

"Yes, Austin, and I shall have to go alone. The Arbuthnots have offered to pull all sorts of social and political wires for me, and in that world I must not even seem to be organizing my own publicity. I am as well advertised now as I need to be, until the theater is a fact."

"Can I do nothing to help you?"

"Not a great deal, for the present, Austin."

He thought it a favorable moment to tell her about Laura's play and his wish to help her as a friend. Charlotte knew that they had seen each other since their meeting at her apartment. He made the whole thing appear very casual on his part.

"I believe I could get her into the newspapers on her scheme to act the part of a chorus girl, written by herself, for herself, and based on her own stage life," he said.

Charlotte's steady glance held his eyes as he talked. "I see no reason why you should not do it," she answered warmly.

"It is not to be thought of, if you think it would conflict with the publicity I have been doing for you."

"But I do not think so. How could my plans suffer by the success of a light Broadway comedy? I am fond of Laura Beltrán and would be happy to see her get ahead. You are clever enough to launch her. Please do it."

"All right, generous person."

"I am not so generous. She is a friend. If you keep in practice while I am away, do I not benefit? You know, I hated to tell you too suddenly, but I am going on to Washington tomorrow."

Austin was saddened by the imminence of their parting. He had hoped she would stay for at least a few days. Subconsciously, he had wanted an opportunity to besiege her with a renaissance of devotion, to cancel thereby in part his having deceived her with Laura.

Their hours together seemed to flow at triple speed. So soon, it was time for him to go with her to the Pennsylvania Station, to put her on the Washington express. And the day was not propitious—a gloomy, raw day that was neither winter nor spring.

They got out at the Seventh Avenue entrance, and walked between the enormous gray columns into the main corridor with its shops on either hand, busy and glowing under artificial lights like the shops in a hotel arcade. The rotunda, illuminated from above through glass, gleamed wanly at a distance; it was, in fact, half a crosstown block away. The feet of travelers and porters, going and coming, made a continuous shuffling, punctuated by clicks—the tapping of the occasional cane and iron-shod heel upon stone. There was a sense of surging movement, but no crowding. The corridor was too wide, too lofty, for its capacity to be taxed. And it was a mere artery for the central hall, or rotunda, the passenger level that stretched from 31st Street to 33rd.

As he and Charlotte reached the head of the flight of plunging stairs, and his eyes could take in the whole, Austin perceived as never before that this was the most stupendous and beautiful interior in America. Here the architects of a new civilization had created and triumphed, instead of adapting some ancestral model. The outer shell of the Pennsylvania Station was that of a Greco-Roman temple, impressive only because it was big, as anachronistic as a thousand banks and city halls throughout the country. But inside a flame of genius had been at work. Space greater than that in a cathedral had been walled and roofed for a modern purpose—the handling of rushed, unthinking

American crowds, streaming day and night from city to city, to and from homes and offices and theaters. The space in a cathedral was designed to foster meditation. In a railroad terminus it was used for action, and in an intangible way the architects had combined all their effects to make that felt. The diffused, hard light, the preponderance of rectangular lines, the elimination of supporting pillars, the parsimony of decoration other than the glitter of metal and stone surfaces, even to the embossed maps that took the place of conventional frescos under the high, shallow dome. Here was a monument—more than that, an integral part of New York, that would not be remodeled because in it a form had been perfected.

Far below Austin, thousands of people wove a complicated pattern on the floor. Several trains had just arrived, and their passengers were pouring through the gates and spreading in fanshaped currents. Queues were collecting in front of other gates, pushing forward restlessly as they awaited the signal that would let them through to their seats in expresses, in locals. An extraordinary number of detached figures scurried here and there on long trips without apparent aim, yet did not destroy the harmony. A jet of energy was blowing steadily like a great wind.

He thought suddenly of the girl Beatrice Purcell, whom he had met at Theresa Glenn's luncheon. She belonged in the midst of throbbing life like this, he did not know just why. But she passed out of his mind the next moment. It was time to put Charlotte on her train.

He bought a ticket to Manhattan Transfer, so that he

would have the right to pass through the gates. Then there was another descent, to the platform this time, where the electrified trains glided in and out with terrible efficiency, smokeless and clean in the half light.

A porter located Charlotte's seat in the parlor car, and she was barely settled in it when the conductors were shouting, "All aboard!" Her farewell to Austin was smooth and hurried, the unemotional farewell of public places.

"Good-bye, Austin, I shall telegraph you from Washington this evening."

"Take care of yourself, Charlotte."

He flowed with the human tide up the steps and through the reaches of the station. His thoughts were not specific. Charlotte and her going dominated them, but already Laura was reasserting her sway. It was of Laura, perhaps, that he was thinking at the moment, when toward the Seventh Avenue end of the main corridor he ran into Eustace Lloyd.

The poet was wearing a black velours hat with a brim curling up behind and sharply down over his forehead. He was swinging a cane, with eccentric, vicious strokes as he walked. He came to an abrupt halt.

"Hello, Pierrot!" he exclaimed, smiling. His mustache and little beard gave a sinister character to his smile.

"Why 'Pierrot'?" retorted Austin, a trifle irritated.

"You've forgotten what I told you? But it doesn't matter. How are you getting along? Are you happy?"

"Nothing to complain of," said Austin coldly. He could not resist adding, "And you?"

"Now what does that mean? Obviously that you think I am jealous of you, and would be gratified if I showed some sign of it. My dear lunar compatriot, I am one Pierrot who is never jealous. I was quite young when I read in a book by an Italian named Sera that jealousy was a symptom of the disease Inferiority. I suppressed the symptom, and so vanquished the disease."

In spite of the equivocal situation between them, Austin responded secretly to Lloyd's banter and would have liked to make friends with him. But he knew that, other considerations apart, they were both far too interested in women to have time for one another.

"I congratulate you on your neat, shiny suit of armor," he said, and held out his hand.

Lloyd responded briskly and without apparent malice. He then waved his hand toward his hat in the way of a final salute, grinned at one corner of his mouth and turned to lose himself swiftly in the crowd.

Chapter 12

AS A first move for Laura and her play, Austin wrote a biographical sketch in which the high lights were adroitly overemphasized, and took it to his old Sunday editor on the Forum. Saylor was glad to see him.

"You've been making good, hey!" said the ancient turtle, withdrawing his head from the recesses of his roll top desk and squinting upward. "There's money in that publicity game, from all accounts."

Austin agreed that his calling was profitable. He produced his manuscript with photographs of Laura, and got it read on the spot.

"Fine stuff," commented Saylor, after he had glanced through the first few pages. "I don't say I'd bite if it were handed in by any press agent. But coming from you, hey!"

The article appeared two weeks later and attracted no more public attention than the thirty or forty other journalistic hurrahs of that Sunday. It made possible, however, a second article by Austin, in the World, and the Morning Telegraph sent a woman staff writer to interview Laura. She was described in the Telegraph as a sort of literary chorus girl who had done honor to the profession. A good display of pictures compensated for the gush and inaccuracies of the text.

Austin knew that a brief flurry in the Sunday newspapers would not be enough to make a producer want the play. He must follow up with some sensational coup. The latter was hard to devise, and while a number of plans took nebulous shape in his mind, he passed the second April of his maturity in the enjoyment of a holiday from the office, in the fluent pursuit of his friendships.

He called to see Theresa Glenn again, and they had tea together at a Greenwich Village place where the strange, swarthy proprietress proclaimed herself to be the city's most expert specialist in lobsters, but where almost no one ordered shellfish. The customers preferred her pastries and amazingly strong coffee, and endured her tea. They obeyed hilariously the sign above the street door which told them to "follow the red line to the Lobster Trap," and called for omelettes and apple pie.

In this restaurant, Austin heard the full story of the American gypsies. He listened also to the details of a plan Theresa had formed for him. She wanted to see him editor of one of the Cooke magazines. Darcy's Magazine, the oldest published by the house, was facing a crisis, she said. Intended to appeal to women, it had been run badly of late by an editor who featured stories scarcely above the level of the tastes of High School children. He had an incurably juvenile mind, and while he had not ruined the magazine it had fallen off in circulation. He would probably be dismissed. Theresa was anxious to use her influence to get Austin appointed in his place.

"It is not a bad shop to work in. Terribly commercial, of course, but the Cooke brothers don't interfere with their editors unless things are going wrong," she said.

Austin was inclined at first to put the idea aside as one that could not interest him seriously. His connection with Charlotte was all important. But before Theresa had finished talking, he had warmed to her enthusiasm. An editorship was something he liked to feel a possibility for the future.

"Am I tempted? Oh, no!" he teased her, stooping across the table, his chin on one palm, his eyes half closed, and flattering her with the seductive attention he knew how to bring to all women. "But don't hurry it. I have obligations now. Some day, perhaps."

She smiled, and repeated she would not be satisfied until he was editor of Darcy's Magazine. His attitude toward her sex was a light, voluptuous attitude, she said, but she had no doubt that millions of women responded to it. This was not an age of sentiment, like the one in which she had been brought up. There was still a field for monthlies that extolled the virtues of parlor and pantry, but a magazine that wanted to be read by the new generation of girls would do well to be colored by the spirit of an Austin Bride. He was a man for modern women.

He counted hers as a precious friendship, he told her. Insight on a woman's part was as much of a compliment to him as love. Theresa explained that she was also growing to love him in a way, as a sister might. She did not know why, for no one could explain human sympathies.

At the back of Austin's mind as they talked, an audacious scheme for Laura's play had been taking form. It was in connection with Walter Rupert Sloat and his great string of publications. No Sunday newspapers were quite so sensational as Sloat's, and consequently so popular. When they commenced to scream about an individual, it meant that the latter would be discussed by the mentally narcoticized masses from New York to San Francisco, and would be regarded as a celebrity by all professional exploiters of the names of the moment.

Austin knew that Sloat had trained his editors to preserve against the ordinary press agent's story a defense that they themselves would describe as hard-boiled. He was no less sure that the publisher was interested in getting publicity for a certain actress and fumed with vexation if she did not figure every week in mediums other than the ones he owned. Sloat was infatuated with Gina Corelli. He had found her in the motion pictures and had made a double star of her, on screen and stage, by pouring out money for her training, for her clothes and jewelry, for advertising without a limit. He had done this with his usual contempt for what the public might say, providing the public had nothing official to go upon. He was never seen in Gina Corelli's company. Her credit accounts in the shops were in her own name, and she cashed no checks of his. If he made innumerable visits to the apartment house where she lived—why, that was not official. He was still Walter Rupert Sloat, the father of a legitimate family, with a private palace on Park Avenue, and the gossips could mouth as they pleased.

Sloat had featured his beautiful Italian-American actress in every magazine and newspaper he owned. But obtaining space for Miss Corelli—even at a price—in other publications had not been easy. There was little give and take between himself and his business rivals. Many of them hated him, and certain righteous ones looked upon him sincerely as a menace to the Republic. Like his contemporary, William Randolph Hearst, and like Northcliffe in England, he had risen too rapidly and surely not to have aroused a vindictive jealousy.

Weighing the facts, Austin decided that it would be amusing, if nothing else, to see what he could do with Sloat.

"Would you use Gina Corelli's picture on the cover of your magazine?" he asked Theresa.

"I hardly think so," she answered, surprised.

"Hasn't it ever been suggested to you?"

"Indirectly. I didn't see why I should cater to an old scallawag like Sloat, and I'm not the sort who can be bribed."

"Suppose I were to ask you to run Corelli as a favor to me."

She stared at him, a shrewd smile hovering at the corners of her lips: "What mischief are you up to, Austin?"

He made it clear that his scheme was within the bounds of professional ethics, and could do no harm to any one.

It would be valuable to him if Theresa promised a Corelli cover, in case he should confirm the request later.

She considered the matter, moving her head slowly up and down. "There is no reason why I should not do it," she said. "Gina Corelli is really a popular movie star now. The Cookes have no special grudge against Sloat. Very well, Austin."

He thanked her, an affectionate timbre in his voice. "Pull of this kind is the secret behind many a press agent's coup, isn't it?" he could not resist adding.

"Of course, wheedling villain that you are!"

Austin wrote that week an article in praise of Laura Beltrán and adventured with it in his pocket to the house of Walter Rupert Sloat.

Seeing the publisher turned out not to be the easy thing it had been on the occasion when proofs from one of his own magazines had been the sesame. He was busy, and he never received any one except by appointment, the butler said. But he gave ground to the extent of admitting Austin and standing on guard beside him a few steps beyond the vestibule, while the secretary was being called.

That Mr. Bride had once worked on the staff of the Monthly was interesting, but failed to create a claim on Mr. Sloat's extremely valuable time, asserted the secretary sarcastically. If Mr. Bride would state his business, a letter would be written to him, making an appointment—perhaps.

"This is a strictly personal and urgent matter. Will you be so good as to take my card in?" persisted Austin.

"I suppose so," replied the secretary, watching him closely

while he scribbled on the card. It was as if he were suspected of being an anarchist who had come to assassinate Sloat.

Austin had written: "Last year, when you asked me to criticize Sloat's Monthly, you remarked I was 'all right.' Can I see you now?"

The secretary returned, smiling queerly. "Well, you know how to get to him, all right," he remarked, and showed the way to the study door beyond the anteroom.

Sloat was sitting in a stiff attitude at the long table that served him as a desk. His dark chipmunk's face wore a sulky expression, the eyes round above their pouches, the lips thrust forward and clamped to a line. The narrow nose with its rounded tip seemed astonishingly long. He nodded, and continued looking at Austin for several minutes before speaking.

"Yes, I remember you," he said, as if answering a question. "Bride, on the Monthly. What's wrong?"

"I'm not bringing you any trouble, Mr. Sloat. The Monthly and I parted company last year."

"Oh, you've left us! I misunderstood my secretary." Sloat frowned. He grew colder perceptibly. It was as evident as though he had phrased it that he expected a plea for a new job. "Why did you leave?" he snapped.

Without showing it, Austin was a trifle intimidated. This was a bad beginning. On an inspiration, he said he had a most congenial job, and then, in caustic, semi-humorous terms he answered the final question by sketch-

ing the incident of the caption and Guy Bent's lesson to his
three schoolboy editors.

"I hope the word mistress in that number didn't spoil
your day as well as Mr. Bent's," he concluded.

"Ha, ha!" laughed Sloat. His outburst of merriment
was startling. It did not go with the morbid mask of his
face, and was reduced in an instant to a flickering grin. He
stood up and went over to a cellarette, from which he produced a bottle of cognac and glasses. "Let's have a drink
on that."

"You understand, I didn't quit on any issue except that
of comfort," said Austin shrewdly.

"Sure. Bent's my best watch dog. Keeps the magazines
looking clean, eh? My orders. But I'd not care to work
under him myself."

"I prefer the game I'm in now."

"I was coming to that. What is it?"

Austin had hoped the direct question would be asked.
He finished his cognac and raised one eyebrow as he
stared quizzically at Sloat. "I press agent clever women.
It's no secret that I did the publicity for Charlotte Moore.
Now I'm interested in pushing a playwright, Laura Beltrán. I've an article about her in my pocket. If you'll order
it into your Sunday newspapers—" his voice softened to
nonchalance as he observed the publisher's face freezing
again—"why, I can guarantee a Gina Corelli cover on Filmworld, the Cooke Brothers' fan magazine."

"I knew you were here to ask me for something. But of
all the God-damned impertinent—" Sloat leaped out of

his chair and stumbled around the table. Austin thought
he intended to strike him, but did not stir.

"Was Miss Corelli ever on Filmworld? Could you get
her there, Mr. Sloat, except through some one who has
the pull I happen to have?"

Sloat glowered at him. Then a curious, remote look of
infatuation came into his eyes. He crossed his hands behind
his back and began to pace beside the table. "Why the hell
should I get mad?" he said at last. "There are no witnesses.
You fix that for my girl, and I'll run the article about
yours. Give it to me." He took the manuscript Austin
handed him and threw it on a pile of correspondence. "I
don't want to read it. It'll go downtown when Filmworld
asks Miss Corelli for her photograph."

"I'm glad we could agree. Thank you."

"Hm—yes! But don't ever try to get back on one of my
magazines. You know too much about me, young man."
Sloat fell to examining a dagger in damascene work that
lay among his papers. He waved a listless dismissal over
his shoulder with a flaccid hand.

It had been an interview upon which Austin might have
hesitated to venture if he had known his man better. A
contact with a bizarre character, medieval and cruel. But
Sloat had chanced to be in the mood to be seduced. A week
after the article appeared under a hysterical double-page
title, two producers of the Chosen Race were camping with
contracts at the door of Laura's little flat on West Eleventh
Street.

His triumph proved to be another turning point in

Austin's life. As if motivated by this newest demonstration of his flair for working in the interests of women, Theresa Glenn brought fresh enthusiasm to her plan to make him the editor of a magazine designed to appeal to the modern girl. He must allow her to suggest his name for Darcy's, she urged, and although he did not definitely consent, she telephoned him one day to say it had been arranged, and that the publishers would send him an offer in the next mail.

"You will have to say Yes. It is the favor I ask in return for the Corelli cover," she declared, half-humorously.

"I'll telegraph to Miss Moore, and if she can spare me it will be Yes," he replied.

His impulse was all in favor of accepting the editorship. Laura was becoming more and more occupied with plans for rehearsals, and later would be taking her play out of town for a try-out. He could expect to see little of her. And Charlotte had written that she would have to remain in Washington a good many weeks longer, perhaps all summer. He wired her explaining his hesitation, and received a characteristic answer, generous and wise:

"OF COURSE TAKE DARCY'S STEP UP FOR YOU AND SPLENDID FOR ME SEEING YOU CAN SWING MAGAZINE TO SUPPORT OF NATIONAL THEATER NOTHING TO PREVENT YOUR DIRECTING MY PUBLICITY LATER IN SPARE TIME MY BLESSING ON THE NEW EDITOR—
CHARLOTTE"

Austin slipped the telegram into his pocket, and without stopping to telephone he hurried down to Eleventh Street to tell Laura the news. She would be glad to hear about Darcy's, he thought. Her advice from the beginning had reinforced that of Theresa Glenn, though she had found strange the sexless comradeship that had sprung up between him and the middle-aged, half-gypsy woman.

And Laura was genuinely glad. Her black eyes glowed at him and she clasped one of his hands between both of her small brown ones, as she told him how sure she **was** he would accomplish fine ends with the magazine, would rally his own public of feminine readers. But Austin heard her vaguely. His attention was absorbed by the fact that he had found Eustace Lloyd ahead of him. The slight, bony figure of the poet lounged by the mantelpiece, framed by the many-colored backs of books on either side and above him. His favorite place in the old days, no doubt, a place into which he seemed to have fitted himself again with disconcerting poise. He had smiled and bowed when Austin came in, but had proffered no sample of his habitual sardonic banter. Through the talk concerning Darcy's, he had turned softly the leaves of a volume on Goya.

Austin knew intuitively that his presence was significant. Laura had said she would not even answer his letters unless she decided she cared for him again. He was in her apartment now, like a bland cat familiar with its nooks and corners and accepting visitors as an unavoidable annoyance.

Laura talked on volubly, a little nervously, and catching

the note in her voice Lloyd moved forward. "You will pardon me if I run along—a stupid errand I had forgotten," he murmured. "Good-bye, Mr. Bride. I'm glad to know one magazine hasn't gone to the Y. M. C. A. or the drummers' union for its editor." He vanished suavely.

"You're seeing Mr. Lloyd——"

"Oh, Austin, I wish he hadn't been here when you came with your news!" she interrupted. "I'm sorry."

"Don't be. I might just as well find out now as later."

She pressed the palms of her hands together silently, and her shoulders shook.

"Then it is true," he urged. "You like him as you used to do?"

"He wrote me such beautiful letters, Austin."

In his turn, he could discover no words.

"After what you did for my play, I feel as if I'd been horribly ungrateful."

"My dear! What has gratitude to do with love? They belong to different compartments of the brain. I loved you as a lover and helped you as a friend."

"And I shall always be your friend. Nothing can ever shake my friendship for you," she said intensely.

He had an obscure certitude that this was the truth. At the beginning, she had given him the choice between love and friendship. He had taken love, and it was dead. But the thing he had not chosen had germinated between them. An odd dénouement. He was the victor, in a sense, for he had declared friendship to be part of all cerebral passions and she, in spite of her denial, had not withheld it. It was the more lasting part. Inevitable that if one must wither it should be love. Inevitable and sad.

"Can I help about Eustace?" she pleaded. "He is my old, old sweetheart."

"No," said Austin. "These things cannot be helped."

He felt lonely, disillusioned, after he had left her. His self esteem was wounded. But he bore her no ill will. He had known that Laura Beltrán and he would never break one another's hearts.

Chapter 13

FROM Austin's editorial window on Eighth Avenue, the eye was offended by the naked brick walls of a biscuit factory, the only tall building in the westward reach to the river. But he learned to ignore it. There was interest in the glimpses of backyards filled with playing children, in the jungle of low roofs, especially the roof of a Catholic home where nuns and strange old women sunned themselves like rusty ravens. On clear days he could see the bluffs of the New Jersey shore, a narrow ribbon of water and the funnels of the French liners that docked at the foot of 15th Street. In the avenue below him, the traffic growled without respite, a traffic largely of trucks and delivery wagons. The Cooke brothers had scorned a more central location and the proximity of rival publishers; they had built where land was cheap.

Austin's office was one of the dozen or so spaces marked off in the huge printing shop for the use of those employees whom the Cookes understood least—their editors. The classic quip of the establishment was, that the brothers held magazine making to be the buying of paper at a low price, the hiring of a peculiar type of individual known as an editor to do something to the paper, and its resale for more than they had paid for it. Old members of the staff did not fail to tell this tale to a newcomer before he had been at work a day.

But the working conditions were agreeable to Austin. He started with a free hand to make what he could of the magazine. James Cooke, the younger brother, an ineloquent person, had removed a cigar from his mouth long enough to mumble the hope that the administration of Darcy's would no longer be a care to him. He had expressed also a platitudinous confidence in new brooms sweeping clean. The elder Cooke, who concentrated on financial problems, had not even troubled to utter a word of greeting. Conferences had no standing in that practical firm. From Austin's point of view, it was well.

He liked his office, a narrow room finished in dark wood and equipped with a battered desk, bookcases and a safe for manuscripts. An office that had acquired character with the passing of the years. Darcy's had been published for a quarter of a century. It had been edited by a number of clever men, and some fools. Brilliant contributors had come to it, had sat in the old visitors' chair by the old desk. It was a contact with the past of American letters to turn the leaves of its early volumes and discover that Bret Harte had written for it, that it had printed stories by Frank Norris, O. Henry and the great Stephen Crane. The commercial atmosphere of the rest of the building, the stacked rolls of paper and the machines that bound western thrillers by the ton, did not succeed in dominating the spot fenced about by the traditions of Darcy's Magazine.

Austin had a clear policy. He would please the modern woman reader, of the kind who had lost interest in the organs founded by pious Methodists and Quakers for the uplift, instruction and mild titillation of her grandmother. His public would be largely a city public. On the farm, women were still entranced by free dress patterns and homilies on domestic science. But Darcy's had never made a bid for rural circulation. It had been a magazine for the city woman, and its weakness had been a failure to move as rapidly as the times. Its proper clientele had fallen back, for want of something better, on the magazines edited by men for men. An absurd state of affairs, which Austin promised himself to remedy.

His first decision was to encourage the woman writer. The bright young men writing fiction in red-blooded magazines were not to be despised as commercial successes, he admitted. They had invented the Go-Getter as their supreme type of hero, and they were adored by traveling salesmen, by the students of correspondence schools and the noble organization of Boy Scouts. They had their following. Let them keep it. In Darcy's, however, women would be given a chance to interpret America from their point of view. Since the war, they had been splashing their world with color as never before. It was natural that they should have produced writers as well as adepts in passion and jazz.

The technical side of the magazine was fascinating to Austin. He discovered that he had a flair for executive work, for planning and building. He went over the sched-

ules carefully, arranging and rearranging the stories until
he felt that each given number created a definite effect.
He caressed his first printed issue as if it had been a child.
It might be a poor enough contribution to literature, but
it gratified him, while an issue of Sloat's or the Sunday
magazine edited by Saylor had always left him with a
sense of irritation.

Austin's only intimate among his colleagues in the
building was Theresa Glenn. They visited between each
other's offices, and sometimes had lunch together in queer
third-rate restaurants on Eighth Avenue because they could
not spare the time to ride across town to better places.
Their friendship grew. But in the matter of the companionship of women, this was a barren interlude in Austin's life.
He fretted silently at the loss of Laura. He had only commenced to gauge the possibilities of the vivid girl, it
seemed, when the cunning of Eustace Lloyd had taken her
away from him. The emotion was not deep, but it was
haunting. The too-mature affection of Charlotte's letters
failed to be a consolation. If she should return at once, he
would be happy with her again, he thought. But she gave
no sign of returning. Her projects in Washington were
becoming more complex. She believed that there, if anywhere, she would be able to find the support she needed.

So Austin worked and pitied himself, and watched the
summer ripen slowly into mid-July. It was a hotter summer
than usual, a flaming, clear season that was tropical in its
splendor. That, at least, was a sensuous pleasure to him.
He found New York superbly beautiful under the sun-

shine, a holiday city through which he loitered coolly in a palm beach suit while his neighbors gasped and wilted.

Theresa stopped at his desk one day. "I am going to send Beatrice Purcell in to see you," she said casually, as she turned the pages of a magazine.

"Beatrice Purcell?" He repeated the name not because it was meaningless to him, but in faint surprise that so many weeks had passed without his thinking consciously of its owner.

"Yes—the girl you met at my lunch at Laurier's."

"I know. You feel she has real promise as a writer?"

"I haven't seen a thing she has written, Austin. She's modest about her stuff. Knows it wouldn't suit my magazine, I guess. But I've confidence in her personality," she declared with large optimism.

"All right. Send her in."

He was looking over some revise proofs the next afternoon when Beatrice Purcell's card was brought to him. The prospect of a second meeting charmed him. "Interesting!" he murmured. He had feared vaguely that she would not trouble to come, after all. An ardent, fierce girl. A capricious girl, too, as he remembered her.

An office boy appeared at the door, then stepped aside, and she walked swiftly in. Austin got an overwhelming impression of her red hair. She was wearing a low, close-fitting hat of brown straw, with the plaits crossed to give a triangular military effect and with an orange plume curling downward at the back. Her hair dropped free of it in coppery coils on either side of her face. It was such strong,

imperious hair that it seemed as if it would have sapped
the strength of any other woman. He had a fantastic impulse to free her of its virility, to crop it below her ears to
the fashionable bobbed length, and to keep the fallen tresses
for himself. He would have liked to say gravely, "I am
going to cut your hair for you." But he was forced to tear
his eyes away from it, and as he did this he perceived the
beauty of her mouth also, wide and smiling, with teeth as
impeccable as rows of kernels on an ear of corn.

Austin arranged a chair near to the desk for her, and
she sat with her long legs crossed, the skirts of the period
revealing yards and yards of black silk stocking.

"You're two months late in bringing me a manuscript.
I've been an editor for all of two months, and you should
have been in the first day, seeing how we talked of novels
at Miss Glenn's lunch," he reproached her playfully, to
mask the flurry her appearance had caused.

"But I haven't a manuscript, even now," she cried in
the startling treble he recalled as her mannerism at the
beginning of a conversation.

"Haven't you been working?"

"Oh, yes—on the novel! I shouldn't know how to do a
short story."

He had commenced to feel quite professional again.
"Short stories are supposed to be easier. They demand a
form of their own, but it's a simpler form. You should
try one."

"Should I? I'm afraid I'm going to disappoint you, Mr.

Bride. The famous novel is only a false pretense. It kills time for me. But I'm not a writer."

There was a directness about her speech which somehow saved it from the affectation of the neophyte who decries his work in order to arouse interest in it. Austin did not know what to make of her. Curious that she should write at all; she was remote from the professional, much less the would-be professional, type. He conjectured her novel was pretty bad, a personal whim, a sort of substitute for a diary. But he pressed her to let him see it. He was there to give opinions on the work of authors, young and old, he urged.

"Silly of me not to have brought it today," she said, her voice soaring. "Miss Glenn told me to, and I come and waste your time for nothing."

"I am very happy you came, because we are getting acquainted," he answered, half closing his eyes and tilting his head back. He paid a tribute of wordless admiration to the fineness of the skin of her neck and broad, boyish chest, revealed by the deep V of her blouse. It was cream-blonde skin that was touched with pink in the warm weather and showed a few freckles. Her forearms, also, had freckles, clusters of them on the upper sides. "I feel an editor should know as many writers as possible, and talk to them about the work they have done and plan to do, if he wants the best results," he added, while all the time he was thinking of the sweetness of her skin and the tan freckles that were not blemishes to him.

"You encourage me a lot. I was going to tear up what I'd done of the novel. But if you should tell me to, I'd finish it."

"Bring it in, will you?"

"Yes, I'll bring it."

There was no excuse for keeping her any longer. He clasped her thin, firm hand and watched her until she had disappeared beyond the doorway.

He imagined that she would come with her manuscript the next day, but several days passed and there was no word of her. The picture he bore in his memory faded a little. He looked with interest at a sleek brunette who had joined the staff of one of the other magazines. A sudden unjust irritation at the brunette swept over him, however, and at the end of the week he visited Theresa's office and asked her if she had had any news of Beatrice Purcell.

"She has been in once, you know. A mighty interesting girl. I neglected to take her address, but I thought she understood she was to come again with a manuscript," he said.

"I'll see her tonight, and I'll tell her you want to see her," replied Theresa, and at the last word glanced up. "Why not join us, Austin? Dinner is already ordered for a small party. But come in for coffee. At Mrs. Strickett's."

"Where is Mrs. Strickett's?" he asked, emphasizing the queer name.

"That lobster restaurant, where we had tea. Remember?"

The suggestion gave him a pleasure which he only partly

admitted to himself. He wanted to be in Beatrice's company, but he was not prepared to acknowledge that she attracted him deeply. He sensed something hard about her, hard and puzzling to him with all his knowledge of women. He resolved he would make himself equally mysterious to her. He would flirt and yet keep her at arm's length, the fierce, red-haired girl.

Austin mooned about the streets of Greenwich Village until long after the dinner hour. He had dined at the Lafayette. A stroll by way of Washington Square, Fourth Street, Seventh Avenue and Greenwich Avenue brought him back eventually to Eighth Street, and stepping into the hallway he followed Mrs. Strickett's bizarre red line.

He saw Beatrice at once, in profile, and was astonished afresh at the vigor of her young head. Her nose was aquiline, and her chin salient. Too bony, perhaps, her chin. The line of her jaw was sharply drawn. In repose, she had a stern, medieval look, but she spoke across the table and smiled, and in an instant she ceased to remind him of Cecilia or Catherine of Sienna.

He was enraged to note that she was talking to an appalling little man. Since the latter was the only other guest remaining with Theresa, Austin supposed he must be Beatrice's escort. The effect was grotesque. A second-rate person, after all, if she could go out with this snub-featured, badly dressed plebeian.

"Here he is now!" exclaimed Theresa. She raised her hand awkwardly. "We had almost given you up, Austin."

Taking a seat on the opposite side of the table from

Beatrice, he gave a glib, flippant account of himself. Temperamental authoresses had demanded his presence here and there about New York, he said, and he had obeyed in the cause of duty, literature and devotion to women. He played with words as the poet, Eustace, might have done, on the impulse, without knowing why he invented his absurdities.

"The most exigent beauty of them all gave me her photograph," he declared. "Who wants to see it?"

He had in his pocketbook a snapshot he had made of the delicious angora, Grisette. It was this he produced and held so that only he could see the face.

"Show it, show it!" cried Beatrice.

Austin looked at her wide, bright mouth whose smile was contradicted by a momentary hardness in her eyes. "Yes, you shall see it. You first, Miss Purcell. But you must be honest, and if you find her beautiful you must tell me so." He passed the photograph across the table.

An exclamation of pleasure rewarded him. "What a lovely cat!" said Beatrice.

The others laughed. They would not believe it was a cat until they had seen the photograph for themselves. The small hoax had been a success, and Austin talked on, in a mood of light irony. He paid not the slightest attention to the ridiculous man beside him until the latter pushed back his chair and announced that it was time for him to return home to Newark. It became clear he had not accompanied Beatrice. The sudden amiability with which Austin said good-night to him seemed to surprise him dimly. He made a shambling exit, and Theresa identified him as a motion picture fan, a subscriber to her magazine who had written so many letters in praise of articles on the home life of Mary Pickford, Charlie Chaplin and Norma Talmadge, she had thought it a due reward to invite him to dinner.

"But Miss Purcell and myself you invited so that we could talk about novels," said Austin. "With your pet subscriber out of the way, let's talk about them. Why haven't you brought the manuscript to me, Miss Purcell?"

"I've been finishing another chapter," she told him, a sharp, forward movement swaying her torso from its rigidity against the back of her chair.

He was on the point of holding her to an appointment at the office when Theresa excused herself to gossip with Mrs. Strickett at another table, and he altered his plan.

"Tomorrow is Saturday. A bad morning for visitors, because it is so short. We close at noon. But if you'd care to come to the place where I work in off hours! Room Nine, 38 East Sixteenth Street"—it was the number of his little library with its separate entrance—"We could talk without any of the distractions of the Cooke Brothers' factory."

Her humid, gray-green eyes were gay, yet inscrutable. "Wherever you say, Mr. Bride. But it's an imposition, isn't it, on Saturday afternoon."

"I want to see both you and your book," he urged. "Let's set it definitely for three-thirty."

"All right."

They chatted in a smooth transition about the oddity

of Greenwich Village restaurants, where women like Mrs. Strickett made a virtue of painted tables without table-cloths, of cutlery from the ten-cent store and recipes from demoded cook-books. But agreeing that her coffee was good, they encouraged Theresa to order more and the party of three re-formed itself for a brief epilogue of unimportant talk.

Both Beatrice and Theresa had long distances to go home, the one to Brooklyn, the other to the edge of the Bronx. They would not allow Austin to accompany them. They would take the subway, they said, at the same station, though in opposite directions.

But when they reached the street, it was to encounter a downpour of summer rain, unseasonable and swift. They stood laughing in the doorway and signaled to taxis that would not stop. "We shan't need a cab. A July rain never lasts long," declared Theresa in her practical way. She was right. The screen of slanting drops thinned out and subsided, and Austin stepped with the two women on to a sidewalk that appeared to smoke as the water evaporated from the warm stone.

He saw them to the subway station at Astor Place and touched their hands, murmuring traditional words of farewell. He did not remind Beatrice that he expected to see her the next day. His eyes followed her tall, spare figure until it disappeared down the flight of steps.

Turning about, Austin walked slowly westward. An imprecise preoccupation carried him past the crossing at University Place, where he could have taken the shortest road home. He went on to Sixth Avenue, enjoying the cool air after the rain, the aspect of the wet house fronts. The El station at Eighth Street and the avenue crouched fantastically like a great spider, of which its iron stairways were the sprawling legs. Beyond, the Jefferson Market courthouse and prison showed a medieval silhouette, unlighted except for the dials of its clock. An admirable tower, but meaningless in the architecture of New York, a copy of a French donjon-keep, thought Austin, as he circled it and drifted east again. He found the irregular streets beautiful in the summer night. A few hours before, he had loitered through them, his mind on a meeting that might have proved fruitless, his faculty of observation blunted. Now, they were beautiful, beautiful.

Chapter 14

USTIN went to his library immediately after lunch on Saturday. He had become attached to the small room, completing its equipment for his needs with odds and ends of garniture and a steady accretion of books. On the table stood two singular candlesticks. He disliked a crude light, and in experimenting for a way of using candles tall enough to shine down upon his typewriter, he had bought a pair of slender glass vases intended each to hold a long-stemmed rose. He had perverted them to the holding of candles. The grease had flowed over and made lines and splashes he thought pretty on the glass, and he had not scraped it away. For months, he had replaced burned out candles with new ones of a different color. The vases were hidden now by cascades of tallow as variegated as the old-fashioned barley sugar in country stores.

"They are monuments to my sense of color," he reflected gravely, as he fussed with them, and in honor of Beatrice Purcell's hair set gorgeous orange candles in place.

The door connecting with the bedroom was shut. As far as a visitor could have told, the library was an isolated workshop. Austin wanted Beatrice to have that impression, and not to think he had maneuvered her into coming to his apartment. It did not matter whether she had learned from Theresa Glenn that he lived at the same address. The atmosphere of the room where he received her was all that was important.

But would she come? he wondered. He had never felt so uncertain about a woman. Her glittering surface, her light, keen talk, together with a reserve of challenging strength—these were entirely of her generation. Odd that he should find the result baffling. Was he not of the same generation? He felt it would be futile to prophesy she would do this or that, as it would be possible to predict, for instance, that he would respond to a sign given him by a sympathetic woman. Yet she was simpler at heart than he. She would do what she wanted to do, come if she wanted to come, stay away—their appointment notwithstanding— if her inclination had changed in the meanwhile.

He dallied among his books, reading calmly at first, then changing with a nervous inconsequence from the Satires of Persius to a new translation of Oriental poems, called "Colored Stars." He found some admirable renderings from the Chinese and promised himself he would read them to Beatrice. But would she care for poetry? It was astonishing to realize that he could not foretell her tastes. She was unlike Elizabeth and Maude O'Neill, who could be catalogued easily, the one cultivated but unliterary, the other emotionally bookish. Equally unlike Charlotte and Laura with their civilized, their catholic, interests.

"I have only to talk to her alone, about things not connected with business," he thought. "She cannot hide her personality from me—will hardly try to do so. But, on my side, I shall be mysterious. She shall not understand me at once. The effect will be to attract her, to pique her curiosity concerning me."

The system seemed to him to be an excellent one.

He had returned to the precocious Roman satirist when he heard her step upon the stairs. He was sure he recognized it. A firm step with a hurrying run and lift to it, the heels rapping evenly on the naked boards. Austin slipped over to the door and opened it. He saw Beatrice already on the landing, a flicker of excitement on her face, her hair flaming.

"Oh, is that you?" she cried, and the triviality somehow did not sound banal.

"This is the right person and the right place," he answered, smiling. "Did the dark stairs confuse you?"

"No, but I smelled ether or something, and I almost turned back. I thought I was in the wrong house, a house full of queer doctors, perhaps."

They both laughed. "I've yet to discover what chemical it is they make on the ground floor," he said. "It haunts the stairs like a ghost. I'd miss it now, if it disappeared."

"It's nice and mysterious, all right."

She entered the room, carrying a brief case in black leather that was rather battered and distended with papers showing white at one carelessly strapped corner.

"Your manuscript?" he murmured, glancing at the brief case.

"Yes, but don't suggest looking at it while I am here, Mr. Bride. I couldn't bear to watch your face. You'll likely hate it as much as I do."

"It's pretty bad, then?" he remarked, coolly impersonal.

"Oh, I don't know! You must decide." She took out a mass of typewritten pages, assembled haphazard, unconfined even by a rubber band, and laid them with a gesture of finality face down upon the table. "That's that!"

Austin made no further reference to the manuscript. He gave the divan to Beatrice and seated himself in a rocking chair opposite her, between the work table and a shelf of books. His narrowed eyes studied the triumphant severity of her features, discovering new details. The height of her forehead was dissimulated in part by loops of hair. The plucking of her eyebrows into long arcs had a subtle note of austerity. But always there was her smiling mouth.

"Will you answer some personal questions?" he asked abruptly. "Where were you born, and things like that?"

She said, her tone negligent, in no way reproving his curiosity, that she had been born on Brooklyn Heights, in an old street which she liked to revisit because it was still unspoiled. But her family had moved years ago to Sheepshead Bay. She loved swimming, the sea, and did not mind the distance from the center of town. Brooklyn, anyway, was a more interesting place to live than Manhattan. Her father had thought so, too. He had worked up to the moment of his death on a Manhattan newspaper, but he had never cared to move across the river.

"Why is Brooklyn more interesting?" demanded Austin, in surprise. It had not occurred to him that there were people of that opinion.

"Why? Because it's the part of New York where most New Yorkers live. And especially if one was born and went to school there—it's natural we should think so, I suppose."

Brooklyn suddenly seemed less of a desert of mediocrity than it had been in his imagination. Amazing! He wondered whether her novel was about Brooklyn. Local color by a journalist's daughter. It would be logical. Fumbling for her secret springs, he asked: "Did your father's work give you the idea of writing?"

"I don't think so. He was sporting editor of The Chronicle, and he never tried to do fiction."

"You are Irish, of course?"

"Of course—with the name I have. But my father and mother and my grandparents were all born in Brooklyn."

She had begun to grow faintly restless. His manner of showing an interest in her had seemed too editorial, thought Austin, and he shifted suavely. He read her a dialogue in poetic prose on which he had been working and which no one else had heard. The hero was the god Pan, a whimsically anachronistic Pan who held sensuous converse with mortals on a strange road. The lines sounded well in recitation, better than he had supposed, and created an atmosphere of glamor. Beatrice did not interrupt him, but he could see her features relax, her mouth soften, and a green flame add ardor to her eyes.

"Oh, it's a lovely thing!" she said when he had laid the manuscript down.

"You really mean that?"

"Most lovely," she repeated.

He thanked her softly, and in reaching for the book of translations which he had replaced on its shelf he came so near to the divan that it was the inevitable thing to sit beside her. Almost imperceptibly, her body swayed toward him instead of away, as he had feared. But he opened the volume and shared with her the beauty of Chinese verse. He read some lines about a mandarin who, leaning on a jade balcony, observed mournfully the flawless monotony of spring. An exquisite ennui, an old sophistication, had survived in the English words. Austin could see that Beatrice found them no less beautiful than he did.

He asked himself how she would take it if he should kiss her. There was little doubt that he could have a premature kiss. But he resolved that it must not be. Much better that she should sense his desire and the check he put upon it. He intended not even to touch her, yet his hand strayed toward her lap. For a second or two their palms and fingers met. Beatrice neither responded to him, nor showed the least sign of displeasure. He drew his hand away, gently.

"Will you have dinner with me some evening, Miss Purcell?" he asked.

"If you want—want me to. Yes. I'd love it." She was looking steadfastly at the opposite wall.

"What evening shall it be?"

She rose and made a vague movement to pick up her brief case. "Almost any evening you say."

"Next Tuesday?"

Beatrice was walking toward the table, was passing in front of him. She paused, and with one knee bent the lines of her body were those of a lithe dancer. She looked down at him, smiling, her head tilted away. "I have an engagement for next Tuesday, but I will break it," she said, her voice richer and sweeter than he had ever heard it.

He treasured the implication in her willingness to set others aside for him, but he left it unexpressed. More intensely than before, he wanted to kiss her, but he clung to his rôle and saw her to the door, touching her hand lightly in farewell, and murmuring, "Where shall I find you on Tuesday?"

"It's too far out to Sheepshead Bay. I'll come to your office."

"Good-bye, then—until Tuesday."

"Good-bye."

After she had gone, Austin turned mechanically to the disordered manuscript of her novel. But he did not read it. A curious hesitancy delayed him. The girl herself appeared more interesting than anything she could have written. He was afraid of being disappointed, and so wished to dwell upon the certitude of her charm before he became her literary critic.

He sought to analyze her hold on his imagination, and was puzzled. The things she said were not extraordinary, and she was not obviously beautiful. Until that day, if asked for a snap judgment, he would have said she was less appealing than some of the women he had known, less poignant. Odd that he should remember with a clarity new in his experience, every detail of their four meetings, how she had looked in this position and that, the nuances of her coloring, her gestures, the least words they had uttered to one another. He had yielded at all points to her personality, slowly, without knowing that he yielded. If Theresa had not sent her to his office, he probably would never have followed up their original meeting at Laurier's restaurant, sharply-etched memory though it had been. Now, he could not imagine himself enduring a loss of contact with her.

Time dragged for Austin between Saturday and Tuesday. He went for solitary walks. He passed long hours with his books, but he did not read the manuscript that Beatrice had left with him.

She came to Darcy's a few minutes before closing time at five o'clock. It was too early to think of dinner, and in prohibition-stricken New York the natural interlude of cocktails at the Brevoort or the Lafayette was no longer possible. There were no good speak-easies as yet. So Austin made tea on an alcohol burner he kept on top of the safe. He produced biscuits from a drawer of the desk, and rummaged among his papers for queer low cups with solid horizontal ears on either side instead of handles,

cups in a cheap Breton ware he had bought in Paris and
which he valued because he had had them so long. He
laughed gaily with Beatrice over the makeshift entertain-
ment, and the tea was a success. Afterwards, they looked
over back numbers of the magazine together until it was
time to go.

On that day at the height of summer, the sunlight had
scarcely commenced to weaken when they left the building
at six-thirty. The sky was cloudless. A light, tepid breeze
blew from the river. The tropical brilliance, the volup-
tuousness of the air, the very film of dust upon the sidewalks, gave to the city the aspect that Austin loved best.

His hand curved about Beatrice's elbow. They had decided to walk to Houston Street, to a restaurant he had
discovered and had found amusing. The timid Italian
proprietor peered at one around the edge of the door and
admitted only his trusted patrons and their friends to share
the joys of dreadful bootleg whiskey and red wine, he told
her. But the dinner was good, and the place had not yet
been swamped by the rag-tag of Greenwich Village and
automobile parties from uptown.

Austin recalled later that they evaded the topic of
themselves as they strolled by way of Fourteenth Street
to Fifth Avenue and through Washington Square into the
shabby Italian quarter. Their flippant talk about nothing
in particular died down, however, when they were in the
restaurant. They had been put at a round table intended
to seat four, and taking chairs on the same side they turned
half about to face each other. Too many forks and spoons,

plated and shiny, were ranged on the white cloth. A basket of bread-sticks and a vase with jaunty marigolds stood between them. Daylight still streamed under the slanting roof of this backyard extension where they had come for their first dinner together.

As if by a complicity long since determined, they entered upon a discussion of love.

"I've been thinking so much about your Pan play," said Beatrice. "It's poetry all right, but I wouldn't like it as I do if you hadn't put something of yourself into it. Writing has got to make me feel the author, or I don't care for it usually."

This was the first literary judgment he had heard her pass, but a sure instinct taught him that the lead he should follow was not that of literature. "Tell me why I remind you of Pan?" he asked.

"Your forehead runs up into your hair in two points, and your ears slope back a little. Ah, yes!" She nodded gravely. "And you've had many, many love affairs, haven't you now?"

"Not so many as you imagine. I've loved women all my life, but if I'd had the vanity of numbers I'd not have found time to understand any of them, to learn anything worth learning about either women or love." A swift calculation had guided Austin's answer. Beatrice found him interesting because he adored her sex, he thought; but she would despise him if he seemed a mere collector of love affairs. He was glad it was not necessary to lie to her, while admitting to himself that had his record been that of a Casanova he would have lied eloquently.

"I've never flirted seriously with a woman I didn't think the most exquisite woman in sight, and I've never gone into an affair without being in love," he went on.

"You're a wise Pan," she murmured. "But what is being in love?"

"It's being absorbed in the other person, not necessarily for a lifetime or any set period, but as long as the mutual charm lasts. There should be no heavy tragedy in love, no jealousy and cruelty. The one who loves longest should be ashamed to put a blot upon the beauty that has been by tormenting the other. He should understand the time has come to look for a new love, that is all."

"A nice, wise Pan," repeated Beatrice. "You see it in a perfectly ideal way." Her eyes were impenetrable, because if there was mockery in them it was subordinate to her youth. But Austin was certain that her mouth, at least, was free of irony, that the intangible hardness in the ensemble of her features had melted.

It came over him like a revelation, almost naïvely, that she was playing the game of love with a hand less experienced than his, no doubt, but still experienced. She had been already wooed by some man—successfully wooed; he would have sworn to it, and for an instant it rendered him miserable. He wanted to commit the folly of questioning her. The mask of his own face, however, became more impassive, and he observed silently the seductiveness of her body. Cheeks flattened under high cheek-bones, a neck that sloped into the shoulder muscles of a swimmer, the delicate swelling of breasts on a strong torso, the exultant fire of her hair.

How life rejoiced in repeating its situations! he thought. But only its situations; all else was invariably different. A few short seasons ago he had taken Maude O'Neill to an Italian restaurant, had schemed to have her go home with him. Now Beatrice sat across the table—in an Italian restaurant, she too. And the drama bore no resemblance to the one in which he had played before. He was an older Austin, for one thing, and the personality of Beatrice was such that, in the last test, he must gamble for her rather than scheme. Nothing he might tell her in the future could ever make clear the terrible importance to him of the next few minutes.

"You remember the photograph of the haughty beauty I showed you the other evening?" he asked, quite calmly.

"Of your cat—yes," she answered, her eyes brightening.

"I'd like you to see herself. After dinner—would you care to drop in at my place?"

Beatrice's noncommittal smile flashed at him. "I think it would be nice to do that. I want so much to see her," she said.

They walked out into the garish turmoil of streets where fruit stalls and the stands of dealers in colored syrups and ice cream were busier than in the daytime, where children tumbled on the sidewalks and adults stood in front of show windows that flaunted shoddy suits and frocks and hats at derisory prices. Houston Street, Macdougal Street,

Bleecker Street. A fantastic road to Cythera. Austin noted
every turn that he and Beatrice took. His hand tightened
on her arm. They paused to laugh at a photographer's
display: rigid bridal couples, barbers and waiters in the
attitudes of grand opera tenors, dignitaries of the neighborhood with mustaches like the horns of buffaloes. Then
they crossed Washington Square and sauntered up Fifth
Avenue.

Beatrice made no comment on the direction they were
taking. Her pace slackened as they approached the house
in 16th Street, and she swung without guidance up the
steps. Beyond the vestibule, she whispered in a little, dry
voice, "You had better go first." Austin was sharply aware
of her heels rapping behind him on the uncarpeted stairs.
The same firm step for which he had listened the other
day. He fumbled somewhat as he unlocked his door and
showed her into the large room. Nicer if he should leave
it in darkness, he thought. But that might startle her. So
he turned on one dim light only, and a little absurdly,
pointedly, he called at once to Grisette. The cat failed to
come, because of a stranger's presence. She settled comfortably in his arms, however, when picked up and taken
across the room to greet Beatrice.

"See, Miss Purcell, isn't she beautiful?"

Grisette's eyes shone enormous and golden, and her two
silver forepaws hung guilelessly below her cloudy ruff.
Beatrice caressed her with ecstatic stroking.

"Oh, beautiful, beautiful!" she said, a catch in her voice.

"She's making friends with you more easily than with

most people," observed Austin, pleased. Nevertheless, he restored Grisette to the cushion where she had been sleeping and turned about, his heart beating. Beatrice was at the extreme edge of the couch, a seat chosen at random because he had neglected in his confusion to bring up a chair for her. Her body was straight, though leaning sideways on one palm. The upper part of her face was veiled from Austin in the uncertain light, but he was acutely conscious of her lips, red and parted in a tremulous smile.

He said something he was never able to recall, because it was meaningless and did not demand an answer. Ridiculous to make conversation, he thought, when the thing he wanted above all else in the world was to join his mouth to hers.

He moved swiftly and took her in his arms, aware intuitively he would not be repulsed. But after their lips had clung together once, she threw her head back, her throat quivering.

"No, no! Ah, no! I must go home," she gasped.

"But you want to stay. You know you do," he urged, in avid tenderness.

She found no words to answer that. Her body became miraculously supple, adjusting itself to him as his arms closed about her more completely, as his lips trailed from mouth to eyes, from her closed eyes to the hollows of her neck and back to her mouth again. He lifted her on to the couch and lay down beside her. Her flesh burned against him, a heat of life, a conflagration of the senses. Her hair had come down immediately, in great auburn ropes that unplaited on her shoulders and glittered with ruddy high lights. Austin buried his face in her majestic hair. It was virile against his cheeks, and its odor like the bark of a slightly resinous tree intoxicated him. His arms tightened in a new affirmation of victory until their bodies were locked together. The pounding of her heart was in his ears.

"We have given the oldest answer on earth to all hesitations," he thought, at the high tide of emotion. "But have there ever been hesitations? None on my side, perhaps none on hers. Love . . . fatality . . . destiny. . . ." His thoughts trailed away nebulously.

They fell, later, to touching each other gently, with inquiring finger tips, with warm palms halting for immeasurable instants. Their faces nestled into a contact that had no urgent need of kisses, and their muscles relaxed, lulled by the rhythm of their breathing. An exquisite peace possessed them. When Grisette slipped like a gray ghost across the room and joined them on the couch, purring, their glances met in a smile, as at a good omen.

They got up and made tea, speaking of commonplace things in low, faraway voices. Some relatives would be coming to Beatrice's house the next day, she said. She was going with her uncle to the races. She must remember to buy a new hat in the morning, and a pair of gloves. And the talk of buying things reminded Austin that he should call at a shop on Thirteenth Street to get a volume of Swinburne's "Chastelard" he had left to be rebound.

"Won't we see each other at all tomorrow?" he asked, worried.

Her face fell. "I'm afraid not, with my uncle coming."

"The next day, then?"

"Of course, the next day. And, you know, I must start for home very soon now. I hate to leave you, but I must."

Standing by the door, they embraced in a feverish exchange of kisses, each one of which was to have been the last. It seemed impossible to say Good-bye. Yet the words were said, and they went down to the street. They walked shoulder to shoulder, her hand clasped warmly on Austin's arm. He expected to ride out in the subway with her to Sheepshead Bay, but when they reached the station Beatrice would not allow him to go any farther. She was accustomed to making the trip alone, she insisted, and did not want him to have the discomfort of the long ride back. He was forced to yield to her. She had gone through the turnstile and was swallowed up in the waiting crowd of passengers before he fully realized she was no longer with him.

He comforted himself with the promise that he would read her book when he got back to the house. He found his rooms, however, alive with the memory of her physical passage. His body ached subtly and deliciously. It was sweeter to sit by the open window, with Grisette on his lap, and dream of Beatrice.

The next morning, instead of going to the office, he read her book. He began it hopefully, a little suspiciously. After he had turned a few pages his hand trembled as it touched the paper and his eyes were alight. It was a first novel of extraordinary value.

Chapter 15

A FEW hours before he was to see Beatrice again, Austin remembered that he had promised to speak that evening at a literary club in Brooklyn. He had been invited as the editor of Darcy's, as an authority on the fiction requirements of a popular magazine. It had amused him to picture a group of men and women earnestly awaiting a message on the earning of checks. Probably, they would not be at all interested in the subject of writing well. He wished now that he had not agreed to go. He was furious at the complication, until it occurred to him he might ask Beatrice also to be at the High School where the literary club met. They could leave early, as soon as he had finished speaking.

Austin telephoned to her house, and was greeted by the same voice that had answered his calls through the past two days. A grave, equable voice. Her mother's, no doubt. He felt a tenderness for her mother, and tried to imagine what she looked like. As he mused, Beatrice herself came to the telephone—a young, soaring voice, almost a treble, as she spoke to him clearly, a trifle distantly because of her mother's presence.

Yes, she would be glad to hear his speech. She would

meet him at the school. Surely, she knew where it was. The Boys' High, at Marcy and Putnam. Until eight o'clock, then, at the main entrance.

He pushed the instrument aside, relieved, and forced himself to get rid of a tag-end of work awaiting him on his desk.

On the purely critical side, Austin was possessed by the memory of the manuscript Beatrice had left with him. Its excellence stunned him. He had discovered faults of construction, but none in the more difficult art of using the right words to make her characters live, her settings real. A fresh, limpid style. Where had she learned it? No influence of the work of any master was apparent. She had written about a girl who had been born about the time she was born, had lived, had loved, had married. The old chronicle of human existence. Yet she had made of it a generalization of her times, her city. A New Yorker in her capacity for all the emotions, this heroine of hers was as hard and glittering as New York. She moved to the music of a jazz band, an unsentimental hedonist, terribly civilized, but without traditions. She was presented as a matter of course, brusquely, a girl who had been made to step out of the ranks of the five million and strut her stuff in a show window. At no point was she self-conscious. She was absorbed in the lurid round of life, and did not perceive even that she was a type. Beatrice had avoided the error of giving her the powers of observation with which her chronicler was equipped.

Futile to try to pin such writing down to models,

origins, Austin decided. It was plainly spontaneous. The average good novelist achieved style at the end of a long apprenticeship, in which his problem had been to eliminate the florid, the artificial, to discover how to be simple. Beatrice's was a form, if an unfinished novel could be said to have form, that had been reached by the short cut of genius.

He was glad that he had fallen in love with her, had wooed her at the frontiers of the flesh, before he read her manuscript. He would always have questioned otherwise whether he had not been more enamored of her talent than of herself. Delighting in the combination, he believed it had been her mind that had first attracted him, but subconsciously. His theory about the mental and physical oneness of intelligent love was justified. The influence, however, of a marvelous product of her mind—the book—would have been beclouding.

After a hurried dinner, Austin set out for Brooklyn. He knew little about the geography of the huge borough, and looking up a route on the Eagle Almanach's map he ended by taking the one that proved to be the most roundabout. He changed at the Bridge to an antique Elevated train crowded with homegoing burghers. The car in which he found himself was shabby and ill-lit, a flimsy thing that looked as if it were constructed of wood, though no doubt it was of steel painted a long time ago to imitate a shade of wainscoting in old-fashioned houses, he thought. There was a long run through a wilderness of poor streets with a provincial air compared to the streets of Manhattan, and many stops at dingy stations which stood higher than the houses around them. Myrtle Avenue, Duffield Street, Franklin Avenue: they were only names to Austin.

He got off at the Nostrand Avenue station. The neighborhood was a superior one. As he walked towards the High School, he looked down vistas of perfectly tranquil streets, some of them old, with trees growing in front of the brick houses, others modernized by blocks of apartments light-colored and uniform. He found the school easily enough, a building that stood in a square of its own, a rambling, somber building, suggesting in the dim light a Norman castle such as one sees in history books, its turrets draped with ivy. Dating back only to the last generation, it appeared hoary, indefinably Brooklyn.

A few persons trickled through the gates. The school was closed for the summer vacation, but the Board was benevolently disposed toward special activities of an uplifting nature and set aside rooms in the hot weather for literary courses and literary clubs. Austin entered, his glance eagerly searching for Beatrice. But it was not until he had penetrated beyond the vestibule that he found her, the flaming, proud one, her green eyes glowing for him, her body all boyish planes and lines and alert as that of an athlete.

"I've kept you waiting," he said, in reproach of his tardiness, when his secret longing was to greet her with passionate words, to put his arms about her, there in the middle of the barren corridor.

"No, dearest. A minute or two is not waiting," she murmured.

He was stricken voiceless. She had used the most exquisite term of endearment, had called him "dearest." It must remain the name of names between them, the simple, the only possible superlative. Touching her elbow, he guided her past the numbered doors toward the room the letter of invitation in his pocket had told him how to find.

The club of aspiring writers was composed of about twenty young people of both sexes and half a dozen old maids. Its chairman was a Jewish teacher, clever and sanguine, a man who showed the pleasure he took in inspiring his little world. Flattering phrases flowed readily from his tongue as he introduced the guest of the evening.

Austin began his address with his mind elsewhere. But it was not so difficult as he had feared. The club members were full of enthusiasm: a cluster of faces with intent eyes and parted lips. All details of editorship were mysterious to them, and, thought Austin as he talked, it is a poor magician who cannot warm to a chance to display his legerdemain before the uninitiated. He was glad, however, when it was time to stop, when he had answered the last question from the audience, and could again give himself wholly to Beatrice.

They left the school and walked beside the iron railing on the Marcy Avenue side of the square. Austin had no idea where they were going. This was Brooklyn, Beatrice's Brooklyn, and she must lead the way. But the moment had come to tell her about her manuscript. A sudden panic harassed him, lest she should think his criticism insincere, the too-friendly opinion of a lover.

"Dearest, you know, I have read your book," he said, restraining himself from caressing the arm that lay on his.

"Ah, yes?" she replied on a questioning note.

"You must believe that what I'm going to tell you is what I honestly think. Where work is concerned, I'll always be as straightforward with you as with a stranger."

"I want you to be."

"Very well. It's good, Beatrice. It's good enough for me to class it among the two or three best unpublished manuscripts I've ever read."

"Good!" Her step faltered oddly.

"I mean that. There are some blunders in the way the plot is built up. You know very little about technique." His tone was deliberately judicial. "But it is written brilliantly, with real talent."

"I had no idea—I thought you were going to say it was terrible. I wouldn't have minded—not in the least, no matter what you had said, dearest."

"It's wonderful when the truth can be so nice," he answered complacently. "You have it in you to be a great writer."

"But I don't want to be a writer," she cried. "I can't bear to think of myself as one."

Austin was overwhelmed with astonishment. "Impossible," he muttered. "Your talent is out of the ordinary. Impossible that you shouldn't want it."

"While I have beautiful things to do, why write?" she protested. "Don't you understand? I have you now. We've only just begun together."

Her fiercely modern ego prohibited the suspicion on his part that she wished to immolate her mind for domesticity, as her grandmother would have done. Austin stared helplessly. "Don't you understand?" she repeated. "Life doesn't exist in order that there may be literature. The lucky, strong ones live and the disappointed make novels about it. Of course, if my life becomes empty again, I will want to write.".

"I've always been guided by a sort of worship of books," he said.

"You are you. I read for pleasure, but I started to do my book because I was unhappy."

"Unhappy in what way, dearest?"

"I'd been married for several years, and it wasn't a success any longer. We spent our time quarreling because there was nothing else to do—nothing for me, at any rate, until I thought of writing."

The knowledge that she had been married shocked Austin unreasonably. Terrible that she should have belonged to any one else so wholly, he thought. He made no comment, but she sensed his feeling.

"You didn't know? Ah, but it doesn't matter about him! He has gone away from New York. I had left him before he went, and I took my unmarried name again. But I should have told you sooner!"

"Who was he?" asked Austin steadily.

"Blaise Doyle, a Dublin Irishman. A fanatical republican, dearest. He could talk of nothing else. He is over there now, fighting the Black and Tans."

"Weren't you in sympathy with Irish freedom?"

"Ah, yes, I was!" she answered gravely. "But it was only sympathy. I wasn't born as he was in the middle of that war. Our lives came together for other reasons and broke apart because there was no more love."

"I'm not jealous, really. That would be idiotic. The past doesn't matter, as you say."

"Neither your past nor mine," she declared, her supple body moving in closer to him. "I love you, and you must love me—a firm, strong love. And if you think I should finish the novel, I'll finish it."

"I do think so. You have a wonderful start. Please work it out, please," he urged.

"It's a promise," she told him, a lilt in her voice.

They had turned at the first crossing beyond the school and had reached a busy shopping avenue not unlike the Main Street of a provincial town. Women's dresses hung in brightly illumined shop windows, modest little dresses posing as Paris models, gaudy dresses, plebeian summer frocks, dresses for all tastes. A double window at a gore was filled with straw hats for the compliant male, stiff hats of an identical pattern, which held the eye on the sole basis of quantity. The three drug stores in the block were gay with old-fashioned revolving globes, blue and carmine and mauve; they had gilded mortars and pestles above their doors. Restaurants named unpretentiously after their owners crowded one another in a succession of artless displays of shellfish, uncooked steaks, salads and fruits, and many pies.

Austin and Beatrice entered a place that advertised its superior merits by calling itself a pastry shop. They sat at a little marble-topped table at the far end, and had coffee with oblong cream-layer cakes that purported to have been made according to a French recipe. Youths physically awkward and verbally bold leaned across the other tables to girls with shrewd, bright eyes and bantered their way through the intricacies of an old game. A place of middle-class flirtations, a rendezvous without aesthetic beauty. But every detail of the room, the bare walls, the tall glasses of ice cream soda garnished with straws, the cakes, the tea-pots and coffee-pots, impressed themselves on Austin's brain. He knew he would never forget them. That once only, were he and Beatrice likely to come there. But they had come on an evening of sweet poignancy in their lives, and through the naïve chatter about them they had sought for definitions of love.

It sounded clever to call it this and that, yet there was no definition, really, they concluded. There was the paradox that the sexes were eternally at war and eternally uniting—little else that could be put into words, despite the fact that subtle lovers wooed the mind first, the senses afterwards. The final point had been made by Austin, and she had agreed with him, smiling tenderly and inscrutably.

They loitered away from the restaurant in the warm night, their hands seeking each other out and clinging, without shame at the occasional glances of passersby. Crossings taken haphazard brought them at last to another long, wide avenue. It was Bedford Avenue, Beatrice said, and began lightly to point out familiar places. She had lived for a short while in the apartment house at a certain corner. The grocery store in the middle of the next block had been where she had done her marketing. Associations from her years of marriage, reflected Austin, wounded; but a pleasure in looking at spots that had known her presence was keener than the wound.

If they wished to walk on the avenue far enough, they would come to a trolley line she could take home, she said. They did not discuss alternatives, aware without putting it into words that any modification of their course would profane the charm that hovered between them. It was delicious to go forward slowly, without regard to time, talking of trivial, intimate things unconnected with plans for the future. They were astonished to reach the trolley line so soon.

Beatrice made a gesture of farewell, brief and mournful, yet definite, as she got on to her car, and Austin did not try to accompany her. He watched her until she was out of sight, then turned away to look for a subway station.

A resolution that had been forming at the back of his mind swelled into major importance on the trip home. He must write to Charlotte Moore and tell her about Beatrice. A difficult necessity. He would have undergone any physical punishment rather than face it, but this was one of life's stern decencies from which immunity could not be purchased. He was supposed still to be the lover of Charlotte, and he loved Beatrice. Odd that in the case of Laura he had felt no compunction about playing a double rôle. His highly artificial affair with Laura had scarcely seemed an injury to Charlotte, and Laura herself had been indifferent to his amatory complications. It was much of a question now whether honesty with Charlotte or a repugnance for even nominally withholding a part of himself from Beatrice were the stronger motive. The latter, probably. His confession, at all events, must be made at once.

Austin tore up several letters before he found the right note of sincerity. Keeping clear of a pretense of tragic self-reproach, he phrased his remorse analytically, a little wistfully. He spoke of his adoration of women, of how Charlotte coming into his life at the moment she had come had ripened his spring into summer. He admired her deeply and unalterably. The words in which he expressed his admiration of her were subtly passionate. But another woman had sounded another chord in him. Shallow of him, no doubt, to be able to love so often; but he was as he was. He said almost nothing about the personality of Beatrice, allowing her to remain a symbol of the change in himself. His final paragraph was a plea for friendship as an aftermath to love.

Two days later, he received his answer:

"If I had thought I could have held you, dear," wrote Charlotte, "I would have married you. Do not deny me the small vanity of believing I could have done so. A woman can generally marry a man while he is in love with her. While he is in love! But I remembered I was forty-three—yes, three years older than I used to pretend to be—and that you were thirty. I took all that I could fairly take, and held back nothing that you wanted me to give. I wept when I read your letter, but you are not to blame for that. The ruthless years that have carried me beyond the arms of a last lover are to blame. I shall not weep again.

"Friendship? It is not possible that it should ever weaken between us. I sense a capacity for friendship in you, and I know myself. We shall work better together, Austin, because we have been lovers."

He was fiercely grateful. What a contrast, he thought, to the way Elizabeth Curran, in the same circumstances, had rejected friendship. The saddest thing in existence, nevertheless, was this amputation, this overt act of putting a waning love to death.

Chapter 16

AS THE weeks wore through late summer and autumn, Austin's life merged itself with that of Beatrice in a tacit compromise of devotion and incompleteness. They did not seriously discuss living together, though both desired it. It was all very well to hold opinions about the freedom of love, the right of the individual pursuing his own happiness to ignore the prejudices of society. But Beatrice had a mother she did not wish to hurt, who regarded her as being still the wife of Blaise Doyle. Doing what she pleased in essentials was compatible with keeping her home intact. The generation to which she belonged attached little importance to the gesture of housekeeping with the beloved, if that involved family strife.

Beatrice came to 16th Street with a liberty that appeared to be quite untrammeled. She never stayed overnight, however, and she did not ask Austin to visit her at Sheepshead Bay. The latter reservation astonished him slightly. He would have liked to know every detail of her background, but assuming that she had her reasons he checked his impulse to angle for an invitation. It was sufficient that she loved him.

He burned continuously before her the incense of a supreme flattery that consisted of an avid observation of the least, last nuances of her appearance, her temperament. He was glad she was not beautiful in the conventional sense. Her vitality was more piercing than a beauty that would have softened her arrogant profile, the austere unity of her frame and her white flesh, the red thicket of her hair. His Celtic blood responded to her as a crystallization of the fair Irish strain. She must stem back to the mother and the mate of Brian Boru, to Deirdre herself. Yet in this modern American world in which she moved, how utterly modern she was.

Seeking for a single word as a key to her temperament, he decided that the word was Clarity. She was not perplexed about life, because she saw it as a succession of experiences that were stimulating to the strong, poisonous to the weak. She rejoiced in beauty, but she had no gods —as Austin had, with his worship of women and books. Counting herself, as a matter of course, among the strong, she evaded nothing that was plainly one of the conditions of the richest fulfillment. Hers was a materialism that a touch of fatalism rendered almost mystic. The excellence of her novel was due to the same sure vision, the directness, that governed her acts. All of the phases of the spontaneous hedonism she described were interesting to her. She clarified motives and used inevitable words. Clarity! In her case, it was rather a hard quality: not that of water or light, but the translucency of certain colored stones. A piece of jade without flaws in it, thought Austin, drunk with admiration.

From his analysis of Beatrice, he passed on to the formulation of a theory concerning their love. He was sure he loved her more deeply than any other woman he had known. They were ideally paired, because over and above the allure of passion there was racial and intellectual kinship between them. But it was a love that should be nurtured in special ways. Beatrice was hard, so he must never be sentimental. He must be ruled by reason, and never quarrel or exhibit jealousy. An amorous loyalty, freed of exigencies, was best for them, as for all lovers not to be classed as primitive. Into these terms he translated his own tendency of earlier years toward making a cult of fundamental indifference.

Choosing phrases that would not sound too arid, he explained his ideas to Beatrice.

"I guessed that was your point of view. But it's not important what you think or I think love should be, dearest," she surprised him by answering. "Just tell me again that you do love me."

"Beatrice, you know I do! Of course I do—beyond everything."

"You don't make it very convincing."

"You are really doubting me!" he cried, hurt.

She locked her arms about him, and her mouth quivered against his neck, half laughing and half sobbing. "Foolish one! I only meant that your voice is unconvincing, it's so bland and calm. If I doubted you, I'd want to die. And I agree with all your ideas about love."

Their evenings and holidays together which they did not spend at 16th Street were a series of adventures in adjustment to Austin. Beatrice and he had the same artistic tastes, similar reactions, superficially, to the enjoyment that could be had from watching the human comedy. But he discovered there were many pleasures in which she liked to be active, while he had merely thought about them. She was a superb dancer, a tireless swimmer, and Austin neither danced nor swam. When he talked of learning how, in order to be more of a companion to her, she smiled and said it would take him too long, that they could spend their time in other ways. Beatrice enjoyed the races, tennis tournaments, baseball—all the sports, but especially baseball, which Austin despised. Boxing was the only sport in which he took an interest. He followed the careers of the good boxers of all nations, and at long intervals he took in a bout at the old Garden in Madison Square.

"But if you like to go to prizefights, why should you snub poor old baseball which draws the biggest crowds of all?" asked Beatrice.

"Is popularity a reason for getting excited over a sport?"

"In a way, yes. Especially for you. I know you so well, dearest. You think New York is a continuous motion picture for your amusement, and yet you turn your back on some of the best scenes. Baseball is part of the life of our day. Tell me, why don't you like it?"

"It's always seemed to me an impersonal sort of thing," replied Austin hesitantly. "Rigid and mathematical. I suppose team work doesn't appeal to me. A lot of men moving about on the diamond in obedience to a complicated set of rules are not so dramatic as two pugs who win or lose as individuals. I pick the one I think ought to win, and his fortunes provide me with thrills from the start."

Beatrice burst out laughing. "That shows you don't understand baseball. If you ever saw a close pitchers' battle, you got nothing from it. Dearest, the sporting writers have had to invent a patter of their own to do justice to the pep in baseball."

Austin's complacency about the games that were banal and those that were not was unexpectedly disturbed. But he did not become an habitué of the Polo Grounds. As Beatrice had said, there were other things they could do together. The first time he suggested taking her to the theater, a challenging flicker appeared in her gray-green eyes.

"Not to one of the regular shows, please. They're usually dull. But I'm in the mood for vaudeville."

"Vaudeville!" He was delighted. "You're the first woman I've ever known who shared my low, cheap taste for vaudeville." Perversely remembering at that moment the music hall actress, Erna Ull, with whom he had once had an affair, he smiled and refrained from naming her as the single exception.

"Vaudeville may be low, but it's not cheap," said Beatrice. "It's gorgeously satirical."

"Of course it is. Our alert intellectuals fail to be alert enough to see it, that's all."

It was Saturday, and they had just returned from luncheon to the little library on 16th Street. They bent over the theatrical advertisements in an afternoon newspaper.

"Dearest, we're in luck," exclaimed Beatrice. "Ted Lewis and Ruth Roye are both at the Orpheum."

Wedged in with a Brooklyn matinée crowd, they reveled from a balcony box in the spinning of the American kaleidoscope that the variety bill afforded. A soloist, described on the programme as "A Ray of Western Sunshine," carolled songs that moved plump matrons audibly to inform their spouses that she was sweet. Incredibly muscled acrobats dived from cross-bar to cross-bar, built and unbuilt their monotonous pyramids, and bounced away into the wings, flourishing their right arms fatuously at the audience as they went. Three youths with foreheads pinched at the temples and hair slicked back, proved their right to be called "The Whirlwinds" by careering and dancing on roller skates around a hardwood platform. Then Ruth Roye slouched on to the stage, ugly and magnetic, a bob-haired flapper from the world of walk-up flats and two-family houses.

Kissing, according to the unreticent damsel of her first song, was something too nice to be missed. "It's like a shot in the arm," she shouted in one of the choruses.

Beatrice shrieked with laughter. "Listen to that. The creature is the funniest ever. What she doesn't know about low-brow girls!"

But Ruth Roye had only begun. Her songs and the comment with which she pointed them were a crescendo of humor as pungent and brutal as that of the Restoration dramatists, as up to date as the almanach. She performed magic with the hackneyed interjection, "I Thought I'd Die!" Each time she chirped, gurgled or gasped "I Thought I'd Die!" she fixed some mercurial emotion of a daughter of the people—ineloquent surprise, or fleshly ecstasy. Her mouth was slewed to one side as she sang:

"You must be hard-boiled, to be good in this woild:
I'm astin' you, ain't it the truth?"

"A genius, in her way," murmured Austin, his pleasure in Ruth Roye enhanced by the discovery that he and Beatrice could go to music halls together, as well as talk literature and exchange kisses.

"Oh, she's a clever interpreter—hardly more than that!" she answered sensibly. "Now for Ted Lewis. He *is* a genius, perhaps, because he's caught the little black-and-white notes that have been flying about in America without a leader. Dearest, do you get jazz?"

"Music is not a passion with me, but I surely get jazz. It's our national symphony."

"Symphony! It's just jazz. We play it and like it for the same reason that the French Court danced the minuet. It expresses us."

"What is a symphony except the musical form taken by a complex feeling?"

"I know. But the word makes me think of the old, great symphonies, which I appreciate in their place and you do not. Pedant!"

They were interrupted by the appearance of Ted Lewis from between the folds of a heavy black curtain. A bizarre, a mocking and a sinister figure, wearing a cloak and a wrecked silk hat, it was his whim to introduce his jazz band with a prologue. He chanted verses of a malicious naïveté that foretold the orgy about to begin, and he flourished a slender wand. The curtain, parted brusquely and hauled up into two giant loops, revealed a contorted pianist and an array of phlegmatic blond confederates behind cymbals and jeering saxophones. High lights flashed from the polished brass. The oval shirt-fronts had the pallor of chalk. Prancing in and out among his minions, Lewis conducted a preliminary massacre of music. It was a swift, screaming death, and the way was cleared for jazz. The instruments hooted and blared in a monstrous new rhythm. Number after number made articulate a life of hard surfaces, of energy seen as beauty, of joy in a mechanical rather than a spiritual civilization. The American bacchanale of work and play identified in a single cult of action. The afternoon of a Wall Street broker, the day and night of the pleasure-seeker at the contests of champions, at summer beach resorts, in dance halls, cabarets and skating rinks. The century was shown dancing to a cakewalk become ineffably sophisticated.

The finale of the act was a darkened stage and a clash of whirling spotlights of different colors. The musicians

left their gilt chairs and paraded to a measure grown suddenly sad, like a ragtime funeral march.

Austin and Beatrice had heard Ted Lewis before. Theirs
was not the surprise of discoverers, but a recognition re-
newed. Leaning to one another in whispered comment,
they agreed that the rest of the programme would seem
flavorless after the jazz band, and they rose to go.

It was four o'clock, and Fulton Street surged with shoppers in the pleasant sunshine of the Fall afternoon.

"The Saturday mob is always worse on this side of the
street. Such a mob!" laughed Beatrice, jostled against her
companion. "What shall we do? Tea?"

But the moment for a pilgrimage he had long planned
seemed favorable to Austin. "We're not far from the
Heights. Take me over there and show me around."

"Haven't you ever been to Brooklyn Heights?" she
teased.

"Oh, yes!" he answered gravely. "But not with you.
I want you to show me the places where you used to live."

She stroked his arm lingeringly. "All right, romantic
one."

They took the subway and got out in a few minutes
at the Clark Street station, miles underground, it seemed,
with its interminable passageway leading to elevators that
rose sluggishly to the surface. Then they stepped into
mild, decorous streets, less touched by progress than any
other quarter of the city. Basement houses of the middle
of the last century stood in orderly blocks, dotted with the
spires of many churches. Brownstone had shaded off

suavely to gray, and brick had mellowed to an old maroon.
There was ivy above the lintels, ivy on the windowless side
walls of some of the corner dwellings. The backyards were
thick with sumachs, and here and there a maple survived
at the edge of the sidewalk. A steady flutter of dead leaves
came down. On the blackening branches sparrows flocked
and quarreled plaintively in premonition of the cold.

It might have been a corner of London, or even of some
staid New England town. In no way did it suggest the
New York of Austin's daily existence.

"And this is really where you grew up?" he asked softly,
caressing her with his eyes, obsessed by her glowing vigor
and modernity.

"Of course. Don't I fit into the picture?"

"It proclaims loftily that it's more your mother's Brooklyn than yours."

"Don't you believe the old humbug. It's scarcely jazzy,
but it did produce my generation as well as the last one.
Those sober-faced houses are full of wild girls, if you only
knew it, dearest."

She led him to the street called Columbia Heights, and
through a break in the mansions on the groomed and
tranquil bluff they looked across to the phantasm of lower
Manhattan. Skyscrapers built without a plan to shape the
whole were merged by distance into a strange harmony.
They appeared to form a single structure, like a sprawling
citadel with innumerable towers. The Woolworth Building
was a white Gothic spire overtopping all. To the right, the
cables of Brooklyn Bridge made a delicate tracery against

the sky. It was crystal weather, and the last sunbeams flashed on the stone battlements and the passing ships.

Austin and Beatrice turned back into streets that had begun to darken. Shivering briefly and without discomfort, they drew closer together as they walked. She pointed to a plain brick house on a corner.

"That is the house where I was born."

He could see her instantly, as she had been such a few years ago, a child with red hair down her back, a lanky child, no doubt, and very freckled. She had run up and down that high stoop and played on this sidewalk, calling to her friends in a shrill treble. The years had passed. She was his lover now, the fierce, sweet one. His fingers closed and unclosed upon her arm.

At the Montague Street crossing, she gave him a still more vivid picture of her childhood. They had reached a hump-backed wooden bridge curving over the cut down which the trolley cars run to the ferry. She had adored coming there with her sister, she said, because it had seemed to them the largest, the most formidable, bridge in the world. They had dared each other to dash across it, and it had taken a lot of courage to make the journey alone. The Penny Bridge, they had called it, for no reason that any one could discover.

Austin felt sentimental over the vanished child, to the point of tears. He was amazed at the emotion, and concealed it with a studied nonchalance. Was this the result of being in love? he asked himself. If so, he had never been in love before, and it would not be well to confess it. Beatrice took love on a hard Twentieth Century note. So must he. But his tenderness found expression in a move toward greater intimacy.

"Dearest, I wish we could go away together for a while," he muttered. "We should have whole days where we've only been getting hours."

"Yes, dearest. Oh yes! I'd like to. But you know I can't quite break with my people," she answered.

"Wouldn't a week-end be possible? Couldn't you invent some story to explain it?"

She considered this with frank eagerness, her eyes alight. "I can do it, of course," she said at last. "I have a friend in Jersey I can pretend I'm visiting. It'll be necessary to let her in on the secret, but she won't give me away."

Austin bent his head and shamelessly, like a cat, he rubbed it along her shoulder and neck. "Let's do it soon," he pleaded.

"Not very soon, I'm afraid. I'm usually home Sundays, and to make it seem natural I ought to set it ahead and do some talking about it. In about three weeks, dearest."

"It will be winter by then."

"Does that matter? We'll go somewhere by the sea. I like the seashore in winter."

They made their plans in low, bemused voices as they loitered up Montague Street.

Chapter 17

BEATRICE had telephoned him there would be a surprise when she came to meet him for the week-end trip. She was pleased about it, yet it was something he might not like, she had said, her voice nuanced with excitement, silvery and far upon the wire. No, she would not give him a hint. An unimportant thing, really. But his judgment would be important. He would understand as soon as she arrived, and be glad she had not told it too early.

Sitting in the small room at 16th Street among his books, Austin wondered what surprise his lover would bring. A new dress, perhaps? It had sounded like that. A bottle of wine? Or an absurd toy to make them laugh in the way they had found it was delicious to laugh, making merry over nothings that were amusing because of the associations they had built up around them? He told himself, with a deep, static passion, that he had found in Beatrice the incomparable companion, the more than sweetheart. Their minds as well as their senses were one. Stirring in him, there was the belief that they would write together some day. He had not thought of himself as a writer since his boyhood disillusionment in connection with newspaper work. Now he saw himself as the collaborator of Beatrice Purcell.

He waited for her eagerly, amorously. Week-end trips he had made with other women acquired the aspect in his memory of banal adventures. He brought an almost adolescent delight to this one. It was charming, he thought, that they had concluded to go no farther than Staten Island. The atmosphere of a big hotel, of the Atlantic City boardwalk, would have intruded upon their intimacy. They would go to a little French place he knew, not far from the beach, and without even leaving New York City they would be more absolutely hidden from the people who knew them than if they had traveled hundreds of miles. A marvelous subterfuge. Nobody would picture them, separately or with one another, on Staten Island. Nobody else would go there.

A chill day, a wan, snowless day of early winter, filtered its light through the curtained window beside which Austin sat and dreamed.

He started to his feet when he heard Beatrice's step hurrying up the stairs. She entered jauntily, wearing a short coat and a flat-brimmed beaver hat, and he perceived at once the surprise of which she had warned him. She had cut her hair. It flamed on either side of her face, with locks pulled forward to cover her ears, and behind it luxuriated in a thicket of curls. Austin got a first impression of beauty, then gasped with a shock of regret for the splendid orange ropes that had been severed. The barber who had done that might as well have violated the Golden Fleece with his shears.

"Don't you think it's nice, dearest?" she cried, panting.

"I—I don't know yet. Take off your hat," he begged.

Her head had lost a certain imperial quality, but it had gained in magic. The stern outline of her features, composed as she postured for his judgment, was rendered Florentine by the bobbed hair. But the instant she smiled, she appeared more modern than Austin had ever seen her, more subtly Irish-American, more candidly the child of her virile day.

He buried his face in the cropped red hair, and rubbed his cheeks across her curls, tingling at the contact with the fine bristles on the nape of her neck.

"It's terribly exciting. I'm going to prefer it to the old way, I know. Give me time to get accustomed, that's all," he whispered.

She laughed victoriously. "You can't imagine the freedom it means to me. In swimming, especially. But I was so afraid you'd hate it."

"Would you have grown it again, if I had?"

"But of course. I'm in love," she bantered.

Packing the week-end bag, he could scarcely keep his eyes off her hair. She had brought the essentials—a filmy, apricot-colored nightgown, a change of stockings, handkerchiefs, and a disproportionately large selection of face powders, creams and rouge. Austin put them with his own things, because they did not want to be troubled with more than one bag. He got a secret pleasure from mingling them with his heavier toilet articles, from laying the night-gown in the folds of his purple kimono embroidered with yellow dragons.

"What books shall we take, dearest?" he asked.

"George Moore and Conrad," she replied promptly.

He made places for "The Story Teller's Holiday" and "Tales of Unrest," then suggested:

"Swinburne, too?"

She nodded.

"And some French poetry?"

"I don't read French well."

"Never mind. I'll translate for you."

"All right."

He added volumes of selections from Swinburne and Baudelaire, and the bag was ready.

They clung together, kissing, at the door, before they opened it and walked gaily down the stairs and away from the old house. The journey was to be a bohemian escapade throughout, it had been decided. They would not bother with taxicabs. They would take the subway to the ferry. And at South Ferry they joined the stream of dull-visaged residents of Staten Island bolting home from their offices, and climbed to the green-and-white waiting room of the upper level.

"None of them have the same lovely reason for their trip that we have, dearest," murmured Beatrice, with a touch of romance. "I'd like to thrill them. I'd like to call out loud, 'We're not married, and we think it's nicer that way!' Only I'd be arrested under the Mann Act or something, wouldn't I?"

Austin's hand burrowed into the folds of her coat, pressing her arm through the fur, and they jested about the solid virtues of the Staten Islanders. When the ferryboat came into its slip, they joined in the rush for places and found seats on the bench against the rail. It was warmer on the water than it had been in town. A pale sunshine tempered the sea wind, and snuggled against one another, their hands clasped out of sight, they took joyous breaths. The waddling motion of the staid craft, as its paddle-wheels churned, seemed admirable to them.

The harbor was beautiful under the winter sky, thought Austin. It had not occurred to him to sail on it in cold weather, except as a bored passenger in the smoking-room, and he felt like a discoverer noting the contrasts of steel-blue and gray, the murky black of smoke streaming in plumes from the funnels of liners, the pallid, flitting gulls. The surface of the harbor was streaked with foam. In its faint agitation, it looked wider, cleaner, than in summer. He sensed the ocean beyond.

At St. George, they laughed at the dingy terminus, the quaint, old-fashioned train, of which every car was of a different model as if picked up at second-hand, and the engine a fussy, small affair, as archaic as the engines one sees in pictures of the Civil War. Debating solemnly whether it were best to take seats covered with red plush, with green plush, or with leather, they decided on the green. A dubious choice, because it placed them among

Italians with highly brilliantined mustaches suggestive of the inner councils of the Mafia.

The train waited for three ferry boats, but Austin and Beatrice did not mind a delay that in any other circumstances they would have found exasperating. Everything amused them. This was the ideal way to go for a week-end, they said, gossiping in muted voices. And when the train finally pulled out of the station, they perceived charm in the ragged landscape. Glimpses of provincial streets with frame cottages. Lumber yards on the outskirts of Stapleton. Wide fields savoring of the sea and waiting resignedly for the near future when they would be cut up into building lots. Cows tethered in hollows. Leafless orchards. The golf links on the near side of Dongan Hills.

They were going to Grant City, a township which Austin declared was by no means so ordinary as its name. A sort of residential hinterland for Midland Beach, he said, and besides that the northerly limit of a very old French settlement that took in New Dorp, Great Kills and Huguenot Park. The descendants of the Huguenots were not much in evidence, but they had founded a tradition, and people with European tastes patronized the French hotels of the neighborhood.

Beatrice smiled her willingness to be taken anywhere that pleased him, and at Grant City he showed the way across the railroad tracks, up the sharp incline of an unpaved street to the Richmond Road Tavern. The latter was a spreading two-story frame structure, with dormer windows and a sun parlor in the rear. It was like a thousand other American country hotels. But the man who received them was a diplomatic Frenchman, a dapper fellow, resembling an American host only inasmuch as he had shaved off his mustache in order to appear native. His manner expressed a discreet approval, an almost affectionate complicity, as he showed Austin and Beatrice to the best room. He bowed himself out.

"What an absurdly delightful room. Dearest, look!" Beatrice had started on a tour of inspection. "The pictures! A stag at bay. Different kinds of fish with every scale painted in. And there's a huge rope coiled up here by the window. The Staten Island substitute for a fire escape. It's unbelievable!"

Austin crossed over to her, caring little for the fittings of the room. He took her in his arms with a sense of exultant possession, kissing the adored hair, her cheeks, her mouth. Her body responded swiftly, molding itself to his, then relaxing as her head fell back upon his arm. A sweet, lost look was in her eyes.

"I do love you. More every day. Never more than today," he muttered, as if answering a faraway question.

"Love me a long, long time," she answered, her lips scarcely moving.

"All my life, dearest."

"I don't believe that," she said, and placed her hand over his mouth, to stifle his reply.

Their kisses banished the question to the limbo of irrelevant things.

A good part of the afternoon remained when they agreed

it would be pleasant to walk down to Midland Beach before dinner. They could take the trolley back. It was nicer on the beach in winter, Beatrice said, than a hothouse creature like Austin might suppose. He retorted that he could only take her word for it, but before they had covered half the distance he was admitting that an unforeseen blandness lay upon this remote corner of his world. They were sauntering down a long earth road that the absence of frost made springy under their feet. A soft mist hovered in the denuded woods on either side. The windows of the tranquil houses they passed were half open to the weather, as on an autumn day.

Staten Island was really part of the protected Jersey coast. It was infinitely milder than Manhattan, thought Austin, astonished. But he said:

"If either of us were here alone, he would find it boring instead of beautiful."

"Of course," she murmured.

As they approached Midland Beach, the road merged into a paved street. It was bordered with summer cottages, flimsy and inconsequential, deserted now, with mosquito netting hanging in shreds around the porches, and broken panes of glass. The cottages had naïve names, like "Ozone Villa" and "The U-Come-In Club," lettered on dangling shingles. Drained suddenly, at the end of the season, of an ephemeral life of boys and girls in bathing suits, who had kept house on canned food, had danced to phonograph music, they remained dusty shells. No one had inhabited them long enough to give them personality.

The beach itself was more subtly desolate. An empty boardwalk swept clean by wind and rain. A carrousel stricken immobile, faint sunlight glinting on the manes of the lions. The undulating skeleton of a scenic railway in the background. The serried ranks of booths where gewgaws had been sold, clumsily boarded up, their protruding counters still covered with stained oilcloth. A memory persisted, somehow pathetic, of the holiday crowds that these had served.

But Austin and Beatrice were not sad. An immense tenderness glowed between them. They rejoiced in the isolation that made it possible for them to stop and kiss beside the silent bandstand, to walk with their fingers intertwined, their thighs and shoulders touching.

"It's wonderful, as I told you," she said gently, expecting no answer.

The tide was coming in, but a strip of dry sand enticed them. They sat, warm in their overcoats, their backs supported by a pile, and watched the foam breaking on the pebbles. The falling breeze was almost suave, and the sunlight seemed shaded to a brighter gold. After a moment, Austin changed his position wordlessly. He stretched out upon the sand, then drew his knees up and laid his head in Beatrice's lap. She looked down at him, her eyes misty, her lips parted, and her hand caressed his face.

"I feel as if everything were happening between us— now—every possible, exquisite thing," he breathed.

Her body quivered. "I—I, too."

Austin had never been so happy.

High tide reached them in a long ripple and expelled them from the sand. They mounted the wooden steps to the boardwalk and walked toward the turnstile, their mood insensibly altering. Their capacity for being gay together with a touch of irony for the rest of the world, reasserted itself in their hearts. They joked about the pretentious names of the beach hotels, the formidable columns in front of a certain hostelry that were nothing but painted wood. As they waited for the car to take them back, the local sports gathered about an ice cream soda counter impressed them as being priceless clowns. They were lucky, they agreed, to be staying at the sympathetic Richmond Road Tavern, instead of at an American place where the host would have questioned their morals.

They had been sentimental, and now Beatrice was glittering, a little hard, and Austin sheathed in his habitual veneer of dilettante cynicism. He had a vague impulse to combat their flippancy, to become articulate in a dedication of his life to her and a plea for the supremacy of glamor between them. But he feared that she would laugh at him. Nor would the attitude have gone with his theory concerning intellectualized love. The moment passed.

Dinner was served at the Tavern with a note of middle-class French ceremony that charmed them. The sun-parlor was being prepared for a dance, and they sat in a high-ceilinged room adjoining. Tableaux of the chase adorned the walls. Their table was fantastically wide, as if meant to hold great trenchers of venison or roasted geese for an entire family. Austin put his elbows on the board and leaned across it as he talked. It was impossible to deal fairly with the many courses. The wines that should have gone with them were lacking because of prohibition. A mournful state of affairs, the proprietor admitted, shaking his head. He pointed to a sign which threatened drinkers with horrible penalties, but he ended by smiling paternally and bringing two small cups of home-made claret.

At the other tables there was a scattering of solemn diners—old Frenchmen with white mustaches, and their corseted wives; an occasional American couple, a smug pride in their suburban homes imprinted on their countenances.

"Dearest, think of it. Those are people who've lost all interest in love. It's just a Saturday evening feast at two dollars a plate for them," whispered Beatrice. "We're the only happy ones here."

They invented bizarre raillery with which to mock their unsuspecting neighbors. According to Austin, one of the decrepit Frenchmen was dining with another man's wife. He had ordered flowers for the table, he pointed out, and he kept his eyes fixed on the expansive bosom of the lady. Frenchmen were never too old to have a zest for amorous intrigue. But Beatrice would not have it so. The flowers, she said, were wild flowers, which had been picked because ancient couples would do anything to pass the time. And the man's gaze was merely held by the most prominent object in sight, while he was thinking of the rank cigar he intended to smoke after dinner.

"You are merciless with the old," said Austin.

"It's a question of capacity for life," she answered. "I have no use for those who are burned out, any more than nature has. They should die."

"You'd find it hard to convince them of that."

She shrugged her shoulders. "I don't try. I'll know what to do, though, when I begin to shrivel. Stay in hiding, at the very least." A fixed, meditative look crept into her eyes and her lips curled. "The worst cases, of course, are the under-equipped ones who can't get what they want, even when they're young. There was a man last year—a good-looking, feeble object. He wanted to make love to me, but he simply couldn't convince me of anything. I was furious, dearest, because I was unhappy with my husband, and physically the creature had seemed at first to be all right for a lover. Do you know what I ended by doing? I gave him an appointment at our flat one afternoon. He thought I was providing him with his chance, but I'd asked Blaise to be there too. And I did nothing but kiss Blaise shamelessly. I pretty nearly seduced my husband under the other one's eyes."

"Did he kill himself?" asked Austin, half seriously.

"Not enough nerve for that. He was weak. But I've heard he's in a madhouse now," she replied carelessly.

Austin was amazed at her cruelty. There was something feral in such a rending of the heart of one who had offered tribute no matter how punily. What unimagined Beatrice was this? A shadow of alien feeling loomed for an instant between them. It was dissipated as the first guests arriving for the dance in the sun-parlor attracted their attention.

Grant City boys and girls, chaperoned by a committee of mothers and a priest, and accompanied by their own jazz band.

"It's a Catholic club, dearest, and the dance is chiefly a match-making affair," chuckled Beatrice. "The priests believe in jazz, because it promotes marriages."

They looked on, amused, but they hurried over their coffee when the invasion became more pronounced, and went upstairs. From their room in the front of the house, only faint echoes of the music reached them.

A closer intimacy wrapped them about. This was to be their first night together. All of Sunday, too, would be theirs, and Sunday night; but, hoarding their fortune, they were leisurely at the door of love. Austin read aloud the incident of the tempting of the young priest, from "The Story Teller's Holiday." His voice assumed easily a flavor of Irish brogue, and he brought out the racial verity of the tale with a humor that enchanted Beatrice. When he turned to the loftier prose of Conrad, she agreed with him that "The Return" was probably the greatest psychological short story in the language. They glanced at their books of verse, but before they had chosen one the desire for reading had given way to a storm of kisses.

They lay warmly in each other's arms, awake, long after the light had been turned off for sleep. Austin's lips wandered tirelessly over her face and neck, and the fingers of one hand were plunged into the curls and marcelled waves of her short hair.

"Dearest, what have you done with the hair that was cut off?" he asked suddenly.

"Done with it? Why, it's at the house."

"Will you give it to me?"

"Some of it, if you like, romantic one."

"No, all, all," he urged.

"But it's a huge mane. Unless you hung it on your wall, and so advertised me to your visitors, I can't imagine what you'd do with it."

"I'd keep it in a special box. It's so much a part of you that having it would mean having you always with me."

She did not answer for a while.

"I'm still interested in looking at it myself. But I'll give it to you one of these days. Not now," she murmured at last, sleepily.

Chapter 18

AUSTIN had been editor of Darcy's Magazine for a year and a half when he admitted to himself that he might not be able to carry out his policies and please the Cooke brothers at the same time. As Theresa Glenn had promised him, there had been at first a strict neutrality on the part of the publishers. Their interest was wholly commercial, and they maintained the sound view that an editor had not proved or disproved his value to them until the reports of newsdealers showed that sales were steadily increasing, or steadily falling off. Darcy's had been losing circulation under the old management. It was inevitable that Austin's appeal to a modernized public should alarm the readers who liked the magazine as it was. Further losses, however, had been halted in six months. An accretion of new subscribers had begun.

The statistics incited James Cooke, the brother to whom Austin was responsible, to read a number of issues. An essentially conservative soul, he had found much to startle him. Without arriving at snap judgments as to whether up to date fiction could be made more profitable than the old fashioned kind, without hastening matters in any way, he had acquired the habit of summoning his editor for frequent short interviews.

Austin disliked explaining himself to James Cooke. An unreasonable feeling, he admitted, since the man was the owner of the periodical and naturally took an interest in its fate. But he did not like him. Cooke had a stolid manner and a congested face. It was difficult to believe he understood any phase of publishing except the activities of the cashier's department.

The interviews had resulted in a widening breach between them. And the last interview had been the most unpleasant.

"Look here, Mr. Bride, what are you trying to do with Darcy's?" Cooke had asked.

"Please women," replied Austin, ennuied at having had to make the statement countless times.

"You're going about it in a funny way. Women will be shocked at some of the stories in this advance number I've got on the desk."

"What kind of women?"

"Well, decent women. There's a story about—um, about a girl who divorces her husband so she can live with him and not feel tied. I had Mrs. Cooke read it, and I tell you she was shocked."

"That story was entirely satirical."

"Um—well, there are others."

"They wouldn't do for The Ladies' Home Journal. But they picture life as it's lived by our present day flappers, and the flappers will read them without turning a hair."

"How many flappers? The Ladies' Home Journal has a

circulation in the millions, young man, and Darcy's has barely a hundred thousand."

"Do you want to compete with The Ladies' Home Journal?"

"N-no. It would cost too much," Cooke had answered literally. "We've got a special public, all right. Go after it. But find stories that are more romantic and sweet."

"This is not an age of sweetness. I refuse to try to make Darcy's both modern and sweet. It can't be done."

"If next month's report shows a big gain, I'll let you ride. I'm not hard set. If it doesn't, you'll get a memorandum covering a change of policy," mumbled Cooke, his bloodshot eyes distinctly unfriendly. "I believe in sweet stories," he added, with sudden truculence.

The situation was upsetting to Austin. He liked being an editor, and had come to look upon Darcy's as a career he would not willingly have exchanged for any other. But if his freedom were to be curtailed, his interest in the work would vanish. He had gathered a special group of writers about him, had trained them to sound a certain note. The magazine he was making would justify itself, if let alone. The immediate handicap was, that it was an old magazine rejuvenated, and it took some time to convince the public that it had become clever. Unlike Smart Set and Saucy Stories, for instance, it had to live down some of its own traditions. Cooke knew it had been gaining a little; the slight hope existed that he might conclude it would be wiser, commercially, not to interfere.

Lounging by his office window with its outlook on the

barren roofs between Eighth Avenue and the Chelsea docks, Austin made plans for Darcy's that were, if anything, more positively along his chosen line. His thoughts turned then to Beatrice Purcell. They had been lovers for more than a year. A year had passed since they had spent the week-end on Staten Island, their first full, tender days and nights together. They had found ways later of snatching other week-ends, even of contriving fictions for the benefit of her family which made it possible for her to stay at 16th Street at odd times with him. They had filched an entire week once when she was supposed to be vacationing at Cape Cod. But on the whole their manner of living was as it had been. Neither of them had swung the other into his pathway, had imposed the forms of material permanence. To a singular degree, they had remained the amorous friends of pagan tradition.

Austin was certain that he loved Beatrice more deeply than any one who had been in his life. He could not imagine himself desiring another woman beyond her. The circumstances pointed straight to marriage. He had often thought of urging her to divorce Blaise Doyle and marry him. But she had taken it lightly when he mentioned the subject, had mocked him playfully, declaring it would be a crime to muddle his decoratively selfish life, and that for herself she knew from experience that she made the worst wife in the world.

He had debated these statements frankly, acknowledging that he had always shrunk from responsibilities. And Beatrice had said:

"You see, you would be making a sacrifice. I don't want you to make sacrifices for me."

"But, dearest, I haven't really been in love before. That alters the case."

"You might fall out of love. Believe me, we're both happier this way than we would be married."

With his temperamental bias in favor of those rewards of the worship of beauty to which the price of struggle is not attached, he accepted Beatrice's answer as a decision. It was no doubt better, he thought, that they should avoid a move involving the wearisome legal process of divorce and on the necessity of which they were not fully agreed. Their companionship was exquisite as it was. Emotionally perfect, its mental phase seemed to provide a certitude of loyalty that passion alone would not have given.

They had made writing an important part of their welded existences. Beatrice had gone on with her novel, improving the early chapters and progressing slowly toward a stronger climax than the one she had planned in the beginning. There was still much of it to be done. She had argued it would be practical to interrupt the work and to experiment with shorter things, for the sake of acquiring technique. And this had led to a literary partnership between Austin and herself. The result had been excellent. She wrote a notably purer prose, created characters more deftly; but his feeling for the sequence of events that made a story was sounder. Under their double signature, they had submitted a number of their collaborations to magazines and had been accepted with flattering promptness.

Austin wondered, as he mused on that winter day in his office, what difference it would make in Beatrice's life and his if he should be compelled to resign from Darcy's. He would not care to look for another job. It would be interesting to see what he could accomplish as a writer. And if his days were to be free of office work, it would surely be absurd to pass them in isolation from Beatrice, when he and she could be happier together, could be of constant aid to one another. The evenings and holidays they shared now would no longer be the most they could expect, would become a parsimonious allowance.

He thought suddenly, for the first time, of getting her to leave New York with him. Why should they not go to Paris, and so evade the scandal that open union within sight and sound of her family would mean? She was probably as determined as ever against the latter course, but she might agree to Paris. Austin had spent a few months before the war in Paris, and had more than once toyed with the idea of returning there for a visit. He would not have gone alone, but with Beatrice it seemed a glamorous prospect. Though it depended upon a crisis that no more than threatened—his failure with Darcy's—he decided to ask her about it, and telephoned to her to meet him later in the afternoon at 16th Street.

When he left the magazine building, he turned up his collar against the penetrating rawness of a premature winter. It had been snowing, and the glooming sky indicated more snow. Hating the cold, Austin nevertheless walked from habit. Even on such a day, he preferred not to miss in a taxicab the varied aspect of the streets—the turmoil of bargain shoppers on the pavements of Sixth Avenue, the lunging current of traffic up the broad sweep of Fifth.

Beatrice and he arrived at the door of his house at the same moment. She was wearing a gray astrakhan coat of the short length that was fashionable that season, and a perfectly plain gray felt hat rolled up in front. Austin did not care for such masculine hats on her, but she had developed a fad for them and he had failed to comment.

They greeted each other with the affectionate, "Hello!" of old friends, and he led the way up the stairs. The large room was chilly, the dead, gaunt fireplace discouraging. As they often did on bad days, they went into the library, drew the curtains, lighted the candles on the varicolored pyramids of grease that now hid the candlesticks, and set an oil stove going. The room became a cosy and unhygienic refuge, a place of flickering shadows and a hothouse atmosphere that invariably tempted them to remove unnecessary garments and curl up together, like sensuous cats, on the divan.

He told her about the happenings at Darcy's. Realistic and direct, she advised him instantly:

"Get free of it all. There are other things in life for you."

"But, dearest, I don't want to quit unless I have to," answered Austin. "The magazine doesn't bore me, though Cooke does. I'll be satisfied if the circulation goes up and he stops interfering."

She shrugged her shoulders. "Once he's started to fool

with ideas he thinks better than yours, he'll always be
tempted to force them on you."

"I'm afraid of that, too."

"Things generally stay right for just so long, dearest.
When they spoil, they spoil. Why cling to corpses?"

"I'd like to believe I could run a magazine indefinitely."

"It would have to be one you owned, then. You know
you're not in sympathy with our grand and glorious publishers."

She explained him to himself, Austin felt, and the flame
of her own vitality stimulated him. She was right, of course.
It would be surprising if he did not soon break with Cooke.
And recalling the main reason for his having taken the
afternoon off to see her, he said:

"Dearest, if I leave Darcy's, will you go to Paris with
me?"

Her eyes flashed in swift response. "Yes," she answered
impulsively. But an odd, cryptic smile tightened the corners
of her mouth the next minute: "Why did you think of
that?"

"We can't live together in New York. At least, you
won't for the reasons we've often discussed. But in Paris
we could do as we pleased. I want more of you, much more
than I have now. And there's our work. Going away somewhere seems to be the only solution."

"It does, doesn't it? Is Paris all it's made out to be?"

"It's marvelous," declared Austin enthusiastically. "I was
hardly a sophisticated person when I was there, but I
brought away a memory of life lived gracefully, of pic-

turesque cafés and beautiful vistas that can't be due altogether to kiddish romanticism. We're both fond of New
York, but we'd enjoy Paris as a change."

"How would we go there, dearest?"

"Why—I don't know. On the French Line, I suppose."

"On the same boat?"

"Surely."

"Oh, no! Not surely. My people would come down to
see me off. They'd want to visit in my cabin. I'd never be
able to explain myself to them."

"Well, on separate boats," said Austin easily. "We'd be
cheated of the voyage together, but we'd meet in a few
days on the other side."

"Would there be no other way of doing it?"

"Hardly," he answered, a little mystified.

She laughed softly. "Paris hadn't occurred to me as our
substitute for marriage. It's a nice dream. Make it come
true, dearest," she murmured, crushing her mouth against
his.

The afternoon slipped away. Their mood was a holiday
mood, and they treasured the bland hours in the library,
where no one was permitted to intrude upon them. Austin
was deaf even to the ringing of telegraph messengers and
tradesmen when she was there. They talked desultorily of
their work, and of trivial things they had laid away in
their memories to tell each other. But their silences were
more eloquent, the long silences they gave to the perennial
magic, the tireless service, of love.

At five o'clock, they made tea, and very late they left

the house for dinner. Beauty in an unexpected, harsh guise awaited them. The snowstorm must have started again soon after they had drawn the curtains. It had swelled into a blizzard, the last flakes of which were dancing in the still air. Sixteenth Street was banked with almost impassable drifts, and Union Square ahead was under a level white blanket that seemed to be a yard deep. The few trees had had their raggedness swathed in a fantastic foliage of eiderdown. Each street lamp glowed at the heart of a yellow nimbus.

Austin and Beatrice struggled forward gaily. They had found it amusing one winter night the year before to call Union Square the Nevsky Prospekt. Now they revived the name.

"Dearest, it's what Russia must be like. Just look at the Nevsky Prospekt," cried Beatrice, hanging on to his arm with a real need of help.

"China lies beyond it, and we've got no sleighs," answered Austin laughing. "Come on. That chop suey restaurant on 14th Street is about the only one we can make tonight."

They were ankle-deep in crisp snow. It took a quarter of an hour to reach the south side of the square, where they fetched up against the statue of Lafayette—an amorphous mound, from which the oratorical arm of the hero protruded. The whitewings had been at work on the 14th Street sidewalk, and it was easier walking there. They arrived panting at the door of the Great China Restaurant.

The gaudy room one flight up was a place where they often came, for the novelty of exotic foods and unapproachable tea. They went straight to their favorite table, in a corner alcove with scalloped wood partitions, and at a reasonable distance from the brass-lunged mechanical piano. Twisted gilded dragons with darting tongues met to form a conventional archway in the middle of the room. The pictures were strips of silk, with birds, rushes and gnarled tree trunks in needlework. The proprietor at his desk and the padding waiters were small yellow men with the faces of Buddhas, Third Avenue haircuts and utterly commonplace western clothes.

The restaurant was almost as warm as it had been at 16th Street. Austin and Beatrice ate "shrimps sweet and pungent" and drank "Imperial No. 1 tea," while they looked comfortably at the clouded windows and talked about nothing in particular. It was not the least triumph of their relationship that they had never bored one another, or had known a moment when they would have preferred to be alone.

They lingered in the Great China long after dinner, grateful for the storm, because it provided Beatrice with an excuse to telephone home that she must sleep with friends, and so make possible a night unhoped for with her lover.

Chapter 19

USTIN read in the Tribune of the death of Blaise Doyle. He had been killed on the republican side in a skirmish in Ireland. There were no details. The name was noted simply because it had been that of an Irishman who had lived in New York.

What would the effect be on Beatrice? Austin wondered. He telephoned her, and her voice came back hard and clear on the wire. Yes, she had seen the newspaper story and knew nothing beyond what it had stated. When he met her in the evening, he found her quite self-possessed, his own lover and not the widow under the spell of renascent sentiment whom he had feared to find.

"Doesn't it hit you at all?" he asked.

"Not as a loss to me," she answered steadily. "Blaise and I had cut each other out of our lives. There was no love left. But I am sorry he should have died so young." Her eyes became moody. "I thought well of Blaise—that, at least, to the very end. He was admirable, in his way. He always tried to get the whole of everything he wanted. He rejected happiness that had been compromised or diluted. This business of fighting for a republic instead of accepting the Free State was like his constant quarreling with me because I was giving him less than he'd had. He—but why talk about a man you never knew?"

"Go on. Tell me about him," urged Austin.

"No. He's dead. The living are foolish to discuss the living who've ceased to influence them, much less the dead."

Austin's concern was, indeed, candidly personal. He would have liked to plead afresh with Beatrice to marry him. It might seem too precipitate a reaction to the news from Ireland, he thought, though she had made a point of not mourning and would undoubtedly have heard him with as much readiness as at any other time. He postponed it until a few days later, when he said, a little indecisively:

"Dearest, you'd no longer have to be divorced to marry me. I wish you'd reconsider."

She gave him a keen, smiling glance. "Have I suddenly come to need legal protection? Is that it?"

"No, no. But we're not so free to be together now that we can afford to be prejudiced against an arrangement that would make it easier."

"We know we like being lovers, but existence in a flat might be too much for us. We're neither of us really domestic."

"There'd be advantages, especially if we go to Paris," argued Austin.

"What are they, dearest?"

"With passports as a man and wife, we can occupy the same cabin on the boat."

"But you agreed we could go on different boats."

"In hotels, then. Even in Paris, where they don't care much about morals, I assure you it would be more convenient."

"Those reasons aren't good enough. A romantic journey should be taken romantically—like our trips to Staten Island. I've had one husband, dearest, and you're lucky, perhaps, that I won't let you have a wife."

Austin decided to drop the subject. If they were to marry, it would come about inevitably some day. In the meanwhile, he was not so sure he did not prefer a love that absolved him of responsibilities. It made him feel pleasantly spoiled, implied the flattery that Beatrice would not have changed him if she could.

They had been talking at luncheon, and were to meet again that evening to go to a private dance in a Westchester County suburb. A woman who contributed to Darcy's was giving the affair, and had persuaded them to come. Generally they refused such invitations, because Austin did not dance; but it had appealed to them to accept this time. For a change, they said, and as an answer to friends like Theresa Glenn, who had been teasing them about their exclusiveness.

Hurrying to meet her at the Grand Central station at eight o'clock, Austin remembered with a faint surprise that he had never been out to Beatrice's house. Queer that that should be so. But Sheepshead Bay was far from Union Square, and she had always taken the initiative in planning that she should come to him, or that they should meet at halfway points. He must ask her flatly to invite him, he

mused, for he would like to know her mother. The thought
was dissipated as his glance roved among the thousands of
passing faces, in search of the beloved face.

She joined him on time and they boarded the train. A
very different train, they commented, laughing, from the
haphazard collection of cars on which they had traveled
from St. George to Grant City. They sank down upon the
soft, wide seat, their hands clinging, and scarcely perceived
the motion when the electric engine pulled swiftly out of
the yards. At New Rochelle, they climbed the long flight
of stairs to the street and took a cab. They were at the
house of Mrs. Thornley, their hostess, in a few minutes.

The dance proved to be one of those overcrowded functions to which suburban more often than city hostesses
are given. The rooms could hardly have held another person. Innumerable young women and men Austin had not
seen before occupied the chairs and divans in the living
room. The ragtime of a three-piece orchestra in the room
beyond was strident in the service of a prancing mob. He
felt an amused tolerance of this gregarious fashion of
pursuing pleasure. Not so bad for the occasional onlooker,
he thought, but stupid for the people who made a round
of such parties all winter long. They poured out energy
crudely, dispersed it among scores of casual acquaintances,
and minimized their chances of forming charming friendships.

After he had reviewed the faces of the guests a second
time, Austin discovered in odd corners a scattering of
women he knew. Theresa Glenn was talking to Mrs.

Thornley, a person whose voluble and boring conversation contrasted unfortunately with her ability to write. A clever Russian girl employed by a new art theater was flirting with a set of diamond studs in the worst taste, rather than with the man who wore them. Surrounded by a group of sophomoric youths, Stella Grant lolled on a settee near by.

Austin rather admired Stella Grant. She was a handsome, extremely carnal-looking girl, with quantities of pale gold hair. Her body was strong-limbed and vigorous, toned away by an active life from any tendency to fat. An Anglo-Saxon type, but with a bold note of temperament which New York sometimes adds to the Anglo-Saxon. She was intelligent, too, a writer whose work he had been featuring of late in Darcy's.

Smiling at him over her shoulder, and with a half humorous gesture of apology, Beatrice had rushed off to dance. It would be an orgy for her after long denial, he knew; she would not omit a single encore. Indolently, perversely, he evaded the nuisance of making talk with a succession of strangers, and turned all his attention to Stella Grant. He insinuated himself among her callow satellites, and in a short time had her listening to him at their expense. The youths gave ground awkwardly. Their faces marked a discomfited surprise when they found that their merry sallies were no longer received with gratifying laughter and were answered, if at all, with monosyllables. One by one, they drifted away.

Austin was never able to recall more than the broad lines of his verbal dalliance with Stella. He first led her on to talk about herself, and dealt craftily with her incomplete sophistication. She had known him theretofore only as an editor. At his office, they had discussed manuscripts in a professional spirit, but he sensed in her a secret impression of Austin Bride as a remote, romantic figure. He worked now to give definite color and body to that impression, and seeing she clearly thought him a man of many love affairs he incited her to question him about love. His answers were cynical, and the bright eyes of Stella expressed the time-worn reaction that she would have known better than others how to cast a spell upon the cynic. He did not mean half that he said. But his insincerity amused him and created an atmosphere between them.

At eleven o'clock refreshments were served. Austin rejoined Beatrice with the idea of coaxing her to leave. The dancing, however, had stimulated her, and she wanted more. She had had some good partners, she declared, and that was a stroke of luck not to be taken lightly. Austin should be willing to be a wallflower for once, she bantered, her cheeks glowing. They were in a corner, hidden by a potted plant from the crowd. He brushed the upcurled tips of her red hair with his lips, laughed tenderly and went back to Stella Grant.

The handsome girl had reached the point of expecting an open flirtation. The place she made for him on the divan was just roomy enough to be decent, but seats were at such a premium in Mrs. Thornley's house that the two were not conspicuous. Austin played the game with a sharper interest than he had imagined likely.

"I've often wondered whether love should be ruthless," sighed Stella, a few minutes before the party broke up. "A good Christian would say No. But you're a pagan. Tell me, what do you think?"

And Austin replied carelessly: "It very often is. That's the significant thing. Should and ought are words that don't have much importance in love."

The women streamed upstairs to their dressing and cloak rooms. Making an early capture of his coat, hat and stick, Austin waited for Beatrice in the diminutive hallway between the front door and the foot of the stairs. A babble of conversation, of chuckling laughter and treble cries floated to him, as the women restored their make-up. He stood with his head tilted back, and presently saw Beatrice and Stella coming down together. He was conscious of giving separate glances to them. Both were lovely, he mused, but only one was dear. That was the difference.

He had to share a taxi with another party of guests. In the train, however, he and Beatrice were lucky in getting seats at a distance from chattering acquaintances. She was tired, limp physically and suddenly depressed. For a while, she showed a disinclination to talk, resting her head, with her eyes closed, against the plush-covered back of the seat. Then she looked up, smiling.

"Nice dance, though the floor was too small. Jack Kiimer and I were quite stunty. Did you notice?"

"Jack Kilmer?" he repeated. The name meant nothing to him. If he had been introduced, he had forgotten.

"Yes, dearest. The lad I danced with half the time. You know!"

Austin did not know. He had a confused impression of many youths with Arrow-collar faces and patent-leather hair, some blond, some dark. Youths whose feet had been active, and brains apparently dormant. Polite, genial, innocuous youths. Beatrice had flashed by over and over again in the clasp of a composite partner, a type, as far as Austin had been concerned. He was not in the least interested in the males one met at functions of the kind.

"I'm afraid I don't place him," he murmured.

"You mean, not by name. What does that matter? But you must have seen us on the floor."

"I saw you, dearest. The men were blanks."

"I wonder whether I should be pleased at that. Is it a compliment?" Her eyes were narrowed. "I gave an outrageous number of dances to one partner, and you didn't even notice."

"Oh, but Beatrice! What are you getting at?"

"It didn't miss me that you found an entertaining companion."

Austin started. He was horrified at the threat of a grotesque, unnecessary passion like jealousy between himself and Beatrice. The possibility of it had not occurred to him.

"Dearest, I was killing time with Stella. I don't dance——"

"And love is the sport in which you're an expert," she interrupted. "That's all right, too. Only, you should finish the job. I saw the way you looked at her as she came down the stairs."

"Love! The words and looks Stella got from me had nothing to do with love."

"You flirted, then. And I danced. She was O.K. as a flirt, and Jack Kilmer was a grand dancer. Nothing wrong with our intentions, dearest, but not so good that I was the only one to do any noticing." She brought out the words in little, dry jets.

Austin moved his shoulders unhappily. This was the first misunderstanding that had arisen between them, and it was difficult to tell from Beatrice's face how seriously she took it. The mold of her features was subtly hard, as severe as fate; but her eyes and lips had never ceased to smile. At times when they had been absorbed in work, she had worn the same expression; it had seemed to divide him into two parts, toward one of which she was judicial, and toward the other unchangeably the lover. A short silence fell between them now.

"Don't you ever quarrel?" she asked abruptly.

"Never," he answered fervently. "I wouldn't bore myself quarreling with people I dislike, and I hate to evoke that sort of cruelty when I'm in love."

"It clears the air sometimes. But you're right not to. You are you. I shouldn't have known you—you'd have been a stranger—a stranger, dearest, if I'd succeeded in making you quarrel. It would have been terrible."

He stared at her intently and amorously, and took her hand. Her fingers twined about his, and their palms rubbed softly together. There had been no breach, after all, no violation of the beauty they had shaped, thought Austin, with overwhelming gratitude.

They commenced to talk about their plans for the next day, the next week. The rest of the journey to Grand Central station was no different from the other happy journeys of their friendship. An impossible hour in the morning, they agreed, laughing, to hope to find a taxicab, but they caught the last one at the stand and rode down to 16th Street in the mood of favorites to whom the gods are always good. It was exquisite to know that kisses and sleep in one another's arms were waiting for them.

Toward noon the next day, Austin got up without disturbing Beatrice, drank a hurried cup of coffee and went to the office. He found on his desk a memorandum from James Cooke ordering the change of policy with which he had been menaced. He read it slowly, rapping with his finger-tips on the blotter in front of him. There could be no more magazine, as he was content that Darcy's should be. It was like a death. But Paris drew tangibly nearer. Paris with Beatrice! His breath caught, and a quiver of delight ran through him.

He wrote out his resignation, with the traditional two weeks' notice, and sent it to the publisher.

Chapter 20

A FLOODTIDE seemed to have detached Austin's life from its moorings and to be carrying it along with a swiftness he had not foreseen. When he told Beatrice about his resignation from Darcy's, it had been the natural thing to assume he would leave for Paris as soon as possible. Equally natural, since their many talks had placed a seal of decision upon the course, that he should suggest no alternative to his going alone. She should follow in a few weeks, he said, and agreeing to everything she had helped him with his preparations. A note of excitement, of longing for the new adventure, pervaded her manner and his.

But the second week in February, it shocked Austin to realize he was booked to sail on the French boat, La Touraine, on the 24th. A farewell and a lonely voyage lay immediately ahead of him. There would be a month or more in Paris, which museums and cafés would not suffice to fill. He must close his apartment on 16th Street, must find a guardian for his cat. It all suddenly acquired the character of a disruptive effort, a dangerous, suicidal thing to do at a moment when he was happy. If only there were to be no separation, if Beatrice could go with him. But she

was to be left behind, and the days were clicking themselves away like the yards on a speedometer.

He wondered if she felt as he did. A change had come
upon the impulsive pleasure with which she had learned
that this plan of theirs was to ripen. She was fatalistic
now, a little hard and glittering. Why not? That was the
way in which she took all pleasures.

He hesitated to ask questions that might sound ridiculous, and it startled him when she reopened the question
brusquely.

"You know, I shall hate to travel alone. We ought not
to have to do it that way. It's a weakness—a sort of failure
on our part," she said.

"What else can we do, dearest?" he cried, distressed. "If
I wait over, will you go with me later?"

"No. There'd be the same drawbacks. Can't you think
of a new solution? You're the active one in this move, and
you should compel things to be right. It would be up to
me if I'd thought of Paris instead of you."

"Do you want me to stay?"

"No. That would be quitting," she replied impatiently.

"Then I must go ahead. No matter how difficult it is
for us now, it's simply good sense, isn't it?"

"Of course, dearest. I suppose I'm railing at life, not at
you or myself. You must go—yes."

He felt relieved. The possibility of rebelling against the
whole programme, of crying that unless she brushed away
obstacles and went with him he would remain with her,
of refusing on the ground of realism to put the Atlantic

Ocean between them, had not really imposed itself upon his conception of their love.

Austin grew almost gay toward the end. He had dismissed as a futility his shrinking from the journey, was impatient to start. The more miles there were behind him, the more sunsets and dawns, the nearer would he be to a reunion with his lover. The present must be immolated for the sake of tomorrow.

On the afternoon before he was to sail, he said his adieus to Grisette. She was to be lodged in her old home with the Boissys, and Austin had already brought down one of the ark-like valises with a grilled window at one end, in which cats travel when they must. He laid the bag aside, and sitting in an armchair he called her by name. The cloudy, gray one was curled on her favorite cushion near the bureau, and a shaft of winter sunshine fell palely upon her. She looked up at his voice, extended her forepaws with the toes spread wide, then rose fastidiously and arched her back. Her eyes were globes of amber, the pupils narrowed to threads. In leisurely anticipation of delight, she stared at him and clicked her jaws in a faint mew, dropped to the carpet and advanced, her tail waving. She loitered by his ankles, choosing the moment, then leaped on to his lap and flattened herself, purring, against him. Under each caress of his hand, her body stirred sensuously. The quivering in her throat was interrupted at times by a catching of the breath, like a human sigh. A rhythm of affection beat its measure between them. A shrewd psychologist would have adjudged them to be creatures by no means so disparate as superficially they appeared to be.

"My dear, this is very nice," Austin said aloud, a little wistfully. "But you're booked for somewhere else, and so am I."

He lifted her in his arms and carried her over to the bag. It was astonishing how quickly she perceived its purpose. A memory of its unyielding narrowness, of the alarming sounds and motions she had experienced on a former occasion, seemed to stir in her, and she shrank back, trembling. But there could be no reprieve. Austin forced her to enter the bag and snapped the lid shut. He carried her to West 29th Street, and when she was in Madame Boissy's care he permitted himself to stroke her once only before he turned away.

Beatrice joined him later in the afternoon. An especial tenderness, a studied optimism, reigned between them as they clutched at the galloping hours. They would not have been able to endure otherwise the steamer trunk supported on two chairs like a coffin, the pile of hand baggage on the floor. Short though this parting was to be, its spectre of desolation had to be conjured and jested about, so that it should not break down their morale.

They had dinner, and spent the evening, the night, together. Storm after storm of passion wrenched poignant, bitter kisses from them. After he thought she was asleep, Austin became aware that Beatrice was crying. He had never known her to shed tears. It shook him to the verge of weeping himself. In default of useless words, his hand found hers and clasped it convulsively in the darkness.

But they were light-hearted the next morning. It was a day of ice and sparkling sunshine. Snow from a recent fall was heaped in pyramids in the streets. The cab for which they telephoned was a luxurious, heated one, however, and they nestled closely among its cushions, their shoulders and arms rubbing through the sleeves of their coats, their mouths turning to each other sweetly and shamelessly. The straight run down 16th Street to the French Line pier was over in an instant. They had deliberately come early, in order to visit Austin's cabin before the arrival of a number of friends who were expected to see him off.

They hastened up the gangplank and penetrated to the somber interior of the boat, where small men with nautical caps worn at a coquettish angle darted here and there in that attempt to seem rushed which is habitual to stewards just before a ship sails. With the help of one of them, Austin found his cabin and was disgusted to note that another passenger had already left his suitcases there. But the cabin-mate presumably would stay on deck for a while. Austin closed the door behind himself and Beatrice.

He took her desperately in his arms. "Dearest—dearest," he cried, stammering over the words. "I must know exactly when I'll see you again. Dearest, tell me."

"I—I can't," she answered, moved. "The agency was uncertain about bookings. I haven't bought my ticket yet."

"I know. But it'll be soon. You'll be over in a month, surely."

"A month or six weeks," she said in a controlled, flat voice. "The way my people take it will have something to do with the exact date, dearest."

"Not later than the first week in April. I implore you. We must have all spring in Paris."

"I'll try."

He ran his fingers among her red curls, displacing her hat. Their clinging lips almost stifled the words, as he muttered, "You'll write me everything?"

"Of course, I'll write."

An obscure need of an exceptional, an unforgettable embrace made Austin slip to his knees and lay his cheek against her thighs, while his arms were raised to her waist. He was on his feet again and was kissing her for the last time when a hand fumbling at the door arrested them. They glanced at one another with mutual, self-pitying smiles, and drew apart. Beatrice had straightened her hat before the man who had the upper berth entered. Stepping aside for him, they went up to the promenade deck.

Theresa Glenn was waiting there, with Austin's former assistant from Darcy's and two of the associate editors from other Cooke magazines. Some women writers whose work he had published made their appearance a little later. The group at once became talkative, exchanging banalities about the joys of ocean travel, the thrilling prospect it must be for Austin to revisit Paris. His manner was easy and no less happy than his friends expected. His face wore its usual mask of unmalicious, contained irony. Beatrice beside him gossiped effervescently.

It was very cold on deck, and the boat had a weather-stained wintry look, with icicles on the rigging. The saloon would have been more agreeable, but it was overcrowded with French people who were making a noisy fête of the departure. Austin's group shifted to a spot where the sunlight promised mendaciously to be warmer. They walked up and down. Cigarettes were lighted. Visitors would be allowed to remain on board about half an hour longer.

Suddenly, Beatrice said Good-bye. The inflection of her voice took in the whole party, then she faced Austin and gave him her hand. He held her eyes with a brief, intent glance and understood that she did not wish to linger among these comparative strangers, to stand at the end of the pier and wave to the disappearing boat, as they would do. She was altogether right, he thought. He would have felt as she felt. All that was possible for them was a hand-shake, and she was gone. Disappearing beyond the gang-plank, she turned and gestured with her hand toward him. He caught the flashing of her teeth, the note of flame that her hair made. A lump came in his throat at this farewell glimpse of her supernal hair.

It ceased to be of importance to him when the others left. He returned their salutes mechanically as they went ashore, and afterwards from the rail. The pier receded into the distance. Fluttering his handkerchief any longer became pointless. He strode two or three times around the promenade deck, scarcely observing the glacial beauty of the river as La Touraine edged into midstream. The surface was partly covered with thin, broken sheets of ice, and where the ploughing ferryboats and tugs had heaped them into shoals they glinted a pale blue. Snow lay upon them in patches. From the funnels of craft of every description, plumes of white smoke streamed northward horizontally before a biting wind. The majestic skyline of Manhattan was etched with a frosty clarity. Austin would have rejoiced in it on any other day of his existence.

"I'm being childish," he thought. "Beatrice will be with me in a few weeks. I'm going to Paris in order to make it possible for her to follow. Ridiculous, insulting to her, to mope, as if I doubted whether she'd keep her word!"

He went down to his cabin, and discovered that mail and telegrams had already been distributed. There were telegrams from Charlotte Moore and Laura Beltrán. Short, stereotyped messages, except that both of them, in acknowledgment of days gone by, ended with the salutation, "Love." He read them, smiling gratefully, and then ran through a number of steamer letters from friends. He must answer them, he told himself, and he would write to Beatrice several times. But what else would he find to do on the voyage? Certainly, he would not care to make any acquaintances among the passengers. "Books," he muttered. Books! No matter what happened to one's heart, there was always the unassailable cult, the secure consolation, of books.

He opened a suitcase and took out his Swinburne and a bulky historical novel, called "El Supremo," which he had postponed reading because of its length until he should have a period of leisure. "El Supremo" dealt with the dictatorship of Dr. Francia in the early days of the republic of Paraguay. A curious, exotic theme. Austin felt his interest rise sharply. With the two volumes under his arm, he mounted to the smoking saloon, and selected the corner seat where he was to spend the greater part of the next ten days.

Chapter 21

USTIN reached Paris on a day in early March. A
precocious blooming of Spring, impermanent
and bland, touched the city with a holiday air.
The sunshine was filtered through a delicate
haze that wrapped the whole valley of the Seine and softened
the contours of distant objects. The flower stands were
laden with crocuses of many colors, with forced violets and
roses. It was too warm to wear the overcoat that had been
none too heavy at sea.

He took a taxicab and drove to a small hotel in the
Rue Vavin that had been recommended to him. He remembered vaguely from his former visit that this was in
the Montparnasse quarter, the quarter to which Americans
with bohemian tastes dart from the Gare St. Lazare like
birds to their nests. The Café du Dôme and the Café de la
Rotonde must be around the corner. Austin looked forward
to being amused by these resorts with an international
fame. They had changed, he knew, and probably represented the life of Paris less—much less—than a chop suey
restaurant represented that of New York. But in the old
days they had been frequented by artists and writers, by
picturesque girls in search of engagements as models, and
against the tolerant French background they had had

their charm. The latter, no doubt, was heightened by their greater cosmopolitanism.

He glanced about his sordid little hotel room, grinning at the bloated eiderdown cushion under which French people stifle happily in bed, and shrugging his shoulders at the absence of an ordinary convenience like running water. It would not do, except as a makeshift while he looked for something else. He could not imagine Beatrice in lodgings of the sort.

After he had brushed up before the full-length mirror that formed the door of the wardrobe, Austin descended to the street. The Boulevard du Montparnasse, which he reached in a few steps, played on a reminiscent chord in his brain and moved him to a thrill of pleasure. Its tranquil breadth, flanked with chestnut trees, their twigs naked and black from recent frosts, had an authentic beauty. But architecturally, it did not amount to much. An avenue with a faintly provincial air, definitely of the outskirts rather than the heart of a capital, he thought. The banal apartment houses were like those of Upper Broadway. Older and grayer; that was all, except for the cafés that occupied every well situated ground floor. Austin found he was challenging Paris with New York equivalents, and smiled at his having reversed so promptly the usual tendency of the traveler. Certainly, the cafés with their cheerful display of sidewalk tables were different and alluring.

He sauntered over to the Dôme and made a circuit of the interior before he sank comfortably on to a wicker chair beside a round-topped table on the terrace and ordered

a vermouth-cassis. The place was crowded with hard drinking Americans and flamboyant girls. That was his first
impression. The details could not be isolated in a moment.
But on all sides of him sounded the jerky sibilance of the
English language, with an undertone of feminine voices
using French, and the occasional flat stammering of a
foreign youth employing phrases from the conversational
manual in an attempt to talk with a damsel of the quarter.
The countenances of the men were of a familiar stamp,
and did not interest Austin. He focused his attention on
the French girls, predisposed to give them a favored place
in his gallery of women. Ten years before, they had seemed
lovely to him.

The mass effect was of ebullient creatures of a low order
of intelligence—jewel-eyed squirrels, or gaudy birds, on
exhibition. Their cheeks were rouged with cunning, and
their lips were sanguinary. They waved their hands, flirted
their heads, as they chattered, and the whole of their bodies
was constantly in minor motion. When one looked closer,
he observed disparagements both physical and temperamental. Most of these girls were ill-shaped, with thick
bodies, coarse hands and opulent, sagging breasts. Their
clothes were deplorable, less on account of poverty than an
indolent failure to be clean and trig. Only those who were
frankly bizarre in the bohemian tradition, who flaunted
blouses of futuristic cretonnes, bandanna handkerchiefs,
gay blankets folded into shawls, could be called effective
from the point of view of dress. And all were females
governing their conduct according to the whims of the

pascha. The ones who had men were engaged in holding the latter's routine or sated allegiance, and the unattached ones were dangling their charms before men in the hope of exciting them. A few were obviously decadent and found men repugnant; yet they, also, with a grimacing, wary bitterness, were competing for the attention of the male.

A nuance of scorn colored Austin's interest. He understood remotely the change that had come over the Café du Dôme. It was no longer a resort of working artists. The girls were not models, nor were they prostitutes in a strict acceptation of the term. They were idlers who managed to live by means of temporary alliances, to which they brought their sex as their single stock in trade. No doubt, they bluffed at being selective, created a skeleton illusion of pursuit and capture, while all the time they were calculating how quickly they could get their bills paid and start a new lease of credit. After New York, where women in need of money worked and had freedom for virtue or love, this was a gruesome, old-fashioned state of affairs.

Austin returned often through the next few days, and his early impression crystallized. He began to watch the American habitués. They were exiles determined to make themselves believe that they were neither futile nor disoriented. The very young among them hailed Montparnasse as the aesthetic center of the universe and were persuaded that the girls with whom they frolicked were grisettes from the pages of "La Vie de Bohême." The older men had abandoned such fancies in favor of a theory that life in the

Dôme was freer and larger than in the entire United States. They rushed every day to the Dôme and spent their best waking hours there. The cheapness of drinks, the joys of sex, and sporting gossip from the American newspapers provided them with topics of conversation; it was held to be in rather bad taste to discuss the arts they were supposed to have come to Paris to practise. A poker game started up every night. They were an amazing crew.

Wearying quickly of his compatriots, Austin turned back to the feminine adepts and established a speaking acquaintanceship with some of them. They bored him. Utterly like little animals, he mused, and wondered why he felt so contemptuous of their patent vacuity. They were only café girls going through their paces, and he should accept them as making a vivid patch in the decoration of existence. But he could not believe they manifested an inevitable, racial type. Vitiated by contact with foreigners, they were surely not the café girls that had been painted by Steinlen, Forain and Toulouse-Lautrec.

He developed an extreme distaste for Montparnasse, and set out one morning by way of the Luxembourg Gardens and the Odéon to look for a new quarter in which to live. He found himself in another world.

The venerable, narrow streets on both sides of the Boulevard St. Michel had the flavor of literary Paris. The shadow of the Sorbonne fell across them. Students dominated the life of such cafés as the Soufflet and the d'Harcourt, aggressive, green youths who clamored about their courses and the fêtes they were planning, and who made clumsy love to

girls wiser-seeming than they. Austin was too old to think
the students picturesque; but at least they had the air of
doing something with their time, of exploring the age with
a certain logic and harmony. Their mistresses entertained
him. Queer little odalisques! Not so voracious as the girls
at the Dôme, seeing they were sharing the fortunes of children who had little to spend on them. Equally subject to
the male, however. Their point of view separated them by
generations from the vital, lawless flappers, for instance,
whom Ruth Roye mimicked in her vaudeville act at home.

Drifting down to the quais, Austin gasped with pleasure
at the silhouette of Notre Dame against a sky in pastel
shades. The low bridges arching over the pale green Seine
enchanted him. He wandered along the river front, stopping frequently to turn over the books and prints in the
boxes of second-hand dealers. At the Rue Bonaparte, he
doubled back through the tangle of medieval byways in the
direction of Saint Germain des Prés and Saint Sulpice. The
displays in countless windows arrested him. He had forgotten the wealth of pictures and first editions, of objets
d'art, contained in the shops of this quarter. He paused
more than once to admire a hoary façade, or a grouping of
mansard roofs a mere photograph of which would have had
some of the tonal values of an etching.

And suddenly Austin experienced a wave of intense
happiness that he should be in Paris. He rediscovered Paris
as incomparably the capital of art, the modern Athens. It
was not dynamic like New York. Beauty here had taken
another, older way of expressing itself. The very body of

Paris had molded itself into suave lines and delicious vistas. Craftsmen whose feeling was for exterior aspects had responded to the prevailing rhythm, creating with a profusion and excellence unknown in any other place. The phenomena of foreign colonies and their manner of amusing themselves were of small concern to artistic Paris.

In his mood of exaltation, Austin told himself that he would know now how to pass his time buoyantly until Beatrice came. He would explore the city and find marvels not in the guide books to show her. The celebrated monuments he would save unvisited until they could see them together. It was only a question of a few weeks. She would arrive with the first leaves of Spring.

He decided to search for a hotel in the Latin Quarter, and eventually found one at the corner of the Rue Racine and the Boulevard St. Michel. His room was noisy. Autobusses raged past on both sides of the building, and honking taxicabs destroyed the quietude of streets that had not been designed to accommodate motor traffic. But the view from one window was charming. It took in a corner of the Musée de Cluny, the 14th Century abbey that had housed the monks of Cluny; the ruined arches of the Roman baths and one of the great trees in the surrounding park.

During his second week, Austin commenced to haunt the American newspaper office on the Grands Boulevards which he had given as his address. Letters from Beatrice were overdue, but he was aware that the forwarding of transatlantic mail was irregular in the winter. He had

chosen the Brooklyn Eagle office, because of its pleasant
reading room and because the correspondent in charge had
once worked with him on the Forum. A seat by a window
that looked down into the turmoil of the Boulevard des
Capucines and the Rue Caumartin established itself as his
favorite.

He watched covertly the girl who distributed the mail
in a set of pigeon-holes every day, and at last he saw her
slip into the compartment marked B a buff-colored envelope
of the shade that Beatrice used. He hurried over and
claimed it. It was from her.

Beatrice had written the evening of the day he had
sailed, but the postmark showed, disturbingly, that the
letter had not been sent until a week later. Austin read it
avidly and swiftly, then dwelt upon it line by line. It was
a lament in the beautiful, austere and limpid prose she
found spontaneously for letters as well as fiction. She had
known a crushing desolation that day, she wrote, a sense
of loss more immediate than she had forecast. Austin could
not upbraid her with a faltering love, for love rang sternly
in each line she had written. But it was a letter, of which
the burden was, "You are there, and I am here." The
phrase was like a knell. The grievous knell of their life in
New York, which had been given up for something else—
surely no more than that, Austin told himself. It was
natural that she should gird at fate, he said, should mourn
on the first evening of their separation. He, too, had
mourned. A doubt gnawed at him, notwithstanding. She
had let her trip to Paris stand in this letter as a thing

assumed, but she had not restated it. An oversight on her part, no doubt, a small omission she had not realized might worry him.

He wrote her an answer full of his eagerness for her coming. But his letter seemed weak in comparison with hers. He had never been good at expressing his own emotions, and reading over the pages he recalled Beatrice's old charge that his words as a lover were unconvincing and frail. Never mind, Beatrice understood him and would perceive the passion behind this letter. He felt happier after he had sent it.

No more mail would arrive from America for a few days, so Austin abandoned the newspaper office. He loitered on the terrace of the Café de la Paix and watched the world go by the corner which the world is said to pass more persistently than it passes even the crossing of Broadway and 42nd Street. Late in the afternoon, he strolled down to the Place de la Concorde. A light rain, scarcely more than a mist, was falling. The patrician gas-lit square where the guillotine had functioned glowed at the heart of a false dusk, and its wet pavement seemed pellucid as a lake reflecting the quivering flames. A double row of lamps soared up the Champs Elysées, between the trees, to the Arc de Triomphe. Automobiles, swift and silent because of the clear speedway, wove about the square and debouched into the avenue. The sky was somber and near, tinged with burnt ochre in the west. This was an urban panorama without an equal, casting a spell upon a New Yorker precisely on account of its beauty being so different from that of New York, thought Austin, as he roved the broad spaces.

Paris continued through long succeeding days to capture him with new fascinations. He adventured to distant quarters, and experienced the pleasure of a boy when he stumbled upon places bearing as little resemblance to each other, for instance, as the restored Roman arena off the Rue Monge and the modern park of the Buttes Chaumont. He chose to make his discoveries without the aid of a guide book. A Baedeker would have given him the hurried psychology of a tourist.

But when he saw from the papers that American boats were in, he returned to the Brooklyn Eagle bureau. Theresa Glenn had answered a letter he had written her at sea. There was mail from lesser friends like Frederick Hagen and his assistant at Darcy's. Only Beatrice had not written.

A preposterous fear clutched him. Was it conceivable that her first letter had had a blacker meaning than he had read into it? If so, what meaning? He could think of none that at all fitted the loyalty of lovers. She was making her final arrangements for the journey, he said, and her silence signified a postponement until she could give him details. He wrote to her, nevertheless.

How to spend his time became, mysteriously a burden and a quest. Sightseeing was an outlet from which the edge had suddenly been taken. He felt an impulse toward strident, modern pleasures and commenced to make a round of the theaters. The Casino de Paris, the Palace, the Concert Mayol, the Folies Bergère. He deliberately chose the musical revues, seeking a blunt, material stimulation. But they were more interesting than he had supposed. Like vaudeville in America, they beat the measure of the millions that care more for life than for art. A pungent commentary on politics ran through them, and France was a country where politics had been developed to the magnitude of a national sport. The tableaux of nude girls were not flaunted solely to catch the dollars of tourists on a libidinous spree. The boulevardiers, also, delighted in female nudity; they occupied a fair portion of the front seats. And the tableaux were beautiful. The fact that breasts and loins could be uncovered here had resulted in a different technique from the one which prevailed at home. It was neither better nor worse.

Austin was sketching his random criticisms at a performance at the Folies Bergère when the curtain rose on the American dancer, Nina Payne. Her slender, virile body, her long legs and her bobbed brown hair transported him in an instant to New York. She was of the same mold and mood and generation as Beatrice. He leaned forward, entranced. For fifteen minutes, Nina Payne interpreted jazz to an audience that received it as a curiosity, a clamorous exotic. But Austin adored her for the embodiment she was of the rhythm he loved best, when all was said and done. She was an admirable artist. He promised himself to see her dance again.

The next evening, however, he went to a music hall in Montmartre. He did not go again to the theater for a long time. For a letter from Beatrice arrived, usurping his interest in matters unrelated to his love.

It was a curious, hard letter, little more than an analysis of Austin's character. It told him nothing about her own emotions, gave him no hint of her plans. It failed even to answer his messages from the boat.

He was an egoist who had mapped out a pathway for himself through life and had kept to it consistently enough, she wrote. But egoism did not necessarily give strength, nor reward with victory. If he desired no more than was brought to him by women because he was charming to them, all was well, and she extolled him for his decorative compromise with existence. There would always be Stella Grants for him. But did not his cult for women include a passion to exhaust their possibilities? Did it not embrace the illusion that he could hold them more successfully than did other men? She thought so, and was sorry he had worked out a system certain to defeat him. And Beatrice illustrated her judgment with the latest chapter in the book of their love. It had not been the beautiful thing for him to go to Paris alone. He had not wanted the separation— she was certain of that—yet power to find the inevitable solution had failed him. What did it matter that she had said she would neither marry him nor travel, unmarried, on the same boat? Without phrasing it in trite questions, he should have been able to pierce to her secret wish, what- ever that had been, and annihilate the difficulties, carry her along with him. That only which imposed itself mutually

—like their first surrender to one another—was worth having. She ended with a salutation of grave and subtle endearment.

When he restored the pages to their envelope, Austin was shaken like a man threatened with the death of the beloved. He decided to rush back to her on the first boat. But he did not act on the resolution. She might consider that the final weakness, he thought. Insofar as she had said anything about their future, she had implied that she would come to Paris to adjust it. With values he had never before been able to give to words, he wrote her explaining the dilettanteism of his youth, beseeching her not to judge him further until she had seen for herself how deeply she had changed him, and reiterating his love.

Then, mail after mail passed without a letter from Beatrice.

Chapter 22

THE cable office in the Avenue de l'Opéra was a small three-cornered room on the street level. An attendant sat at a table, and there was a low, slanting desk built against the wall, with four seats for the public. Austin stooped over a blank, on which he had written Beatrice's name and address. He mentally phrased his message in a dozen different ways, and found them all colorless, curt. It could not be helped, he decided. Cablegrams were like that. He wrote down:

COME TO ME DEAREST ANSWER

and turned, with a physical awkwardness, to file the blank. The impassive clerk counted the words, verifying them aloud. Horrible that they should have to pass by way of his consciousness, thought Austin.

It was eleven o'clock—about six in the morning by New York time. Beatrice should receive the cable before noon, and her reply could be delivered in Paris the same day. Such promptness, however, was not to be counted on. There might be delays in transmission, and unless her ticket were already bought, she might take a day to conclude arrangements, to have a decision for him. Perhaps two days.

Austin weighed the hazards of his message with a cautious, an almost painful, exactitude. It would take her by surprise, and she was not the woman to rush to the nearest telegraph station as soon as she received it. She would dwell upon the state of mind that had caused him to send it, and would meditate her answer. But it would please her. With an inverted logic and a false optimism, he advanced to the theory that she would respond as he would have responded to a cable from her. Actually, he did not believe she would come to Paris; her silence on that point had been too stubborn. But she would tell him to return to New York.

The following afternoon, the answer arrived—a small blue form, folded into a square and pasted down. Tearing it open nervously, he read these words:

CAN'T COME EXPLANATION GOES BY MAIL TODAY BEATRICE

He did not know whether to be more disillusioned or relieved. A Paris of love and work for them had become a vanished idyll. But, at least, their misunderstanding was about to be cleared up. He consulted all the timetables and telephoned to the steamship companies for dates when mail might be received. He settled on a Monday, nine days away, as the reasonable probability. There was a bare chance, however, that the Leviathan had been caught, which would make it the preceding Saturday.

On Saturday, he said, "There will be no letter today." Yet he went to the Eagle bureau and looked through whole files of newspapers and magazines, while he watched the mail clerk and the messengers who slipped in and out. He did not relinquish his slender hope until the place closed.

On Monday he was there early, and passed hours in restless waiting. A portion of the mail had been delivered, with nothing for him. The chattering tourists who shared the hospitality of the bureau irritated Austin. They asked banal questions which any guide book could have answered, and read aloud extracts from their letters. Stupid people. Still, they were happy, he mused, and he could not say so much for himself.

He had dropped even the pretence of finding the newspapers interesting when, after luncheon, the girl attendant turned from the next room and walked straight toward him. She had a long box under her arm. Her plain face with the hair drawn back was set in a smile—the shallow cheeriness of a stranger confident of bringing good news.

"A registered package for you, Mr. Bride," she said.

Austin rose to his feet startled by this unexpected box addressed to him in Beatrice's handwriting. He thanked the girl coolly enough, but his hand shook as he signed the receipt. Moving to an isolated corner of the bureau, he twisted half around to conceal what he was doing from possible onlookers, cut the string and tore off the paper wrappings of his parcel. He raised the lid of the box.

The terrible beauty of Beatrice's severed hair assailed his eyes. Here were the orange ropes for which he had once begged her, uncoiled and heavy, gathered into one great strand and tied with an orange ribbon. He saw a glinting of points of flame. The hair had been cut more than a year before, but it had not lost its lustre. A virile aroma, as of resinous bark—the very odor of her living hair—floated to his nostrils. Part of her was in this narrow casket on his knees. There was also an envelope, containing an engraved card. The latter announced the marriage of Beatrice Purcell and John Stanton Kilmer. No written message for him . . . only the stark card . . . nothing more.

Austin covered his mouth and chin with one hand, and lines appeared on his forehead. Then, with a slightly exaggerated care, he closed the box, retied it and placed it under his arm. He walked out of the office, down the stairs to the boulevard. Mild April sunlight shone gaily on the budding trees and splashed the fronts of the buildings with gold. But the visible world had gone black for Austin. He was like a person under the first empery of a mortal illness. Vast shadows hovered before his eyes and sullied the grace of Paris. Though his step was firm and his body erect, he felt as if he were about to faint. His mind was functioning slowly, in vague, broad terms. He knew that á ghastly thing had happened to him, but no one in particular seemed to be to blame. Jealousy, anger and hatred were far away, futile outlets for his grief. The shade of Beatrice appeared to be moving a little in front of him, as if she were dead.

"What shall I do?" he muttered. The idea of drugging himself into insensibility with alcohol occurred to him as a classic expedient. He turned into a bar and ordered a glass of cognac. But the moment he had swallowed it, he was swept by a wave of nausea. He had always been an epicurean in his drinking, yet had been able to drink much without feeling it. On occasions, he had been lightly intoxicated. He perceived now that his nervous system was attenuated to a point that made it impossible for him to become a sot.

He left the bar, horribly sober and ill. On the Boulevard des Capucines and the Avenue de l'Opéra, he stopped often before displays in show windows, his eyes shifting stubbornly from object to object without recording them in his memory. He did not know what he was looking for, nor where he was going. Any occupation would do, so long as it gave him a reprieve from thought.

The Tuileries Gardens under the sunshine were as cold as the grave. Court ladies and sweet nude marble nymphs were corpses on their pedestals. Austin recognized the Louvre with a frowning astonishment. There was the Louvre, he said to himself, and since he had not visited it this time, since he had been saving it to see with Beatrice, he might as well go in now. But he could not make up his mind to do so. He wandered here and there in front of the building, and found presently that he had entered a circular inclosure with statues set around it. The monuments bore little relationship to one another: The sons of Cain in the wilderness, Houdon and his muse, Time, a nameless barbarian, Corot and his muse, the architect Mansart. What could they be but salvage from various Salons, put here because there was no logical site for them? A pathetic little outdoor museum.

Austin circled the fenced refuge innumerable times, goading himself to observe and to comment. But until he returned later, he could not recall what figures had stood there. He remembered only a proud stone girl, the muse of Houdon, her face turned upward to the sculptor. She had been beautiful.

He went back to his own quarter at last, and sat on the terrace of the Café Soufflet, the incredible box still under his arm. The numbness about his heart had commenced to give way to a mordant anguish. He visualized Beatrice with a totally unrecognizable husband, a symbolic male, a type. She had married Jack Kilmer, the youth with whom she had danced at Mrs. Thornley's house. He had seen Jack Kilmer on that occasion without seeing him, and today he was equally obscured. But she was more vivid than if she had been in the flesh before him.

Why had she done this thing? He fumbled for her reasons, refusing to face them, abandoning a motive the instant it assumed in his brain the accents of verity. He was not ready to know the truth about her marriage—if, indeed, it would ever be attainable, he said.

That afternoon he was obsessed by the appalling magnificence of her cruelty in sending him her hair. She knew what a fetish it had been to him, knew the meaning of her act could not escape him. A gift of all of her that could ever be his in the days to come. A gesture of finality. It was impossible to conceive of more gorgeous obsequies for love. Only she—the stern, flaming one—would have had such an impulse. He understood it—from her, of her. But he felt destroyed, his wound unstaunchable.

He stumbled across the street to his hotel room, and wrenching the cover from the box he took her hair into his hands. He drew its vital weight along his chest and around his neck, where it coiled supplely like a snake. Tears ran out of his eyes unheeded, as he buried his face in the glittering thicket and breathed its perfume. He lay down eventually, stunned, and lost his count of the passing hours.

Austin's physical deterioration through the next few days was rapid. He crept about the necessary business of life, his shoulders stooped, his features expressionless. The hotel had become hateful to him, but lacking the energy to look for another he escaped from it as early in the morning as possible. He went for purposeless walks, from which he brought back chaotic memories without charm. Restaurants and cafés he detested helped him to kill the time.

Mentally, however, he did not give way. With an almost morbid lucidity, he judged the case of himself and Beatrice. He perceived that, despite his sensitiveness to women, he had started to woo her without comprehending that she might influence him more profoundly than others had done. He had built up an agreeable artistry of love, a voluptuous practice, deriving its appeal from the fact that woman was his master passion on a poetical plane that most men did not reach. Any intelligent and reasonably pretty woman had been adequate as a partner in one of his affairs. He had toyed, and the sole virtue in his philandering had been the finesse he had brought to it. Having never been in love until after the coming of Beatrice, he had supposed that civilized beings could always control their emotions; he had used the august name for a lesser manifestation of beauty. Beatrice had known there was such a thing as love. He had not.

What, then, was love? No definition existed, nor could one be framed, decided Austin Bride. At some unwritten moment in their intimacy, he had surrendered completely to a red girl. She had become precious to him in a deep unalterable sense. Nothing could have debased her in his eyes, none of life's mockeries or degradations, so utterly had he made her a part of his own ego. But she had failed to make him a part of hers. It was his fault.

He reconstructed grievously certain episodes of their early days together. He had told her, that first evening they had dined on Houston Street, that lovers should be absorbed in one another, not necessarily for ever, but as long as the mutual charm lasted. He had said there should be no jealousy and heavy tragedy, that the one who loved longest should retire gracefully, acknowledging that the time had come to look for kisses elsewhere.

It had been a fatal thing to tell a woman who was destined to pierce the shell of his complacency. Doubtless she had taken him at his word, and believing him incapable of any deeper feeling she had been the one to hold herself in check.

On various occasions, he had expounded to her his theory that love should be ruled by reason, that a mental sympathy was the only essential. Her acquiescence had never been wholly candid. She had had a way of smiling and adding that it was not important what he thought, or she thought, as long as there was love. She had been the wise one, and had not sought to apply a ready-made system to the heart. But she had not given him more than he had asked. Why should she have done so?

Austin became harder with himself, too merciful to her, as he rang the changes on his irremediable disaster. His love at the end had clearly been greater than hers, for all her scorn of his dilettanteism, of his supine departure for Paris, alone, because that had been the easiest thing to do. But he could not hate Beatrice. He would not condemn her for having sacrificed him. She was brittle and bright, he said, of a temper that refused to compromise, though it might break. Like the clear, green jade to which he had once compared her.

And he stamped out, as a weakness she would despise, the temptation to melt into self-pity. He had his souvenirs of her. Even she could not take them away from him—if she would. They were no cause for becoming maudlin. By so holding on to some of the wreckage of romance, he concluded afterwards that he had probably saved himself from a form of melancholia that must have ended with suicide.

As it was, the inevitable seduction of the idea caressed the outskirts of his brain. He repulsed it ironically. A fine answer that would be to Beatrice's zest for existence, her realistic vigor! Death was a debatable notion if it could be conjured with cunning—but not suicide. Not in these circumstances. He could imagine himself shooting her husband, and then sending a bullet through his own head to cheat the electric chair. Nothing less than that. A primitive, humiliating notion, at the best.

He ranged the streets of Paris, brooding, loathing the things he had found most lovely, too listless to travel on to another city, another country. Paris must do. He would reaccustom himself to it.

Under the arcades of the Odéon one morning, he was turning over the pages of books on a stand, indifferent to their contents, when two lines of verse arrested his attention:

"Maintenant, ballade, recueille des pavots dans tes mains
Et des gerbes d'épines et plusieurs gerbes rouillées."

Swinburne in French! How well he knew the closing stanza of the "Ballad of Death":

"Now, ballad, gather poppies in thine hands
 And sheaves of briar and many rusted sheaves
 Rain-rotten in rank lands,
 Waste marigold and late unhappy leaves
 And grass that fades ere any of it be mown;
 And when thy bosom is filled full thereof
 Seek out Death's face ere the light altereth,
 And say, 'My master that was thrall to Love
 Is become thrall to Death.'

Bow down before him, ballad, sigh and groan,
But make no sojourn in thy outgoing;
For haply it may be
That when thy feet return at evening
Death shall come in with thee."

He remembered that after he had left Elizabeth and
freed himself from his job on the Forum, he had made
a rite of reading with a certain exultance the "Ballad of
Life."

Chapter 23

A MONTH of desolation wrought havoc with Austin. Contorted, gross impulses succeeded one another in his mind, stole upon him unawares. He would return to New York and ruin, by some act of vengeance, the lives of every one concerned in his tragedy, he thought, and the next moment admitted that if he were within reach of Beatrice he would probably grovel at her feet. A thing that must not be. It would be preferable to mutilate himself in some other way.

Jealousy of her unknown, her almost anonymous, husband smouldered at the depths of his heart, like a fire pushing its way through the rubble of civilized pretences he had heaped upon it. Unendurable to know that she had given all to a new lover. He wished that she had died instead.

Turning definitely at last upon his own self, he desired a metamorphosis of horror and lust that would make him unrecognizable, permit him to look back callously at the Austin Bride who had trod sweet-scented ways with Beatrice. He was barred temperamentally from becoming a drunkard, or taking drugs; but there was plenty of mud otherwise in which he could roll. A round of crass fleshly contacts should do the trick. The poets said so, at any rate.

He resumed his appraisal of the women in cafés and restaurants, stonily indifferent to their allures. The prostitutes were much overrated by the tourists who gloated over Paris as a city of superlative vice, he said. They were often well dressed and sometimes handsome, but their professional manner was more dully commercial than that of a bond salesman. Once, in his newspaper days, he had guided a slumming party through the back alleys of San Jose, in California. A houseful of Mexican harlots he had found had been better comediennes than these colleagues of theirs on the Grands Boulevards. The poor little half-cocottes of the Dôme and the students' cafés, the short-term mistresses who had fallen heir to the mantles of Mimi and Musette, he had already classified in days when he had been inclined to be more sympathetic than he was now.

The working women of Paris diverted his attention. He acknowledged they were pleasing now and then, when one found them in the sole milieu they seemed to enjoy—installed as somebody's wife and business partner, behind the counter of a tiny shop. The midinettes were apt to be cute sparrows, as chittering and as brainless. Girls in offices wore clothes at which a New York servant would have hooted, and had evidently been taught that make-up belonged to the commerce of the pavements. Waitresses were peasants in corsets and cotton stockings. It was odd that respectable females of the lower orders should consider it so unnecessary to be chic.

The noting of these differences gave Austin's brain something to work upon, but did not sway him. What did it matter? Prostitute, Mimi or midinette—any of them would serve as a beginning. Yet he postponed the consummation.

He had taken to roving the garish Rue du Faubourg Montmartre and the streets leading into it. An equivocal neighborhood, a tenderloin semi-theatrical and buzzing with rumors of illicit gambling. Racing touts and souteneurs lounged in the cafés. Looking for a place to have dinner, he drifted one evening into a restaurant connected with a bar in the Rue de la Grange-Batelière. The small, square room had six tables, attended by one waiter, who looked like an anaemic descendant of Maupassant's Bel-Ami. Characteristically, the food was good. A French restaurant may be never so mean, and not bring shame on the national talent it serves.

The patrons at Brussier's were thickly painted girls and young men in shoddy imitations of London tailoring. A plump woman, however, who sat facing Austin, was of a somewhat superior type. She was about thirty, a sleek brunette with questing eyes, but free of the cast-iron smirk, the puppet gestures and crude readiness for business of the streetwalker. The maroon silk of her blouse stretched tightly across a large bosom, and bit into her arms half way above the elbow. Her manner was one of unwholesome boredom, the manner of a woman who sleeps late into the day and comes out at night hoping that a fortuitous encounter will bring a truce to her ennui. A widow, or a discarded mistress, commented Austin to himself, without a quiver of human response.

After he had finished eating, he took from his pocket a

volume he had bought on the quais. It was on art, and was illustrated with modern pictures, most of them nudes. With one elbow on the table and the back of his chair braced against the wall, he slouched sideways. The woman could see over his shoulder, and was watching the pages of his book as he turned them.

"You are interested?" he muttered, handing it to her.

She replied that pictures always interested her. Her voice was agreeable, with a throaty Parisian intonation. The Salons at the Grand Palais were her especial delight, she said. But though she exclaimed over the illustrations in the book, she soon wearied of them and turned the conversation into personal channels.

"You are a painter, perhaps?" she asked.

He moved his head ambiguously, not caring to go into details about his work. She took it as an affirmative answer.

"And what country do you come from?"

"America."

"Ah, you rich American painters! You all have big studios in Montparnasse and give gay parties for the models, don't you?"

Austin smiled grimly. If the Faubourg Montmartre could still credit the bohemian legend about Montparnasse, no wonder it flourished in more distant parts of the world, he thought.

"Why do you smile?" she pressed him.

"Because you think I am rich," he retorted curtly.

"You must have money, to live so far away from home.

The exchange makes a poor American rich compared with us."

He perceived it was this that constituted his charm for her. A gleam of cupidity had appeared in her eyes. It was perfectly all right, as far as he was concerned. Had he not decided to purchase a bitter antidote to love? Why not from this woman? If she did not demand her pay by the night, she would take it in some other form. He stared brutally at her. A voluptuous, ripe body, he noted less impersonally than before. The kind in which sensualists are supposed to rejoice. But it would be well to get her to declare herself more positively.

"I'd like to know about you."

The woman responded eagerly enough. Her name was Germaine Lagarde, she said. Until a few weeks before, she and a friend had had a shop where they specialized in painted flowers for hats. But the business had not gone well and they had closed it down. She hoped to start again by herself, and had begun to furnish a flat she had taken on the Avenue de Clichy. The prices of things were terrible. She was living in the meantime with a family around the corner. Not that she liked the quarter, but her landlords were worthy people, distant relatives, in fact, who did not charge her too much for her room.

Austin allowed her to ramble on for a period his wandering attention did not measure, before he interrupted to ask her to go to a café. They walked to a place in the faubourg where Germaine said the music was good. It was a second-rate café, very brightly lighted and panelled with mirrors, yet dingy-seeming on account of cigarette smoke and infrequent dustings. Nondescript creatures at a piano and two 'cellos performed industriously, yielding the honors at times to a long-haired violinist with the mannerisms of a genius and a faulty technique. Minor actresses, cocottes and sports were closely packed about the tables.

"I adore music," sighed Germaine. "For putting one in a happy frame of mind, there is nothing to equal it."

His nerves jangled, Austin endured the café for a half hour. It was difficult even to hear himself talk, but Germaine pitched her voice above the tumult. It would be nice for them to be comrades, and to go often to amusing places like this one, she averred. Could she expect to meet him tomorrow evening, for instance? Would he be going to the restaurant in the Rue de la Grange-Batelière?

He stared at her moodily. He knew that if they parted on ordinarily friendly terms he would never look her up again. A flirtation according to the rules was the last thing he desired. Out of the question to pretend that he was spiritually attracted, that he might fall in love with this woman. If she would agree to an immediate carnal surrender, well and good.

"Don't you know now whether you like me? Why wait until tomorrow?"

She considered him shrewdly, aware of his meaning. "You Americans, you expect everything so quickly! Just like that!" she said, pursing her lips and nodding her head. "You remind me of your soldiers who were in Paris during the war."

Austin was sardonically entertained at being compared to an American doughboy. "It's a good way to be, isn't it?" he mumbled.

"Oh, I don't say no! You have decided, then, that you want a little French sweetheart?"

"Yes."

"And you would be generous with her? You wouldn't be like some men, and expect to have a sweetheart without helping her to get along?"

He grimaced drearily. "I'd certainly expect to be generous."

Germaine's manner changed at once. Growing calfish, she agitated her shoulders, beamed at him, and thrusting one hand into his lap she gave his hand a hard squeeze. *"Mon loup!"* she exclaimed. "My own big wolf! I was right in thinking we would discover a sympathy for each other." A moment later, she put an arm about him and kissed him publicly.

"I'm tired of this café—the noise, the smoke," he said, shuddering. On the sidewalk, he asked her brusquely, "Where is the best place to go?"

"I can't take you to my room, *chéri*. I live right with the family, you understand, and they would not like it."

"A hotel, then?"

"I know of something better than a hotel. A building where they rent small suites by the night. Such comfortable apartments, such discreet arrangements, *chéri!*"

He wished she would not call him *chéri*. A word that

had a tender nuance in English, but here it was the name that prostitutes hissed at one from doorways.

"A suite will be all right. The advertisements in the Sourire call that sort of thing a *garconnière*, don't they?"

"Yes, *chéri*."

Germaine guided him to a house in the Rue de la Boule Rouge, where a rat-faced woman slipped out of an office and started up the stairs ahead of them, wasting no breath upon phrases. She showed them into an apartment on the second floor. After Austin had paid her and the door was closed, he sat rigidly, taking stock of his paradise. The walls were papered in magenta, and there was a purplish carpet, magenta curtains of imitation velvet drawn in front of the windows. All was magenta—even the salient bed with its quilt and feather bolster, like a catafalque stretching almost from wall to wall of the first room. Through a half open door he could see a table where meals were doubtless served, two chairs and a sofa. In there, also, the upholstering, the hangings, were of the color of stagnant blood. The atmosphere was intended to be florid, but it succeeded only in being stark. A grim boudoir for harlotry, he thought. Strangling, hideous, on a warm night especially, such as this was.

His business, however, was with Germaine. What did the setting matter? She was alive and complacent. He looked her up and down, his imagination whipping his senses.

"Take off your clothes," he ordered.

"But, of course, *chéri*."

Ignoring the dressing room, she stood a short distance from him and unhooked her skirt. It fell to the floor, and she stepped out of it. She stripped off her blouse. Wide expanses of a coarse-grained skin emerged, plump shoulders and great, sagging breasts. There were folds on her flanks and stomach. Her hips were enormous, her thighs short between the waist and knees.

Still wearing her stockings and a loose pink undergarment of some mixture resembling silk, she came over to the chair where Austin was and sat upon his lap. Her heavy arms went around his neck, and her eyes of a willing animal, brown and lustreless, found his and sought to hold them.

The blunt contact of her alien body worked on him like a poison. His flesh leaped in consternation at the feast to which it had been called. He shrank back dolorously into himself.

Austin understood that his attempt to destroy the man who had loved Beatrice had been morbid histrionics. He had slunk on to the stage unarmed even with an illusion. Now, Beatrice was interposed, a visible mirage, as she had appeared in their moments of extremest beauty. He could not violate his memories, would never be able to do so. No one who was not like Beatrice could stir the pulse of desire in him.

If he should woo again, it must be because he was drawn by the magic that the Celtic-American woman had for him, her alchemy of dreams though she moved at the vortex of the jazz age, her capacity for being at one and the same time hard and mystical and poignant and gay. If he should kiss, it must be cream-white skin with small freckles on it in summer, a body with long limbs and little breasts, and the royal pageantry of red hair.

He thrust Germaine Lagarde from his knees and paced blindly about the floor. The remote babbling of the woman came to his ears. She was asking him what was wrong, but minutes passed before he could reply to her.

"I am not—not well," he stammered at last. A solution offered itself. "Will you please go into the next room and get me some water?"

When her back was turned and the running tap made sufficient noise to cover his movements, he shut the connecting door. Then he put money in plain sight on a chair, and walked rapidly out of the apartment and away.

Chapter 24

THE brief, hot summer of that year was rioting in Paris when Austin set out for the Brooklyn Eagle bureau for the first time since he had received the salutation and farewell of Beatrice's gift of her hair. He had left no forwarding address, and it had been a matter of utter indifference to him that mail must have been accumulating through the weeks that had lengthened to months. The bureau had seemed the one spot he could not face.

His life had been arid. Adjusting himself slowly to conditions, he had shaped a routine that permitted him to get along without excessive abasement, or revolt against his lack of an occupation. Certain cafés, certain restaurants, had drawn him regularly, though he had avoided the forming of friendships among the habitués. He had read a great many books. The spring had been protracted and rainy, not on the whole a lovely spring. But with the definite blooming of summer, new energy had flowed through him. He had given up the room he loathed and had found a better one in the Rue de la Sorbonne. This change had suggested it was now more than time he should go in search of his mail.

He sauntered under the full-leaved chestnuts of the

boulevards, vaguely pleased by the caressing warmth and the spectacle of crowded blocks of café tables overflowing the sidewalks. The glasses of many-colored drinks gleamed prettily. At the Eagle bureau, the girl attendant stared at him as if he had returned from the tomb.

"Mr. Bride!" she exclaimed. "You should have let us know where you were. I was about to send all your mail back to New York."

"It doesn't matter. No need to have worried," he replied pointlessly, and felt obliged to add, "I've been traveling."

She collected from pigeonhole B a great handful of letters and many newspapers and magazines. None of the superscriptions were in Beatrice's writing, he observed stoically. But every one else, it seemed at the first glance, had been trying to get in touch with him. An incomparable irony.

Already conspicuous in the bureau, he did not want to make himself more so by reading his letters there. So he gravely filled his pockets, tied the periodicals into a manageable parcel, and left. He rode in an autobus to the Place de l'Odéon, where the proprietor and waitresses of a certain brasserie-restaurant had come to know him and looked amiably upon his long tenancies of a corner table. It was called the Grande-Chope—a place of comfortable leather-cushioned seats, of tall windows that on a day like this were thrown wide open on the square.

Austin lounged indolently for a while before he turned to his correspondence. Charlotte had written to him twice, Laura Beltrán once, Theresa Glenn three times. There was a note from Maude O'Neill, he saw with pleased astonishment. His assistant on Darcy's, Marguerite Sims of the Forum, even Madame Boissy, had not forgotten him. Nor had Frederick Hagen and a few other men acquaintances.

Charlotte's letters lay nearest to his hand. "Best of dear friends, I hope you have had enough of Europe," she wrote. "My theatre has been subsidized at last, and I need you now to help me make it a success." She explained the modifications that time had brought to the project they had so often discussed. The realization was going to be more spacious than the dream, she said, because she had hoped for barely five hundred thousand dollars and the timid ones had suddenly taken courage and contributed a million. Her own credit amounted to a third as much again. The foundations of the building were to be laid at once. The interest of the public must be revived, stimulated. But Austin must not think of himself in the rôle of a mere press agent. He could be her confidential director, if he were willing. "You have a special genius for working with women, for women," she told him in conclusion.

It was an odd experience to be restored to contact with one's old life by the generous words of an old lover, thought Austin. It was like waking up in a mortuary chamber and discovering that, after all, one was not dead. Even this would have been impotent to stir him from his lethargy two months ago—last month. But today was today. Stricken and rotting cells had been sloughing themselves off unknown to him, had been replaced. He was convalescent, perhaps.

He opened the letters from Theresa Glenn and read them with a slighter recrudescence of emotion than he had feared. Theresa had known more about his love for Beatrice than any other friend. The stages of his tragedy had been clear enough to her. She had written to sympathize, reticently, understandingly, making allowances for his very failure to answer her letters. A calm, wise woman. Her philosophy, however, would have been useless to him then, and as if aware of its shortcomings she had merged into another theme. Austin should return to New York, she pleaded. The roots of his existence were there. In spite of his superficial preciosity, he beat to the rhythm of New York. He had not been able to work with the publishers of Darcy's, because they were old-fashioned. But he should start his own magazine. She would raise money and help him to do so. He could have a brilliant career as the editor of a magazine for modern-minded women.

Laura gave him the news of her latest comedy, which following the one he had helped her launch had established her soundly as a playwright. She missed him and would give a lot to see him again. Would he care to collaborate with her for the stage? She did not have the glimmer of an idea for another play, and he was good at plots.

And Maude O'Neill held out a branch of peace. She had heard he was in Paris, wanted him to send her his impressions of the city she longed to visit too. Their affair had not been firmly based and so had foundered, she wrote, but was that a reason why they could not be friends? Austin acknowledged with a throb of critical satisfaction that the poems she enclosed were keener music than those early ones he had seen. Clearly, she had grown to be a ripened, stronger Maude. The years had not stood still for her.

He sat back, musing. Of the women he had loved since he had been capable of loving maturely, all had spoken except Elizabeth and the best-beloved. The one he had rejected ruthlessly, and the one who had rejected him. Life never faltered in the terrible logic of its processes; it did not care by which partner a lethal wound was dealt, nor for what greater or lesser reason. Blood flowed out to the lees from such a wound, and there was no resurrection.

But though their relationship had died, sundered lovers lived on and bore the mark of one another. He found that he could examine dispassionately the effect that Beatrice had had on him. To an extraordinary degree, she was of her city, her race, her times. He—women apart—had been a connoisseur of exteriors, and she had carried him along with her toward the cult of ardent living. She had not made allowances at the end for the scales of his old self that still clung to him; they had fallen now. If, as Theresa said, he beat to the rhythm of New York, that had only been fully true since he had known Beatrice. She had given him, also, by some mysterious telepathy, a finer clarity concerning fiction. After the inevitable words she used, her austere marshalling of human motives, he could never again be turgid and journalistic. It might well be that he was equipped to write the novels of his secret ambition.

"What impress of myself have I left on her?" he asked, and was aware without bitterness that the question could not be answered yet. She would complete her book under other influences than his, would do new work at which he could not even guess. She would weave a many-colored pattern, in which he would have his part. The pattern-maker would be lost, lost to him; but the time might come when he could trace the strands that he had furnished.

Austin gathered his letters together, and strolling through the sunny Place de l'Odéon he turned toward the Luxembourg Gardens. He felt relaxed physically, his flesh conscious of a gentle ache as if it had been bruised all over and now was being healed by the warm air of summer. His brain, cleared of a malignant fog, was receptive to the lure of sights and sounds it had long repudiated.

He remembered the dictum of Laura's lover, Eustace Lloyd, who had detected a Pierrot in the man he had been then. "Have a prayer or a pistol ready for the day when you find I'm right," the poet had said. Well, he had laid the spectre of the pistol, and he had said his prayer.

The faces of sweet women detached themselves from the passing throngs. Women who had nothing to do with the fever of the cafés, the trafficking of the boulevards. Unfamiliar types, provocative or grave, exotic books whose pages he had not turned.

He paused to stroke a queenly angora cat that lay blinking in the sunshine on the window-ledge of a shop. Inside the railing of the Gardens, a group of little girls played, their legs bare and satiny, their eyes deep pools of coquetry, their voices high and flute-like. The parterres on the green lawns were a blaze of roses and dahlias and flaunting hollyhocks.

Paris, he perceived, was beautiful. But it was not for him to remake his life in a new world. He must return to his own. Charlotte's theater or Theresa's magazine, a play with Laura or a book by himself: there would be no lack of work for him to do. Doubtless, also, there would be love.

Austin saw already in his imagination the imperial sky-line of New York looming beyond the bows of the ship that would take him home.

THE END

COLOPHON

THIS *book is composed on the linotype in Granjon which was designed by Mr. George W. Jones, one of England's greatest printers to meet his own exacting requirements for fine book and publication work. Like most useful types, it is neither wholly old nor wholly new. It is not a copy of a classic face nor an original creation—but something combining the best features of both. This type face is gradually becoming more and more in favor for fine printing.*

BOOK DESIGNED BY WILLIAM GUYER

SET UP, ELECTROTYPED, PRINTED AND BOUND BY
THE AMERICAN BOOK BINDERY—STRATFORD PRESS,
INC., NEW YORK

PAPER MANUFACTURED BY THE
P. H. GLATFELTER MILL, SPRING GROVE, PA.
AND FURNISHED BY
PERKINS & SQUIER COMPANY, NEW YORK